# MIX OF STORIES

EDWARD MCCARTHY

**Gotham Books**
30 N Gould St.
Ste. 20820, Sheridan, WY 82801
https://gothambooksinc.com/

Phone: 1 (307) 464-7800

© 2022 Edward McCarthy. All rights reserved.

No part of this book may be reproduced, stored in a retrieval system, or transmitted by any means without the written permission of the author.

Published by Gotham Books (September 17, 2022)

ISBN: 979-8-88775-053-8 (sc)
ISBN: 979-8-88775-054-5 (e)

Because of the dynamic nature of the Internet, any web addresses or links contained in this book may have changed since publication and may no longer be valid.

The views expressed in this work are solely those of the author and do not necessarily reflect the views of the publisher, and the publisher hereby disclaims any responsibility for them.

EDWARD MCCARTHY

# THE RINGS

Charles Flannery was his real name, but everyone called him Charley. He became sort of a fixture in his hometown. Every Wednesday he could be seen sitting in the cemetery in his portable chair at the foot of his wife's grave. Charlie was a writer of articles for various magazines. He also had three books published and received checks from his agent every month. When people attended a burial ceremony on a Wednesday, they would see Charlie, and usually ask the officiating minister about him. They would be told that Charley was reading his latest article to his wife of 30-years. He lost her a few years back, but he's never missed a Wednesday since then, rain or shine. There was a time when a close friend of Charlie was attending a service there and someone asked him about Charlie.

"That's old Charlie, a close friend of mine for longer than I wish to recall. Anna was his high school sweetheart. When he returned from Viet Nam and the veterans' hospital, they were married. He came close to losing his leg over there. She prayed for him every night he was gone. That reminds me: when they married,

Charlie had engraved in both wedding rings 'Anna and Charlie Forever.' When his Anna died, Charlie took off his ring and placed it on Anna's right ring finger. I know because I was there and watched him do it. I thought it was a message of his undying love when Anna wore both rings.''

"It was another three years before old Charlie suffered a serious bout of pneumonia and died. I attended the wake. Something caught my eye as I was saying my goodbye to Charlie. It was a movement, very slight. I wondered if it could be a muscle spasm. No, It was too late for that. Just before the coffin was closed forever, I noticed a wedding ring on old Charlie's finger. I talked to the funeral director about this too. No one knew how it got there because it wasn't there before. At my request, the director removed the ring. There was engraving inside it reading 'Anna and Charlie forever.'

# MIX OF STORIES

# WW II
## ON THE MAAS RIVER

My infantry company was at the Maas River in Holland in the early spring of 1945. (It is called the Meuse River in Belgium). Our duty was to protect the area as our crossing place into Germany. It was also a site for American spies to cross back to our lines, and we had to prevent the Nazis from crossing into our lines. There was a fox hole at the river and another about 300 yards back from there. I was in the more distant one from the river. My partner's buddy was preparing to sneak down to the other one with another man. but they had to wait for dark because Nazis were watching from their side of the river. Earlier that day a new lieutenant believed we were too careless with the hand grenades we were issued. We carried them in our field jacket pockets and slung from our webbing. He ordered us to tape down the handle or the cotter-pin with electrician's tape for safety. We had to do it even though we thought it was stupid. Suppose we needed that grenade in a hurry?

Later, after dark, we saw my partner's buddy and another man heading for the river. We wished them luck. A few minutes later we heard a German burp-gun firing, then silence. Minutes later we heard an explosion. Apparently, Nazis had crossed the river for an attack? My partner and I prepared to protect our little hole in the ground.

This is what really happened: Our two men headed for the fox hole at the river, but it was already occupied by two Nazis who had crossed the river during the night and awaited them. When the two GIs appeared, the Nazis opened fire, killing one of our men. The other lay on the ground with out-stretched arms. The Nazis either believed he was dead or they couldn't find him in the dark. He was lying flat on the ground searching with his fingernails and praying to find the end of the electricians' tape on his grenade. When his prayers were answered he slowly undid the tape, trying not to make a sound. If he did, he was dead. He finally undid the tape, pulled the pin and lobbed the grenade into the foxhole, killing both Nazis. We tore the tape off our grenades that night. My partner broke down and cried when told that his buddy was dead.

All of these WW ll recollections are absolutely true.

EDWARD MCCARTHY

# A KINDLY GENTLEMAN
## (TRUE STORY)

Ask a kid today to run to the store for you and he will demand the federal minimum wage, health insurance and a retirement program. Back in the 1930's, teachers, adults and bigger kids bullied small children much more than now. It was common in some schools for teachers to wield a wooden "paddle" against kids, punishing them for being late to class, talking in the hall, and a dozen other violations of their behavior code. When the teacher ordered one to "bend over" we would all witness what today is considered a crime. Believe me, that paddle hurt! We learned to be defiant when we were struck with that paddle. We just turned around and looked the teacher in the eye, even if it was hard to catch our breath. This is why I was surprised when one of my adult neighbors treated me as a human being. Mr. William Smith was different from other adults I knew. He was different because he treated me as an equal, not as something beneath him, not as something to be scraped off the bottom of your shoe, even though I was a mere 13-years old. He must have been about 90 years old because he had served in the Civil War for three years. He lived only four houses up the street from my parents' house, and he never asked me to run to the store for him.

Mr. Smith and I would sit for hours on the front steps of his brownstone house, and talk about the depression, the president, Hitler, the stars, planets, Einstein, etc. It was truly an experience you could not buy and could not afford. Whenever I went out, I looked up the street to see if he was sitting on his front steps. I preferred talking with him instead of riding my bike or playing stickball. He once asked me, "If a tree falls in the forest and no one is there, does it make a sound?" I thought about it, then answered. "I don't know." He said, "Yes and no; sound is a vibration of air impinging on an eardrum. If there is no eardrum there is no sound. Aha, but there are the eardrums of millions of bugs and birds; therefore, there is a sound, to them, but not to us." Mr. Smith was a smart man and an ex-soldier. He had a wound in his leg from a Minie ball, a little bullet invented by a Frenchman named Minie. The wound in his back was from an Indian arrow. He also told me about an entire army unit in which each man was awarded the Medal of Honor during the Civil War simply for signing up for another hitch. Those medals were withdrawn later when the entire list of recipients was revisited.

My friend thought he was born in 1845. He said, "Just about everyone back then was born at home without the help of a doctor or nurse, and few had a birth certificate. The family Bible was where births, marriages, and deaths were recorded. Neighbors often helped during late pregnancy and births." My friend met his wife in Huston, Texas. She was a school marm. At that time, he couldn't even spell "English," but he came to love the written word. He studied and went to school. Previously, he had gone only to the third grade. His wife helped him and he studied hard. He became a teacher. He was living proof that perseverance can win over some shortcomings. The first book he read was the Bible. He was alone now except for his sister. His wife was dead for the past six- years, from a "growth" in her stomach. Mr. Smith was a wonderful storyteller. He could make you feel that you were right there in-side the brown walls of the Alamo mission when Santa Anna and his troops bombarded it. He was born after that happened, but he spoke with men who had seen the carnage a few days after the loss.

I inched closer to him when he told of the Apaches raiding his wagon of army rations. He still had ten miles to drive the wagon when he noticed five Apaches trailing him. They stole some horses earlier and ate one of them. I asked, "Did you shoot any of them?" "They shot the corporal sitting beside me, but only in the sleeve with an arrow. It didn't even touch his skin. Yes, I shot at two of the five and I think I hit one, the one who shot an arrow into the back of my leg a few weeks earlier." I knew Mr. Smith for an entire year. One day he was acting sad and he spoke slowly, "I don't think I will be hanging around for very many more days; let me tell you now, I really enjoyed your company. Your parents should be proud of you." I said, "Those are much like the words I was going to say to you." I felt very sad for the rest of the day and for two more days because I had not seen him on his steps. Then I saw him one afternoon as he sat down on his front steps. I ran up the street, and was not aware that my eyes were filled with tears. He looked so pale and thin. He asked me, "Why the tears; did your frog die?" then he laughed. I wiped my eyes on my sleeves and said, "I never even owned a frog." When he smiled, my sadness evaporated. That day we saw the last train to travel on the third avenue elevated tracks. I recall that it was festooned with red, white, and blue streamers, and inside was Governor Fiorello LaGuardia. When we said our goodbyes that afternoon, we shook hands, and he held my hand longer than necessary. I did not see him after that. Then I saw the funeral wreath on his front door. He never had much in material things, but he left behind a thankful kid with very fond memories of a kindly gentleman who spent his last days with a person whom most people merely ignored. RIP my friend.

EDWARD MCCARTHY

# THE BAILIFF

Linc Chambers, the bailiff, was in conversation with a deputy. He and Judge Matthews arrived in Hillside a day before the trial date for five separate defendants. The judge was studying some of the court preliminaries when he said with some surprise, "You have a girl in your jail? The sheriff nodded his head. "Have someone take her to the hotel," the judge ordered. "That's where she lived, Judge," someone said. "Ok, send her home. Tell her to appear in court at 4:00 PM, and ready to defend herself." Linc offered to walk her home. At the hotel, Linc asked Jane if she had robbed and killed Mr. Sanders. "No. I didn't, of course not, I heard that he fought with his killer. Take another look at me. I weigh 105 pounds." Linc asked why was she arrested. "Because I gave the sheriff some marked bills for change when he bought a beer. Those bills must have been what Mr. Sanders gave me to pay his bar tab earlier that day. The sheriff told me that all of Sander's bills in his pocket were marked" Linc asked if she had a lawyer. "Didn't think I'd need one. Why were the bills marked? I didn't see any marks on them." Linc replied, "The sheriff told me he expected a robbery of the stage coach that carried those bills to the bank here, so he had the serial numbers on the bills written down at the Tucson bank. Mr. Sanders received some of those bills when he cashed a bank draft. Whoever has those marked bills is suspect." He wasn't getting anywhere with the woman.

Linc visited the town shops where Mr. Sanders would likely have visited as he paid off his debts. He finally had success at the stable. Sanders had paid the stableman, three dollars. The stableman still had them in his pocket and showed them. Linc asked if anyone else saw Mr. Sanders pay him the money. "Well, yeah. Billy Mason was here. He even laughed at Sanders when he dropped his money on the floor, a big wad of money. Billy's about 20 years old, built like an ox, but a mite slow." Linc asked, "Can you remember when Billy left the store?" The stableman answered, "Yeah, it was right after Mr. Sanders left." Linc visited Billy's parents and asked to speak with son Billy. Linc and Billy talked on the front porch. Linc asked Billy if Mr. Sanders had given him any money. Billy looked from left to right, as though considering to run. "Why are you acting like that," asked Linc. Then he ordered, "Empty your pockets!" Billy did so, after some hesitation, but refused to empty one pocket until his father shouted at him. He reluctantly placed the contents of his pocket on a chair cushion. There was a bloody pocket knife and $2,343.00 in bills. Billy confessed to his father that he wanted the boots on display at Webbers' General Store. Linc didn't like his job at this moment. He took Billy to jail.

The judge freed Jane and sentenced Billy to twenty-years in prison after a doctor's examination. Linc went back to the saloon later to see if he could milk the hero title he was given. The woman he proved innocent was very grateful indeed; she bought him a drink.

EDWARD MCCARTHY

# WILL COYOTES CRY?

Anyone in Adamdale could tell you about Ron McKenna. He is a friendly type, about 5 feet 10 inches tall, 160- pounds, and about 28 years old. Ron was born in Adamdale. His parents had died in a fire several years earlier. The fire had been set by Apaches who raided his parents' small ranch for the horses. Ron was rebuilding the house and had made friends with some peaceful Apaches, trading horses for furs and hides. This is how Ron made a living, and not a bad one. The Apaches realized they were being treated fairly, even enjoying coffee at Ron's table as they talked business. They appreciated this and took extra care with the furs and hides they traded with him.

The years immediately following the Civil War were hard times for North and South, but were worse in the South at the hands of the carpetbaggers. Ron paid his taxes, but always had a small herd of unreported horses hidden out. Many of the ranchers avoided paying taxes so they could put food on the table. This was the only way they could show a profit too. Carpetbaggers were said to be punishing the people for losing the war. Some carpetbaggers were actually sent south by President Johnson, and the pickings seemed easy. They were traveling from town to town, buying up properties from people who no longer could pay the higher taxes, mortgages and percentages on bank loans. The talk at Johnson's Saloon was usually centered about the carpetbaggers unless one or both of them were present, and then there was silence. Ron enjoyed one drink and left the saloon early. He had business to conduct in Eddington, a small mining town. After conducting his business, he stayed at the Eddington hotel.

At sunup he was on the road back to Adamdale. He rode until noon, then stopped to study a man in the distance who was sitting and leaning against a rock. Ron worried that the man could be hurt, but once he neared the figure, it was plain to see it was an Indian, and he was dead. Ron rode on. Two hundred yards farther on, he found another dead Indian. He checked his .45, making sure it was fully loaded. Farther down the trail he came upon a covered wagon. He shouted for the owner, to avoid scaring him or being shot at. No one answered his calls. He was about to move on when a figure appeared through some brush. He drew his weapon, but holstered it when he saw it was a woman holding a shovel. She was about his age or a little younger. She looked very tired and sad. "I just passed two dead Indians up the trail. Is everyone OK here?" He asked. "No,

I just buried my father; he died earlier this morning, heart attack, I guess; and now I have to get to town. There are still two Apaches skulking around. I shot the two that you found. I better get moving to Adamdale."

    Ron rode alongside the wagon. The woman's two stout horses soon brought them to town. She told Ron her name was Diane Watkins. She drove to the Watkins Gun Shop before pulling up "That's my dad's shop. We went to Eddington to pick up some needed equipment and guns. On the way back, Dad grabbed at his chest, then he turned pale. After a while his lips turned blue. It was terrible. He was dead in just a few minutes." She took a deep breath and continued, "I'll store our purchases inside the shop and hope a thief doesn't make off with them before I can sell them." Ron offered, "I was planning on staying at the hotel, but if you give me the shop key, I'll stay here the night, maybe two nights. I knew your dad; I bought a pistol from him some time back. Anyway, carpenters are working on my house for the next few days." She shook her head, "Oh, I hate to bother you. You've already been so kind. If you could do that, I'll try to sell the shop. There must be another gunsmith around." She gave him the key to the shop. "I'll ask around too, Miss Watkins." Ron completed his business in a few hours and collected $200.00 for horses he had sold previously. At noon he went to the saloon for lunch and a beer. He chose a table and sat down. The sheriff joined him and said, "Been talking to Watkins' daughter. Poor girl's been through hell. She's grateful for any help she can get, and you have my thanks too. Mr. Watkins was a fine man. Sorry to hear he's gone." "I appreciate that Sheriff. Do you know of a gunsmith looking for work?" The sheriff was in deep thought, then he told of a young man who had been apprenticed to a gunsmith in Missouri, but now he couldn't find a job. Ron asked where the man lived, then walked to the hotel. "Is John Randall in his room?" The clerk nodded his head, pointed to the stairs, and said, "106." Ron knocked on the door. A young man asked, "How can I help you?" They talked and Ron liked the well-mannered man and decided to help. "I can do the work," John said, but he didn't have money to buy the equipment. "You look like an honest man, John. I'll lend you the money; shouldn't be more than $200.00. I'll write up an agreement for you to repay me at $20.00 monthly. Is that OK?" John was very grateful, "You bet it is Mr. McKenna." Miss Watkins agreed to the deal. John moved from the hotel to the gun shop to save the nightly $2.00 hotel fee. There was a couch in one room, as well as a bed in the back room. Ron slept on the couch; John had the bed.

    Ron awoke at about 2:00 AM. It was hard to get comfortable on the couch. He rose and drank some water. He took one sip then thought he heard a noise at the back door. He froze and listened intently. He heard it again and tip-toed to his gun belt. He silently slid the .45 from its holster, and squatted to present a smaller target. It was too late to awaken John. The candlelight from the street lamp lit the interior of the shop, but it merely took a small nip out of the darkness. In the dim light Ron saw the figure coming toward him. It was an Indian, an Apache, and he was holding a rifle. Ron said, "Put the rifle down and raise your hands." The sudden rifle blast caused Ron to fire. The Apache fell. The rifle thudded and skidded across the floor, out of the Indian's reach. Ron waited for a response from another Apache. He believed there were two of them, the two who escaped after shooting at Diane Watkins. "Who the hell is doing that shooting?" shouted John. Suddenly an Apache appeared at John's door. The second the Apache showed himself. He was downed by a bullet from the gunsmith. One moment he was silhouetted in John's doorway, the next, he was writhing in pain on the floor. Now the sheriff was banging on the shop door. Ron opened it. "What's the story?" he asked Ron. After Ron's explanation, the sheriff mused, "What the hell did they want?" The Apache lying in the doorway moved. The sheriff said, "Maybe we can get some information from one of them after Doc patches them up. I have a man who speaks Apache." He took the two wounded Indians with him when he left. Diane Watkins was the next to enter the shop. She was breathing heavily after running from the hotel. "I was so scared that you were hurt, or that John was hurt," she quickly added, John told her that they were fine.

It was early morning when the sheriff was back at the shop. He said, "It's a long story, but we found out that the Apaches were searching for Mr. Watkins, to kill him for killing their brother, Long Runner, the eldest of the brothers. Mr. Watkins was returning a borrowed buck-saw one day to his neighbor, Hank Owens. On the way to Hank's ranch, he saw Hank butchering a buffalo. They talked, and Mr. Watkins accepted a hind quarter, which they loaded in Watkins' wagon. After returning the borrowed bucksaw to Hank's barn, Mr. Watkins returned on the trail, but now he saw two Apaches working on the Buffalo. Hank was nowhere in sight. Watkins yelled at the Apaches, and then fired his rifle, killing Long Runner. The other one fled. Watkins searched the area, but could not locate Hank. He didn't know it, but Hank had returned to his ranch by a different route after giving the remainder of the buffalo to those Apaches. This is why they tried to kill Watkins when his wagon appeared after getting supplies. They didn't know he would soon be dead from natural causes." Ron said, "They looked awfully young to me." The sheriff looked puzzled for a moment then answered, "One is almost 16, the other is about 20." Then, Ron asked if the Apaches had to go to jail. "One is barely a man, the other is a child. You know the judge will throw the book at them." The sheriff scratched his head and answered, "Yeah, I guess I could let them both go if no one will charge them; they suffered enough over a series of errors and mistaken thinking. But where can they go? The tribe won't accept them because they broke the treaty, or it looks that way, and the whites would kill them." Ron mused for a while. "I'll take the kid. I can patch up his leg and use his help on the ranch, and he can learn a lot about the ways of whites. By the way, what's his name?" The sheriff thought for a moment, then said, "His name's Little Puma. He's a breed, you know! Ron was surprised, "I didn't know that, Sheriff." The sheriff added, "And he speaks English."

A week later at the ranch, Ron told Little Puma, "The carpenters did a fine job, but they left a mess. Look at it now; this place has never been so clean and fixed up. I think we can celebrate in town today." He opened the front door and was facing Raphael, the spokesman for the friendly Apaches. The Indian had four wild horses to sell to Ron. During the course of business, Ron introduced Little Puma. "Little Puma, is that white name?" asked Raphael. Ron said, "No, that's his Apache name." Raphael seemed surprised, "He not Apache, he son of white man in ranch near river far south. Apaches from south raid ranch long time since, kill others, take baby. Him name Mason. Now I say hello Mason boy." The boy answered, "Hello, Raphael."

## MIX OF STORIES

Ron and the Mason boy were in town in the morning. Mason had his hair cut and Ron bought him some clothes so he would not draw attention. The Mason boy seemed to appreciate the change. They then visited the land office. Ron asked the agent if he had any information about the Mason ranch, who owned it, who lived there, etc. "Well, yeah. The widow, Clara Hastings, lives there since her brother was killed in an Indian raid several years ago. There was a Mason child, but no one could find him. She tried for years, but now believes he's dead." Ron said, "This is the son, standing beside me." The agent reached into a drawer, flipped through some files and withdrew one with the name Richard Mason on it. He scanned through the pages, and then stopped. "It says here that the Mason child was named Bill. He had a burn mark on the back of his left hand and a birth mark on his right shoulder that looked like a sitting cat. Mr. Mason left the ranch to him." Ron asked Bill to remove his shirt. The agent could see the burn mark and the birthmark. "I declare," he remarked. "Looks like he is the child of Richard Mason. Clara Hastings, his aunt, has to come to my office to transfer the land title to Bill unless she contests the transfer."

Ron and Bill rode south to the ranch. Mrs. Hastings seemed happy to see them, and hugged Bill. "I still have letters from your mom, telling me about the burn on your hand. You got that burn from putting the back of your hand on a hot lantern chimney when you were still an infant. Your mom blamed herself for that. She told me about the cat that is sitting on your shoulder too." Bill said, "I was told I was called Little Puma because of that birth mark, but I kept telling them my real name is Billy." When the evening wore on, Mrs. Hastings asked Ron to stay overnight because it was getting dark. In the morning, Ron said his farewell to Bill and Mrs. Hastings because Bill decided to stay at his ranch. Bill thanked Ron for all he had done for him, and for helping him decide to live as a white man. Ron planned to see his friend, the gunsmith, in a couple of days and see how well he was doing in his new business.

John Randall was just closing the gun shop to go for breakfast when Ron arrived. They ate breakfast together and talked. John had all of the money to repay the loan. "Business has been good," he said. "A man bought 40 belts and holsters that I made; said he would resell them in Tucson. The gun business is good too. I'm mighty beholden to you, Ron. I'm making a deal with the owner to buy the building too." Ron faked coyness, "Aw, shucks," he joked. "Eat your food and let's get a drink." John then told him that Diane had been asking about him. "You should visit her before you leave." When they returned to the gun shop, Diane was standing outside the locked door. John whispered, "She's been coming here every day, and I knew it wasn't to see me." Once inside the shop, Ron and Diane sat and talked. "The things I've been hearing about you are hard to believe," she said. "You're a Robin Hood of the West. You're friendly with some Apaches, you've lent money to John, and you've helped me, and took a young Apache to live at your ranch." Ron said he would bring her up to date. They sat for a half hour, sometimes holding hands in silence. Ron broke the silence, "My dad had an expression for when he was complimented. He would ask, will coyotes cry over me?" Diane looked him in the eye as she said, "You're a good man, Ron McKenna, I'm sure they will."

EDWARD MCCARTHY

# ANN MARTIN

Ann Martin was born on a horse farm in Virginia in 1844. She married Lieutenant Benning in 1862. Immediately following the ceremony, he was called to duty. Three days later he lay dead on a field of battle. Then one night the Martin's barn was burning. She and her father fought it the best they could, but it was a total loss. Luckily, Mr. Martin was able to get the horses to safety. As they watched the burning timbers fall, they turned around to watch in horror as their house was also covered in flames, and Ann's sick mother was in an upstairs bedroom. There was nothing they could do, but watch. Neighbors joined them on the lawn. One neighbor cursed the army that would pay spies to commit such atrocities. This was the fourth farm in the area to suffer the same fate. Two men tied Mr. Martin's hands behind his back to prevent him from rushing into the burning and crumbling house.

After the burial of Mrs. Martin, the sheriff told Ann and her father he was convinced that the fire had been set by four union soldiers. He almost caught them. One of the men's left sleeve was smoldering. The sheriff hadn't yet known of the Martin fire. He was trying to be helpful when asking those soldiers what happened to the soldier's sleeve... The four soldiers raced off on their horses. It was too dark for the sheriff to recognize them.

There were sporadic skirmishes around Mr. Martin's farm for a week following the fire. Mr. Martin decided to leave the area with his daughter. He wrote a letter to his brother Henry, who had a horse ranch in Arizona. A reply came a week later by mail. The letter advised him that his brother had room on his ranch for him and his niece. Ann was excited about the move to Arizona Territory and getting back into the horse business "We should buy a wagon and start tomorrow," she said. "Whoa, Ann. Why do that when we can take a train to Missouri and get a wagon there and join a wagon train?" Mr. Martin sold his 47-horses. Seven of them had good blood lines, and they brought in more money. He sold his property and bought two carpet bags for himself and Ann to carry their meager belongings. He also had money from the insurance on his house and barn. They would not be a burden to anyone.

## MIX OF STORIES

They arrived in Missouri in two days and took hotel rooms to catch up on sleep and bathing. They bought a wagon and laughed when tossing in their worldly necessaries in two carpet bags. Later they purchased straw mattresses, blankets, food, and cooking utensils. They paid $300.00 to the wagon master, Mr. John Welsh. This was $100.00 less than the money paid to be taken all the way to California. Mr. Martin's wagon and two others would leave the safety of the train and drive south-west to Arizona Territory. It was an ambitious and arduous journey, but in 62 days the martins and two other families separated from the train. The two other wagons contained six men and boys, and three women. Two of the boys were 18 and one was 16. They could be useful if attacked.

Mr. Martin was looking for a river. Once there, he would follow it south to Henry's ranch, about three days farther on. The river was two-days distant from where they left the train. They reached it and turned south. They camped that night and made plans for driving to Henry's ranch the following night. On the final trek of the journey, the people said their farewells. One wagon crossed the river in the afternoon. The other one crossed the next morning. The Martins were

crossing a wide, grassy plain when they noticed two riders following them. As the riders neared the wagons, it was plain to see they were Indians. Suddenly the Indians fired arrows at the wagon. Mr. Martin raced his horses away, but the Indians soon caught up, and fired more arrows. Ann left her seat and scrambled to the rear of the wagon with her father's rifle. She took a quick aim and fired as an arrow struck the tailgate. One Indian slumped and stopped. His partner stopped to help him. The ranch was in sight when two white men came riding their way. The injured Indian fell from his horse, the other one galloped away. The wagon, escorted by two riders, made it safely to the Martin ranch.

Ann and her dad were warmly greeted by her uncle. They immediately went into the house. Minutes later, a banging on the front door brought the people to rapid attention. Henry answered the loud knocking. Nobody was there, but a wounded Apache was lying on the porch. The men carried the boy to an empty table. Henry held his hand over the wound to stem the flow of blood. Ann prepared a bandage. She spread open the wound and could see the back-end of the bullet. She used a pair of tweezers to extract it, and then she sewed up and bandaged the boy's shoulder, thereby gaining a life-long friend. Henry knew the boy as Jose. "It was probably his brother, Vincente, who was with him, and who left him at the door," he told her.

In the afternoon, about a dozen friendly Apaches came to the ranch. One of them was the boy's father. Henry explained what had happened, and then Henry and the boy's father entered the house. When they emerged, they were smoking cigars. They shook hands and the Apaches left. The boy's brother, Vincente, came to the ranch later that day. His father had told him to apologize along with Jose or go join his uncle who led a war-like band of Apaches. The boy and his brother apologized. Ann said, "I am sorry for hurting you, Jose. Can we be friends?" He answered, "We are friends."

## EDWARD MCCARTHY

During the course of the week in which Jose was healing, he enlightened Ann as to the events that led to the friendship of his father and Henry Martin. It began about four years earlier. Jose's father was being hunted by the sheriff on a murder charge. Henry found him unconscious in his yard one morning and cared for him. The Apache's name was Hermano. He told this story: two days previously, Hermano and his 15-year-old nephew were fishing under the trees when they heard a shot. They investigated quietly and sighted a man leaning over another and stealing what he had in his pockets. The nephew became frightened and began backing away, but stepped on a dry twig. The man heard the snap and fired two shots at the sound. The second shot killed the nephew. Hermano ducked and began making his way back to the horses. He mounted his pony and began to ride quietly, but three bullets were fired at him. One of them went through his side. It wasn't a killing wound, but Hermano could have bled to death if not for Henry. The murderer must have lied to the sheriff because he, the sheriff and his deputy showed up looking for Hermano. "Hermano murdered Jess Wilkerson for his money. Jess had just sold four horses and had more than $100.00 on him. This is Pete Seamour, the witness, and that's what he tells me." The sheriff said. Henry asked, "How would Hermano know that the man had money? He was two miles away from the saloon trying his luck at fishing?" The sheriff thought for a moment, "I don't know." Then Henry asked if Hermano was there when the money was transferred. "The deal was made in the saloon. He can't go in there. He's an Indian" Henry asked, "Do you know who was there?" The sheriff counted on his fingers." There was Jed Wilding and our witness to the crime, Pete Seamour, who happened on the murder scene too and saw the killing and the theft of money" Henry looked puzzled, "Sheriff, if he was a witness to the murder of Jess Wilkerson, what was he doing at the murder scene unless he followed Jess or rode with him from the bar?" The sheriff turned to address the "witness." Before he could ask his question, Pete Seamour drew his pistol, disarmed the sheriff and other men, then rode off. "Pete's not very bright; we'll get him later or tomorrow. How the hell did you know?" Henry told the sheriff that he believed Hermano. "Come listen to his story. You'll believe him too." The sheriff did believe Hermano. "Did they catch the killer?" Ann asked. "Hung him on the following Saturday, recovered the money too." answered Jose.

A stranger rode the north trail. He was Will Hastings, a recently discharged union lieutenant. He was 25 years old, a little over 6 feet, and he weighed about 170 pounds. He had fought in the war since its start to its end in April 1865. He had three battle wounds; one of them would not permit him to stand or walk over extended periods. He arrived at the horse farm at about noon. Ann saw him dismount. She flew from the window to the front door, her heart was racing, then she thought about it and slowed her pace. She had seen the yellow stripe on the man's trousers and for a split second she thought her husband had returned. The man knocked on the door. She bided her time, fixing her hair, pinching her cheeks, and slowing her breathing. When she was composed, she opened the door. "Can I help you?" The man appeared to be very weak "I don't know, Ma'am. I'm looking for a job. I've come all the way from Virginia…." Ann was quick to respond, "Virginia? You really did?" He answered, "Yes, ma'am. My parents own a horse farm there. I was raised with horses." For a moment the man seemed to lose his balance. He held onto the door. "I saw your horses, and it looked so much like home." Ann backed away and told Will, "Come on in. Sit on the couch." He sat as she poured him some whiskey. "I'll make some coffee. The folks will be here soon for lunch, could you stay for lunch?" Will smiled, "Yes, Ma'am." He was very grateful. He was also very hungry. "When did you eat last?" she asked. He replied slowly, "I think it was yesterday. It wasn't much. Some Apaches were poking around too close to my camp. I had to douse the fire." Ann began to put the food on the table. She poured coffee for herself and Will. She also had set four places at the table instead of the usual three. Her father and uncle sat as Ann motioned Will to the table. He sat, introduced himself, and told his story. Henry said, "So, you're Vince Hastings boy? Your Dad had a winner the year I left to come here. Daring Boy, I think it was." Will corrected him, "It was Darling Boy, actually,"

After lunch, the men left. Henry told Will to find a bunk in the bunk house and come to the house at 5:00pm. They wanted to know what was going on in the world. The evening conversation took many a turn. Ann and her family now knew a lot more about this young man. Ann was falling in love again, something she had dismissed from her mind since her husband's death. She rode with Will, showing him the farm, which was, for all purposes, a ranch. There were even 20 or more steers on the property.

Plans had already been made for a trip into Mexico to gather all the mustangs they could. Ann was going, and some Mexican wranglers would be hired once there. Two men were left at the farm. Will was asked to accompany them. He accepted readily. Six days later they had 67 horses penned up in a blind canyon in Mexico. Will went riding one morning. He topped a hill and spotted one of the wranglers overlooking another blind canyon where there was water and about 120 or more mustangs. "Wow," Will said. They left the hilltop and strung rope and limbs across the canyon mouth. Henry Martin rode into town and hired four more wranglers. They set out the following morning for the ranch. Will was asked to ride ahead and enlarge the corral. Will had just completed the job when the horses appeared. He opened the gate and counted 224 mustangs. "Now," said Henry, "we check for brands. I will not be accused of horse theft." There were four horses with a Lazy- S brand. "That's Tom Sullivan's brand," he said. "I'll send him a note, and he can come pick them up." The man who delivered the note to Sullivan returned with a note that Henry read aloud. "You stole my horses, you return them." Henry was truly surprised at such an answer. Henry was selling the horses as quickly as they were broken to saddle. He feared that one of his men would put one of Sullivan's horses in the corral with those to be sold so he wrote another note to Sullivan. "We located your horses in Mexico among the mustangs. Come and pick them up or I will set them free." Will delivered the note to Sullivan as he watched Sullivan's three adult sons eying him as a bug. "There's no answer, now you get off my range," Mr. Sullivan said. He was obviously angry.

Will rode to town the following day to have the soles of his boots replaced. He had a half hour to spare before picking them up. He went to the Big Horn Saloon. Well, that turned out to be very dangerous. He took his glass of beer to a table and sat down. A few minutes later, Sullivan's three sons walked in. There was plenty of room at the bar, but one of the Sullivan's pushed a man aside as he shouted, "You're standing in my place." The surprised man picked up his beer and started walking to a table. Sullivan hit the man's arm; the glass of beer smashed on the sawdust floor. "Now see what you've done," Sullivan said. "I don't want no trouble, Mister," the man said. Sullivan was growing his anger. "First, you took my space, then spilt beer on me. You sure bought into trouble." Sullivan pushed the man hard, knocking him to the sawdust floor. Will was sure that this was all done for his benefit. They were proving what bullies they were. The man on the floor rose to leave when one Sullivan shouted, "Watch that Martin horse thief over there. He's got a gun." One of the Sullivan's drew his weapon. Will was faster. He shot the man in the belly. Another Sullivan drew his weapon and caught a bullet in the heart. The man who started the fight raised his arms. "I aint doing nothin,'" he said just before he was shot, but Will had not shot him. The stranger picked himself off the floor. He held a smoking gun. Will turned to watch the last bully drop to the floor then ran to him and removed his weapon from its holster and placed it in the dead man's hand. "He drew on you, right? I saw it." The man nodded his head.

There were several ways for Mr. Sullivan to react to the killing of his sons. The sheriff made it absolutely clear to him that the fight was started by his sons. Regardless of this, Sullivan could try to kill Will. To everyone's surprise, Sullivan chose to accept what the sheriff told him. Sullivan also knew that his sons went to town with the intention of killing Will and he had tried to stop them. The Martins and Will attended the burial ceremony. Sullivan thanked them for this. He was not the same after that. He was a subdued remnant of his former self. He sickened and died two months later.

Will and Ann were married in June. The family made another trip to Mexico, bringing back 273 mustangs after 6 days of hunting. Uncle Henry died in 1878, leaving the ranch to his brother, who owned it for only 2 years when he died. Will and his Ann had two children. Ann became sick in March, 1897. She died in June. Will buried her beside her uncle and father. Every day after that, Will visited his Ann and shared all the news. Every day the cook made his lunch and

placed it in a shoe box so he could picnic with Annie. When the end came two years later, he was found lying across Ann's grave. He was buried beside her.

# WW II
## NOTES

It has been claimed that there were an estimated 86 million deaths caused by WW ll. Among these were 1 million American casualties, including 405,399 deaths. Adolf Hitler tried his hand at several trades before being convinced that dictating to the world was his choicest role. He had been a paper hanger and artist, but what is little known is that he had also been a Benedictine monk, and Josef Stalin had studied to be a priest. Hitler quit his monk role when he learned he would never be the Abbot, the boss of that group. Hitler's I.Q. was 135. Stalin is said to have murdered as many Jews as Hitler. In fact, he requested Hitler to send them to him. Stalin assured Jews of their safety in Russia, then he set about murdering them.

Russia's revolution of 1917 merely changed the name of the dictator, and each change in government after that brought a new dictator. Before 1917 the tsars ruled Russia for 300 years. Can anyone imagine more than 500 years of dictatorship? And it continues even today.

After WW ll, I was stationed about 20 miles from Paris. I hitched a ride to the city of lights every weekend, then I would ride the subway (Metro) for 2 francs and visit all the places I had read about, including the infamous Pigalle. However, we were warned to stay away from bars where there were Russian soldiers on leave. Our officers didn't want to start a war there. This reminds me of two Nazi, SS officers I had captured in the war. They wanted to sign up in the US army because they were convinced that we would be going to war against Russia at any moment. WW ll was America's last declared war.

I served with the War Crimes Administration for about a year as a field investigator of atrocities. Of the 22 Nazis tried for crimes against humanity, 19 were found guilty, 3 were acquitted. Of the guilty, 12 received death sentences, 3 were sentenced to life in prison, and 4 received varying terms in prison. Even today there are people in America who deny Hitler's wrong-doing, and admire him and his hatreds. All the sick people are not in hospitals. All the nuts are not in candy bars.

# WWII
## DEATH, FOR REAL

    I was a happy go-lucky kid. I loved to walk and run. I would walk two miles on a Saturday to see a movie I waited for. Death was common in the movies. I counted eight killed in one western. They were common in gangster movies also, but they drew little emotion from the audience. We just counted them. Then the war came to my house and I went into the army. Months later my company walked for more than 72 hours (more than 110miles), without sleep, and eating while walking, then we hunkered down for a 6-hour fire-fight. It seems that a battalion of American troops had blundered into that town earlier, believing it had been pacified. On one lawn was an overturned ¾ ton truck and two dead American soldiers. Two other American bodies lay face up in a ditch. We ran forward, firing our rifles as we leaped over the bodies of friend and enemy. We hunkered down, then leaped up and ran forward again, firing as we went. We stopped firing when a Nazi aid man hoisted a white tee-shirt. Then we took over a house and slept where we fell. The sight of dead, young Americans plus the enemies we killed and wounded left an indelible memory. Everyone was sniffing, from the cold weather and walking stiffly from frozen feet. but sleep came quickly. Our captain let us sleep for ten hours before hustling us out on the road again and to another village or city. It's a toss-up on which effects an infantryman more, long marches or lack of sleep.

MIX OF STORIES

# THE BAILIFF

This is the story of how Linc Chambers became a court bailiff. He was aroused from sleep by the jail turnkey who shouted, "Hey you, wake up. You're going to see the judge." A deputy walked behind him down the boardwalk to Murphy's Saloon. Judge Aaron Matthews sat at a table as he watched Linc approach. Linc was pushed into a chair. "Do I know you?" asked the judge." Linc stood. "Yes sir. We met when I was the sheriff in Coby town." The judge asked, "What are you doing in my court?" Linc answered, "I guess I was too loud in the saloon two nights ago. I turned down an offer of a drink from a town citizen. He tried to make something of it by calling me a saddle tramp and claiming I stole my horse." The judge turned to the deputy sheriff and asked, "Is that the truth of it?" The deputy was slow to react, "Well, the prisoner drew his gun. I didn't hear the talking." An elderly man rose from his chair and said, "Your honor, I was a witness. The other man was drawing his gun, but was slower. This man could have shot him, but he didn't." The judge asked, "Do we have any other witnesses?" Two men rose. The judge swore them in and they agreed that Linc beat the other man to the draw. "Why was Mr. Chambers arrested?" he asked the deputy as he was losing his patience. "I was walking past the saloon when I saw the prisoner draw his gun, so I arrested him." The judge tapped his gavel on the table and said, "Case dismissed. I want to speak with you later, Mr. Chambers. Will you be around?" Linc answered "Yes sir."

He was sitting at the back of the court after retrieving his sidearm at the sheriff's office. When the court session ended, he and the judge walked to the saloon. Judge Matthews bought him a drink and they talked. The judge needed a bailiff to keep order in the court, but more than that, the judge needed someone to travel his circuit with him, someone with the authority to arrest, to maintain peace in the court, someone who knows the territory, and someone to talk to. "I'll see that you are made a federal marshal," he promised. "On a more serious note, I know you escaped from a union stockade up north. Don't worry, I'm not screaming for your arrest. You see, when the war ended, the union government was overstocked with prisoners. They offered freedom if the prisoners would join the union army and be sent to the west to rebuild forts, roads, and to fight Indians, and now the population is growing. By taking the job, you are pledging your loyalty to the United States. I have been ordered here to Arizona Territory, and I was promised my own bailiff and I chose you. Say you will and I'll send a wire Washington." Linc thought for a while before answering, "I'll take the job because there are no others." The judge said, "You have to remain in the job for a year before you are officially free of the escape charge." Linc's jaw tightened, "OK, I can't promise, but I'll do my best."

Later that afternoon, the judge's wire was answered. He told Linc that he had been accepted as bailiff, and also had the authority of a federal marshal, but they would not approve of a marshal's badge. One badge was enough. "That's all right with me," Linc said. On the following morning the men took the 9:00 am train to Phoenix, Arizona. Once there, they put up at the hotel and had an extra bed put in their room. Judge Matthews pored over a map as he determined his circuit. The trials were usually over in less than two hours. Linc bought two horses at the Swenson stable. He was given two saddles and bridles by the sheriff. They had been taken in lieu of fines. He then went to the Bird Cage Saloon for breakfast. Judge Matthews was already seated at a table and was finishing his meal. Linc sat at the table where he could face the bar. The judge said, "I've been thinking, Linc." Linc merely said. "Uh-oh." The judge went on, "It took millions of years to produce man as he is today. That must have been too fast even for God, because He had little time to put honesty into them." Linc said, "I think it's the times we live in, Aaron. If we had better times, we'd have better people." The judge smiled, "Maybe you're right. It's something to think on, but I guess the better people are those who are good even in bad times."

A noise at the bar interrupted the conversation. A gun clattered to the floor, a shot sounded, then a body fell heavily to the saw-dust floor. Linc was on his feet leveling his .45 at the shooter. "Holster your weapon, Mister," he shouted. The shooter holstered his weapon, and faced Linc. "Who the hell are you? I don't care who you are; just go away." Linc could see that this man was dangerous. "I can't do that. I'm an officer of the court." As this was said, the wounded man rose to his feet as he held his bloody arm. As he turned to walk away, the gunman reached for his weapon. He would have shot the man in the back. "Draw that weapon and you're dead," Linc said. The man withdrew his hand and reached instead for his beer. Linc holstered his .45 and turned to sit. From the corner of his eye, he saw the shooter face him and slap leather. Linc drew his weapon, spun around, and fired. The man grabbed at his gut. As a look of surprise spread across his face, he fell dead. His gun clattered to the floor. A man down the bar said as he pointed to the dead man, "He was the fastest draw in these parts."

It was not long before the sheriff walked in. He stood talking to three men at the bar before he strode to where Aaron and Linc sat. "Did you kill that man?" he asked Linc. "Sure did," answered Linc. "He drew on me." The sheriff wanted to know if Linc was a law man. Aaron placed his hand on Linc's arm and said, "I'm Judge Matthews. This is my bailiff. Yes, he's not wearing a badge; hasn't received it in the mail yet. The sheriff said, "Fast with a gun, are you?" Linc said, "Fast enough." The sheriff pulled a chair under him and sat. He called out "Barman, bring me a beer. I'll celebrate my new friends." He turned to Linc and said, "Bailiff, huh?" The men talked for an hour. When they separated, the sheriff said, absentmindedly, "Bailiff huh, I think I'll get me one of those."

# MIX OF STORIES

The men slept until about 8:00 AM then went to the hotel desk and asked if there was another place to eat besides the saloon. "There's a restaurant down the street," the man pointed. "You called it a restaurant? What the hell is a restaurant?" Linc asked. "I know it's a place to eat. But it's a foreign word, isn't it?" The clerk answered, "It's a French word. It means rest, restore, replenish." Linc said "Well, Aaron, let's go get restored. I always wondered what that word meant." Judge Matthews just looked toward Heaven and shook his head in wonderment.

There were four trials to be heard in Joshua, a town 35 miles away. They started out on horseback after breakfast. They passed only one small ranch about 20-miles out where they filled their canteens and rode on about a quarter mile where they stopped at a small wooded area and built a fire. They drank some coffee then lay down and slept. Linc would never forget that night. He awoke and walked into the trees to relieve himself. As he was returning, a shot jolted him fully awake. He raced to Aaron. When he reached for his weapon, a bullet stung him in the side, taking his breath, and knocking him out. When he awoke, he saw four men taking all of his and Aaron's belongings. He remembered how angry he was, but couldn't do anything at the moment. One of the men roughly turned him over and took his money from his pocket. Another thief did the same to Aaron. Linc played dead as his blood continued to spread through his shirt. The men took everything, horses, saddles, blankets, guns, everything. When the men left, Linc woke Aaron and half carried him toward the small ranch they had ridden past up the road. They had to rest often and apply pressure to stop the blood loss from their wounds. They were both exhausted when they arrived at the door of the ranch house. Linc noticed that there were no horses in the corral where he had seen eight previously, but from a distance. They reached the porch and stopped. Linc was too weak to stand. He fell to his knees and banged on the door until he passed out.

It was still dark when Linc awoke. He felt a bit stronger as he rose to his feet and opened the door. The stench from inside the house was overpowering. A man and woman in their fifties lay on the floor. Both had been beaten and shot in the head. Linc dragged their bodies outside. He then helped Aaron into the house, but his friend was unresponsive. Linc dragged and carried him inside and into the one bed. He found an unused sheet and tore it into bandages to wrap around Aaron's wound. He finally stopped the blood, or thought he did until he checked his friend. Aaron wasn't breathing; he was dead. Linc cursed as tears filled his eyes. Images of the four thieves were clear in his mind. "I'll settle this, Aaron, I swear," he said as he buried his friend and the man and woman, then fell into the bed completely exhausted. He slept all that day and part of the next. He was roughly awakened by a man who angrily poked a .44 in his face. "What did you do here? Where are my parents?" The young man of twenty or so years demanded an answer. Linc answered slowly, "There were four thieves. They shot us and stole everything we had. They must have stolen from here too; the horses are missing." The stranger asked, "My parents?" He was insistent. "I buried them and my partner out back." The young man ran out to the graves. Linc followed and saw the young man crying as his hands became fists, then loosened to wipe his eyes. The man introduced himself as Jed Walling. He then helped Linc to mount his horse as he led it the two miles back to his ranch. Jed's wife ran from the house to her husband. "What happened?" she asked.

"Looks like the Berman family came back from up north. Mom and Dad are dead." Mrs. Walling was shocked, but quickly recovered after hearing the details. Jed introduced Linc as he helped him dismount, then he explained that the Bermans were a gang that had lived near here but were captured up north, and had escaped prison. Linc sat at the kitchen table and thanked Mrs. Walling for helping him. She insisted that he call her Eileen. He told her and Jed everything that had transpired as he drank cup after cup of coffee. "I'm sorry," he said. "I ran out of water yesterday. They stole our canteens, well… I think that was yesterday." Linc felt safe and slept through the night. In the morning he felt like the old Linc---almost. He asked Jed for directions to town. Jed pointed, but protested. "You can't walk to town, not in your condition; the wound in your back will split open." Mrs. Walling used white thread from her sewing kit to put four stitches in Linc's back and side, where the bullet had exited. Linc laughed, "You sound like I'm pregnant. I feel fine… if I don't have to do any heavy lifting," he joked. Jed answered, "You won't feel so sound after walking 18 or so miles, take one of my horses. Leave her with the sheriff or bring her back if you come this way again."

Once in town, Linc borrowed some money from the sheriff to send a wire to the territorial representative to get him up-to-date and to request his pay. He was surprised to receive such a quick and welcome response. He was sent $101.82. Linc took a leave of absence until he felt well enough to return to his job and reassignment to a different judge. He started his quest for the killers by returning to the campsite where Aaron was shot. He followed the horses tracks in the direction of Phoenix, but off the main trail. From a hilltop he spied a ranch. There were horses, which looked familiar, and cattle in the corral. He walked Jed's horse to a clump of trees nearer to the house, then sat on a rock and watched the house. The only movement he saw was that of a young woman who hung out the wash and drew water from the well. That evening Linc approached the house, noticing his and Aaron's horses in the corral. Crouching low, he looked in a window. The young woman was eating. Linc saw no one else through any of the windows. He recalled a sign on the front door that read, "Williams." Linc burst through the door. The young woman dropped her sandwich. She was frightened and said, "Mister, you don't want to be caught here. There are three graves out back, belonging to the owners and their son." Linc demanded to know where the men were. She pleaded "I don't know, but please leave. You'll get me in trouble, and get yourself dead." Linc asked, "Who are you?" She said, "They're my brothers. They're very bad. I've tried to get away from them, but they beat me when I try. A man helped me once, and they killed him and his wife." "Saddle a horse you're getting away from here now." She shook her head and pointed to the window. "Too late mister, I see them coming down the hill now. You've got maybe a few minutes." Linc cursed under his breath, "All right, but I'll be back when they leave again." He ran from the house. He watched as the four men entered the house, and he recognized two of them. They left in about an hour, mounted their horses, and rode east. Linc saddled his horse with his own saddle, and then saddled Aaron's for the young woman. They rode to Jed's ranch to return Jed's horse. They were greeted by Eileen and Jed and were invited to stay for supper.

After they ate, Linc and the young woman named Ann were ready to leave. Eileen stopped them. "There's some stranger out front just standing there eying the house.

# MIX OF STORIES

I think it's one of Ann's brothers." Linc said he was sorry for getting them involved. He should have known the brothers would follow the trail to Jed's ranch. There was a knock on the door. Linc answered it by suddenly opening it and sticking his .45 in the man's ribs. He yanked the man into the room and asked what he wanted as he disarmed him. "We want our sister back," he said as Linc tied the man's hands behind his back. Linc asked, "Who else is out there?" The stranger smiled, "My brothers, all three of them." Linc opened the door and told the captive to tell his brothers everything is fine; come on in for coffee. The man did just that. A voice came from the brush, "Show us your hands Billy." Billy replied, "Can't do that." Linc grabbed the man, pulled him inside and shut the door. He told Jed to tie the man to a chair then he went to the back door. There was some tall brush about 30 yards from the house. It was a chance, but he made it safely in the twilight. He would have to be very quiet. Linc's anger had never waned since his friend was murdered. He also recalled his promise to avenge his murder. He flitted from tree to tree and tree to tall brush as he slowly approached the three men during the waning daylight. Every now and then, the brothers would fire at the house. Linc used the noise to cover his movements when it became dark. The men also shouted to each other, giving away their positions. A man fired at the house. The brief spark from his pistol momentarily lit up his silhouette. Linc fired. The man fell heavily. Linc hurried to the man, taking his pistol. The man died with a bullet hole in his head.

The odds were being reduced, but it was still two-to-one. Linc heard a movement. He ducked. The noise was caused by one of the brothers who had tossed a stone in front of Linc to distract him as he approached from behind. The man aimed. He could not miss. Linc swiveled about, leveled his weapon, but a shot sounded before he could fire. The man fell. He recognized Jed's voice as he called out, "Don't shoot. It's me, Jed. I couldn't let you do it all alone, Linc." They moved toward the remaining Berman, separating as they approached. "Is that you, Jack?" His voice gave away Berman's position. Linc and Jed fired at the same time. The wounded man fired into the ground, then slumped to his knees and dropped forward. He was dead when Jed found him.

Linc and Jed returned to the ranch which the brothers had taken over. Linc recovered all of his and Aaron's money and property as well as all that had been stolen from others. Now it could be returned. He advised Jed to claim the reward if there was one. Then he visited Aaron's grave to say a final good- bye. After two days of much needed rest Linc rode to Phoenix and wired his boss in Washington, D. C. The reply came in an hour, "You are assigned to Judge William Matthews, brother of Aaron. Meet stage in two days." Linc smiled at the prospect. When he met the stage, he had to smile again. He recognized the judge immediately. Well naturally, William was the twin brother of Arron. They had a lot to talk about, and they did as they wiped their eyes.

# SHERIFF JOE WESLEY

Joe Wesley had lived in High Lake Village for a mere seven months when he decided to run for the office of sheriff. His main purpose in running was to rid the county of its present sheriff. Joe knocked on many doors although he had a slight limp after an auto accident. He was gaining many votes and learning that the public liked him. Joe's bride of four months sold her business in the big city and opened a real estate office in High Lake Village. This was the second marriage for Joe, and Lynn's first. His first wife had died years earlier from cancer. High Lake was a quiet village. Many vacationers, anglers and hunters visited there in the season, making the village a favorite resort for many. During the past year, there were some burglaries, bar fights and domestic quarrels, to put down, but there had been only one murder there in three years. The sheriff's men worked in eight-hour shifts and went home feeling safe.

Joe learned that there had been an increase in the influx of drugs over the past three months although his county was relatively free of them. They came in from Peru and Colombia, through Mexico. Police agencies throughout the state were stymied as to how the drugs were coming in. Border guards said they were locating fewer drugs during the past three months. A search was conducted to find a tunnel that many believed was the source of the increase. People were saying this had to be the answer. It was not. Two tunnels were found, but had not been used for months. Joe Wesley's county did not border Mexico. It was at least 7+ miles from that border. He believed that drugs did not pose a big problem in his county. He thought the drug cartels merely ramped up their transportation systems.

Joe was told by the mayor that he had won the office of Sheriff by a large vote, and then he asked if Joe would take over this Friday rather than next Monday. It seems that the ex-sheriff had left town along with his sergeant, who had also sought the sheriff's office. The first day in office passed without incident, but one concern was that of being accepted by others working at the sheriff's office. Joe could easily be considered an "outsider" even though many people phoned to wish him good luck. He went home that evening feeling quite self-satisfied. He had run an honest campaign and was settling into his new job.

## MIX OF STORIES

It was four am when he heard a noise, or dreamed it. He sat up in bed and listened. Someone was in the hall. Joe grabbed his gun from the side table and a pair of handcuffs. He was a proficient boxer. His six feet and 185 pounds had won him many fights when he served as a detective under the state attorney general. He crept to the door and swung it open as he flicked on the bedroom lights. The stranger in the hall stared at Joe in disbelief and said, "You're not the sheriff!" Joe smiled, "Did you come here to argue that point?" The man said, "No, I mean, you're not the one I was looking for. I came to beat up the sheriff, but you're not him." The stranger's face became red in embarrassment. The intruder was a large man, 6 feet 2 inches and about 200 pounds of muscle. Joe was glad he did not come to beat him. He asked. "Why would you beat up the sheriff?" The man's voice was more relaxed, "He sent my brother to prison, and he knew Eugene was innocent. He checked with my neighbors and found out that Eugene was in my house watching TV with me when the murder of his girlfriend took place 20 miles away, but they wouldn't allow that to be said in court. I don't have any weapon, and I'm sorry I intruded on your sleep. My name is Dan Starr. I'm not really a criminal." Joe let out a sigh of relief, "I am really the sheriff, young man. And I'll have to place you under arrest for burglary." A moment passed, and then Joe said, "Damn, why do you have to be so pleasant about it? Hell, just take off. I don't want to see you looking at me with those big eyes." Dan looked like he would cry. Joe shouted, "GO, and close the door when you go out." He returned to bed after explaining to his wife, Lynn, what just took place. She said, "I'm glad you let him go."

It was seven am when Joe awoke. He showered, shaved, had some coffee, and drove to work. His office was quiet as usual. At about ten o'clock Dan Starr phoned him. "What's up, Dan?" Joe said, "I have a gift for you, sheriff." Dan was not too friendly," Mail it," Dan continued, "Oh, don't get sore, sheriff. I really have a gift for you. Have some of your men at the curb when I arrive in ten minutes. My gift is too heavy for one man to carry." Joe wanted to know what it was. "You'll see." Ten minutes later Dan drove up and parked at the curb. Two deputies immediately grabbed his arms when he exited his car. Joe told them to release him. They opened the rear doors and viewed many small packages wrapped tightly in plastic. One of them went back inside the building and exited with a drug-test kit. A few seconds later, he told Joe, "It's heroin and Mary-Jane and it's high grade. Must be a few hundred pounds. We have to weigh it and notify State." The sheriff's office had no scale, so they carried the packages to Mead's Drug Store, less than a hundred feet distant. The total weight was nearly 400 pounds, but much of it was marijuana. A deputy told Joe, "That's worth many millions of dollars when the heroin is cut, but it'll be cut anywhere from one to ten times. You could live like a king if you had a mind to."

Joe and Dan went to Joe's office. "I gotta hear your explanation, Dan. Where did you get that stuff?" Dan was happy to explain, "Out past Sullivan's General Store. I have a friend who lives about a mile down that dirt road. I went to see him about a job he knew about. I haven't worked since I came home from Afghanistan about 4 months ago. Well, I was half-way to my friend's place when I saw this bundle at the side of the road. I was curious so I checked it out. No one was around. I figured it was drugs. I had to break open the big package so I could get all the smaller ones into the car."

Dan drove with Joe to the spot where the package had been found. They exited the car and Joe noticed that the soil looked like something heavy had been dropped from some height and bounced three or four times. As he was telling this to Dan, a shot rang out from a rocky spot about three hundred yards away. The dirt was kicked up three feet from Joe. He and Dan ran behind the sheriff's car as Joe drew his weapon. To see where the shooter was, Joe fired a shot toward the rocks. There was no response. He said to Dan. "I'm opening this door and getting in. Stay low. I don't think he's there anymore, but stay low and follow me." Joe slid into the driver's seat and waited for Dan then drove off. The brush was so thick, there could be an army hiding out there. On the drive back, Joe told Dan about two openings in the sheriff's department. "The test is next Saturday, take it. I'll see what I can do to put you to work quickly. I'll take a look into your brother's case too." After dropping off Dan, Joe returned to the road where the drugs had been found. He walked to the rocks where the shot had come from and searched the area thoroughly. All he found was a cigarette butt. He put it into an evidence bag to be tested for DNA.

In the meantime, Eugene Starr had filed an appeal based on inadequate counsel. The State Supreme Court agreed and approved a new trial. Joe interviewed Dan's neighbors and found three people who would swear that Eugene was with Dan in Dan's house at the time of the murder. They were willing to swear this in court, but had not been called upon to appear at the previous trial. Dan aced the written and physical tests for deputy sheriff only two days before his brother was released with a full pardon. Joe assigned Dan with a man who had eight years of service. The state was now looking for the ex-sheriff and his sergeant for their possible role in Eugene's court case and conviction, and in the murder of Eugene's girlfriend. Joe spoke with Dan one morning about the drugs. He asked what Dan thought of the situation. Dan said he believed the drugs were dropped from a plane, but more than an hour later than expected. Nobody was there to pick them up. "I believe the same thing Dan. Moreover, the one who should have been there to get the drugs, was the bastard who shot at us. Maybe he overslept or something intervened. Anyway, now they know we have the drugs. I called state and they will take the drugs away. To keep them here makes it too dangerous for the people. I was also given a description of the men who will pick up the drugs, just in case someone else tries to take them."

The men arrived that afternoon and carried away the drugs. Joe felt very relieved. He left to visit a Mrs. Farley, who had called earlier to report that she had seen Sergeant Johnson. She remembered him from when he was in the sheriff's department. She was driving to visit her sister when he passed her in his car. She knew the police were looking for him. She heard it on her police scanner. Joe stayed off the air because Johnson was reported to have a police scanner in his car. Joe phoned nearby police agencies with an all-points bulletin. "Watch for Johnson, but be careful, he's likely armed and dangerous." He then called the state forensic lab for information on the cigarette he had sent them. "We have a DNA profile, sheriff, but there's no match anywhere."

Driving home that evening, Joe heard a loud crack like a rock hitting the windshield. He checked the glass, but saw nothing. He parked in his driveway, and exited

# MIX OF STORIES

the car. As he shut the car door, he noticed the ding in the edge of the roof, above the door. It was not from a stone. It had the round shape of a bullet and it was mere inches from where his head had been. He promised himself, "I've got to get that son of a bitch before he hurts someone, and that someone might be me." Joe asked the people he worked with for any information they could give about Johnson because they had worked with him. One man remembered he had a girlfriend in the village. Joe sent two men to the address and assigned others to 24-hour surveillance on her house. On the following morning the night watch reported that an old man was visiting the girlfriend in the evening and leaving at sunup. Joe asked if he could possibly be Johnson in disguise. "We'll check him out tomorrow morning." Joe warned, "Be careful, he's armed."

When Joe came to work in the morning, he was told that Johnson was in the lockup. "Put him in the interrogation room," he said. Then he asked if Johnson was armed. "Yup, he had a .38 in his belt and no carry permit." Johnson seemed very nervous as he sat. His eyes darted here and there. Joe asked if he was nervous. "You'd be nervous too if the cartel was on your ass, and they've got people everywhere. They know by now that I've been arrested." When he finished speaking, he dropped his can of soda in a trash bucket. Joe retrieved it and held it toward Johnson. "Do we use this, or will you give us a mouth swab to get your DNA?" Johnson nodded his head, "I'll give you a dozen swabs." Joe was quick to add, "You'll sign an agreement first." The swab was hand-carried to the forensic lab; a response was promised for that afternoon or tomorrow. Johnson was surprised because he believed there was no prior DNA record on file. He refused to say any more. Late that afternoon the lab chief called and told Joe that the swab matched the DNA on the cigarette butt. Joe ordered Johnson to the interrogation room again. "We have some more charges against you besides carrying a hidden gun. How about two charges of attempted murder?" Now tell me everything you know about those drugs." Johnson clamped his mouth shut, "Aint talking!" Joe opened the door to the room. "Well, I guess we can't hold you. I'll call the local paper and tell them we had to release you. You're free to go." Seconds passed. Johnson wanted to go, but couldn't. "You know damn well the cartel is waiting for me to walk out of here. They might have a sniper on the roof across the street. Put me back in a cell." Joe feigned surprise, "Innocent men don't belong in jail, you know that." Johnson asked what kind of a deal he could get if he talked. "I can't make any deal. That's up to the D.A." Johnson's voice was pleading, "You don't have to mention the two shots I fired at you," just to scare you, of course." Joe said it depended on what he was told. Johnson told everything. The cartel was shipping drugs on radio-controlled ultralights, about 400 pounds at a time. Because a radio signal carries only so far, there were men stationed along the route to continually guide the ultralights to off-loading sites. When Johnson tested his tracking device the day of delivery, it was out of power. He rushed home to recharge it, but when he returned the ultralight was nowhere in sight. He believed it had returned to its starting point. In fact, it was an hour or so late, and it nearly crashed. It dropped the package a good distance from where it was expected before turning about and returning to its starting point. Thus, the message went out by the cartel to get Johnson. It was believed that he stole it.

Joe notified his friend, the attorney general, of this information. Within a few hours, six men with hand-held radio devices were arrested as they awaited the arrival of ultralights, which the FBI later brought down with their payloads intact. In the meantime, Joe was gathering information on the woman whom Eugene Starr was accused of murdering. The ex-sheriff was located. He was working as a prison guard in Pennsylvania, and could not be connected to any wrongdoing.

As Dan was exiting headquarters after his shift, Joe motioned him to wait. Joe was going to invite him to dinner with him and his wife. Joe and Dan were the last to exit the building. As they walked down the six steps, shots rang out from high up, across the street. Dan dropped in pain to one knee, but regained his footing. Blood oozed from the wound in his thigh. Joe was attempting to stem the bleeding from a wound in his own right arm. Bullets left little concrete pock-marks where they struck the sidewalk. Some people had ducked behind the parked cars, but Joe and Dan ran toward the four-storied building and inside. Joe was in the lead as they painfully climbed the stairs to the roof. Joe exited the roof door and dropped to one knee. The sniper fired. The bullet went high and splintered the door. The sniper lowered his rifle, and then took more careful aim. Joe was lying prone, unable to raise his weapon. Dan saw the trouble Joe was having with his wounded arm. He fired, and killed the sniper with one shot. Joe had tried to pull his weapon with his bloodied arm, but found it was almost paralyzed. Joe tried to get to his feet, but couldn't. He fell to the roof. When Dan tried to do the same, he fell next to Joe. They viewed each other and burst out laughing as two deputies rushed to their aid and helped them to their feet. One deputy said, "Man, you two are nuts." He was smiling. This is when Joe knew he had been accepted as one of them.

At the hospital, they were put in beds next to each other. Joe said, "I was about to ask you to dinner at my place tonight before we were rudely interrupted," Dan joked, "Well, I can't make it tonight, you nether." Joe smiled and said, "I heard that they are keeping us for observation, and not releasing us until tomorrow. They have to check us thoroughly because those nasty buggers in the drug cartel sometimes dip their bullets in feces or poisons. They said that those bullets went through our flesh and muscles without hitting any bone. They're only being careful. Oh, I hear my wife talking out in the hall. Hi, Honey."

MIX OF STORIES

# THE TANKER
## WWII

My infantry company was just about to enter a city in Germany during WW11. The captain called to me and told me to scout out the area. Perhaps he believed the company could take a needed rest, but as soon as I left, artillery pinned down the company. I was far enough away to be safe from the shelling. I walked one block. As I crossed the street a sniper's bullet whizzed past my ear and smashed a window behind me. I took cover behind a concrete abutment about three feet high. There was a similar wall on the other side of the canal that ran down the street between them. I tried to spot the sniper, but all I could see was an open window with a dozen chair legs sticking out of it. I tried several times to get a shot at the sniper, but he was watching closely and sent a bullet my way each time I moved.

A bullet pinged off the top of the wall only a few inches from my head. I hunkered down believing my company would soon arrive and take care of that sniper. Five minutes passed. That is a long time when pinned down by a sniper. A million ways to evade the sniper rushed through my head, but I knew the sniper would win regardless of what I did. There was open ground surrounding my position. Every now and then the sniper sent a shot my way, letting me know he was still there. More minutes passed. Then I heard a tank squeaking and choking like a rhino in labor. I was cussing myself for not being more careful. It was approaching me. I was telling myself name, rank, and serial number, that's all the Nazis are entitled to. I could have kicked myself for the six notches on my rifle stock. If captured, I would be roughly treated, if not shot immediately. When I could see the tank, there was a big man in the conning tower, a big, black man. I told myself, "Nazis don't have black men in tanks." The tank stopped directly behind me. The big sergeant shouted, "Having trouble, soldier?" Hell, there I was, lying prone on the ground, trouble? "Yes, Sarge, there's a sniper in that second-floor window where all those chair legs are sticking out." He answered, "OK, don't go anywhere." The guy had a sense of humor; I had to smile. The tank chugged and revved up, belched black smoke then drove directly to that window, raised its 75mm gun, moved forward until the muzzle actually knocked those chair legs down and was inside the window, then it fired. I leaped up and ran to the tank. The sergeant smiled and asked, "Anything else I can do for you?"

I answered, "No, thanks, Sarge." Then he told me that my company was on another street. He knew because he had been in radio contact with my captain on a different matter. It took me a few minutes to locate my guys. When I did, I bragged about my hero to anyone who would listen. I am more than 96-years of age as I write this, and that tanker is still one of my wartime heroes. I'll never forget him. I cut those notches out of my rifle stock too.

MIX OF STORIES

# JOHNNY O

He was called Johnny O because no one could spell or pronounce his real name. He was seventeen years old and recently fired from his job as handy-boy at the JF Ranch. As one of the ranch hands told it, he was caught kissing the boss's daughter behind the barn. He collected his pay at the main house and said he was grateful that he had earned enough money from Mr. Randolph to buy his horse and tack. "I know there is nothing to be ashamed about, son, but you know if I don't fire you, it might just invite others to do worse." Mr. Randolph wasn't angry. "I understand, Mr. Randolph; you see, I was kissing her goodbye because I planned on leaving tomorrow for a full job and full pay. As Johnny was leaving the yard one of the men asked, "Where did you kiss her, Johnny boy?" Then he and the other men snickered. "On the forehead, you dumb ass; you know she's only thirteen." Johnny had his dad's pocket watch and $18.00 pay in his pocket, but that amount wouldn't last long. He needed a job. It cost 75 cents a day to keep his horse at the livery stable and a dollar a day at the Warner Hotel, and then meals were about a dollar a day. If he had a ranch job, he would earn a dollar a day and his meals would be free, so would a bed. This was better than many jobs in town that paid the going wage of 20 cents per hour for a ten-hour day.

Johnny rode through Silvertown and camped about six miles out toward the Raven Ranch. Mr. Raven had known Johnny's father since the uprising when they fought together until they were hospitalized and discharged. Even in these hard times, Johnny could not count on a job, even from a friend, but he would not be upset if he were turned down. He camped by a stream and heated his can of beans on a hot rock near the fire. When he was finished eating, he poured himself a cup of coffee. When he finished that, a man from a near-by camp called out to ask him if he had seen a wolf. Johnny told him he had not. Then the man cautioned him because a large gray wolf had been spotted near another camp. Johnny thanked the man, and went to sleep. He awoke later as the fire was just about burned out. He put some more wood on the embers and heard a sound in the brush, then saw a gray wolf limping away into the blackness. He wanted to help the animal, but would he be allowed to approach him?

No one knew that a pack of eight wolves was only a short distance upriver. The wolf Johnny saw had been the pack leader until he was injured. A sliver of wood projected from his left forepaw. The pack members had separated from him. This was a bad sign. It meant he was no longer considered the leader. Sometimes when this happens the sick or injured wolf would be attacked, sometimes killed, by the other wolves. The injured wolf made his way to the river. As he washed his injury, he heard the pack approaching. The wolves were on the hunt. The big wolf swam across the river and was carried downstream to Johnny's camp.

In the morning Johnny was rolling his bedroll when the wolf appeared again. The suddenness of the sight frightened him. He straightened up and drew his side arm. "You scared hell out of me, Chief," he said, "I thought you might be an Indian on the prowl. Hell, you're big enough to be two Apaches." The animal was listening, just sitting on his haunches, tilting his head, and listening. Johnny approached the animal with some left-over beans and bread on his tin plate. The animal growled and bared his teeth. Johnny carefully set the plate on the ground. As soon as the beans were eaten, Johnny cleaned the plate, packed everything on his horse, and rode off toward the Raven Ranch. All this time the animal just sat with tilted head as he watched Johnny then he followed the horse. Two hours later Johnny was speaking with Mr. Raven when an elderly man rode up and said there were about 20 head of cattle missing on the northwest range. Mr. Raven asked Johnny, "Think you could round them up? Do that and you've got yourself a job." Johnny was quite surprised, "I'll go right away, Mr. Raven." He galloped away. He knew he was at the right spot when he saw the fence was down. He could see the strayed cattle too. He rounded them up and patched the fence before returning to the ranch. He couldn't swear by it, but he thought and believed there was a gray wolf helping him round up the cattle. He reported to Mr. Raven that the cattle were back and the fence was repaired. "You've got your job just as I promised, but I don't need your wolf on my ranch. He scares hell out of me and Joe." Johnny was surprised, "You saw him?" Mr. Raven answered, "Hell, you can't but see him; he's a big fella. Now go wash up, it's almost time for supper, then go to the bunkhouse and pick out a pad."

Mr. Raven had a middle-aged Apache woman named Reena as his cook. She was an outcast because she had married a white man. Apaches would not accept her, neither would whites. Her husband had been killed while out hunting about six months ago. No one knew who killed him. She did not like many white men, but she liked Johnny immediately. He called her Miss Reena. When they were short of meat, Johnny could be counted on to bring in a deer, antelope or wild boar. Reena would hide the gamey taste of deer by grinding up pork with the venison. Johnny couldn't tell the venison from beef. One morning when Johnny was checking the fence line, he had the definite sense that he was being watched. When he saw Chief, he relaxed. However, he was also being stalked by a mountain lion. Chief ran alongside his horse for a time, then suddenly stopped and turned around. Chief faced the mountain lion that was following them. The lion backed up; Chief stepped forward. The lion stepped forward too, this was a challenge, but so did Chief step forward again. The lion suddenly turned and sauntered off. The game of "I dare you" was over. Johnny couldn't get off a shot because his horse was squirming too much. He wanted to hug Chief, but, of course, Chief would have none of it. Johnny shot an antelope that day and promised a nice slab of meat to Chief every day. He tried to get close to Chief several times, but had to back away.

## MIX OF STORIES

Although Chief stayed away from the ranch yard most of the time, Joe managed to rope him and tie him to the corral fence one day. Johnny found him that way and immediately approached him to undo the rope. This was the closest he had gotten to Chief, and there was no growling. When the rope was untied, the great wolf whined and buried his head in Johnny's armpit, then licked at Johnny's chin. This is when Johnny got a close glimpse of the sliver of wood sticking through Chief's forepaw. He had seen Chief pulling at the sliver with his teeth, but the animal couldn't pull it through his paw. Johnny saw a small side branch on the wood under the paw. It could not be pulled loose from above. Johnny quickly yanked it loose from below. Chief yelped, then licked his paw. Johnny had jumped backed after removing the large splinter, but Chief did not try to bite him. Johnny told Joe how Chief had acted that day, and told him there was no need to tie him up. Chief followed Johnny wherever he went. When Johnny camped out, Chief slept beside him. Johnny appreciated the company, but not the snoring. Johnny noticed that Chief's paw healed quickly. He stopped limping after four days. The pair enjoyed many days together, and Chief was fast becoming a good round-up wolf.

Then the military came to the ranch to sign up all able-bodied men. The uprising was in its second year, but had now caught up to Johnny. He was conscripted. When Chief was seen, he was caught and locked in the barn until Johnny left. Johnny turned and waved toward the barn as he rode away with General Lee's army sergeant and six other conscripts. He received little training and no weapon. When his unit faced the enemy, he was told to pick up a weapon or remove it from the hands of a dead soldier. In his first battle he was wounded in the arm, but remained with his unit. He was promoted to corporal during his next battle. When the war was in its third year Johnny had been wounded twice. Sergeant Johnny was sent home without his horse and penniless. He could no longer stand the rigors of war because of his wounds. He begged rides, but walked a long distance from Virginia. He had a chit for a train, but the track had been torn up. He found a horse where a battle had raged, and he stole clothing to replace the ragged gray uniform he burned. There were federal troops everywhere. He was also afoot again because he saw that this horse was branded with a US. He let it go free. He did not wish to be shot for stealing a federal horse.

It took almost three weeks to reach the Raven Ranch. He told Mr. Raven that his horse had been taken by the army, but he would buy one of Mr. Raven's if given the time to pay for it. He noted the man's white hair and grayed skin. "No, you don't," said the boss. "You go pick one, and a saddle and tack, just don't take mine or Joe's. I missed you, boy." Mr. Raven seemed to have aged a great deal in the time they were separated. Joe later told of Mr. Raven's sickness. "He's just now gotten back on his feet. I like that man, and we almost lost him. He's perked up a mite since you came back. I think you're good for him."

Johnny asked if he had seen Chief. "Nope, been AWOL since you left," Joe said. Johnny did not have to be told what to do. He began by checking the fencing. It was in bad shape, but Joe was getting old and wasn't up to all the repairs needed. Johnny would have to work a little harder. It was good that he was regaining his strength. He was hunting one day when he heard a wolf baying. He called out to Chief, and felt sad all day.

He rode to the north-west and saw some fence posts lying on the ground. On close examination he saw the hoof prints of shod horses among those of the cattle. They led toward the Towner Ranch which had been sold recently. He followed the tracks to a dead-end ravine with ropes closing the once open end. As he turned his horse to report his findings to Mr. Raven, a voice from behind some brush ordered him off his horse. He was roped and led to a barn where he was locked in. Then he heard voices outside the door, three of them. They were deciding what to do with him, and when they could move the 30 head of stolen cattle. Then they went to eat supper.

Johnny was tied hand and foot. He edged against a wall and was able to get to his feet and look through a window opening in which there was no window, but he couldn't climb that high. He searched the barn for something to cut his bonds. There was nothing in sight. He heard rustling at the front door. The door shook. He prepared to face his captors, but the sound moved to the side of the barn. Now it was a sniffing and grunting sound. He believed it could be wild boars that roamed the area. Suddenly, a large body came hurtling through the window opening. It was Chief. He landed on his feet and ran to Johnny, rubbing against his legs. Johnny sat on the floor. Chief chewed at the rope binding his feet. Johnny turned so Chief would see his tied hands. Then Chief tore into the rope shredding it, and did the same with the rope on his feet. Johnny hugged his large friend. "We've got to get out of here now, my big friend." The doors were locked from the outside. Johnny tried pushing against the wall boards, but they would not give. He moved a wooden crate to the window and piled hay atop and around it. It was a simple matter to help Chief and himself through that window opening, Once outside, he and Chief ran to the Raven Ranch. He told Joe what had happened. Joe saddled his horse and rode to town for the sheriff. Within an hour it was all settled. Mr. Raven had his cattle, and Johnny retrieved his horse and Chief.

Mr. Raven was only in his early fifties when he died. A post mortem examination showed that a small piece of shrapnel in his chest had worked into his heart. He had left a will with his attorney. Johnny and Joe stayed at the ranch in hopes that the new owner would keep them on. The attorney drove to the ranch in his new $65.00 Fancy Stanhope buggy and called to the two men to follow him into the house. He sat them down at the table in the living room. "Johnny, you are the new owner of the Raven Ranch. I know it's a surprise. It seems that Mr. Raven took a liking to you. Joe, he left you all the cattle, 72 head I believe. I'll leave these papers for you to sign. Among them is one that combines the ranch and the cattle, making you co-owners, or partners." Johnny and Joe looked at each other, and shook hands. Johnny said, "And you move into the house too partner." Joe was all smiles. "Gladly, Johnny. It gets mighty cold in the bunkhouse on some nights." Before he left the house, the lawyer said, "Mr. Raven had a son who died at age seven from blood poisoning, He had cut his ankle on barbed wire, if I recall rightly. He told me how much Johnny resembled his son, and then he cried for not taking his son to a doctor. He had no family except you two." As he rose to his feet, the attorney dropped a bankbook on the table. "He had a little over $1,000 in the bank. It now belongs to you two. I hope you use it wisely."

MIX OF STORIES

# JASON

Jason's first official duty as Deputy US Marshal was displayed before the folks of Milltown in two propped up coffins. Willie and James McGuire were silent proof of Jason's prowess with a .45. The Milltown Eagle claimed the corpses were compliments of Jason Connor. Following this was the story of how the men met their end. The story embarrassed Jason. It tended to point him out as a role model and hero. He did not believe he was either one. He was a young man, only 23 when appointed to his position. The men in the coffins were road agents and murderers. Jason was a passenger on the M and R stage when the men held it up. They ordered the driver to halt, then to toss down the box of silver ingots and the mail. They shot John Mallory, who was riding shotgun beside the driver, but had no chance to use his weapon. When they shot at John, they did not see Jason. He shot and killed both thieves, then rushed John to Doctor Hastings in time to save his arm and his life. Jason stayed off the street as much as he could. Somehow it seemed to him to be improper to be thanked for killing others. He rose later in the day and visited the Stellar Saloon. He played penny-ante poker and he was a very good player. While there, he actually drank more coffee than liquor.

The Milltown Eagle had a story on page one that took the people's minds off Jason. It was a story of March 1, 1867. It read: "We now have 37 states in this union with the addition of Nebraska. Our great flag will have to be amended again to depict 37 stars." Because this became the topic of conversation, Jason was out of the limelight." "Someone should write a song about us being 37 in '67," the mayor offered. On the corner of Lee and Main Street was the Westwood Gun Shop. The owner was a young man named Henry. He sold, built and rebuilt and repaired guns of all makes and types. Jason's .45 needed some work to take the free play out of the trigger housing, so he visited the shop. Behind the counter was a young woman. Jason was pleasantly surprised. "May I help you?" Her voice was very pleasant. "Yes ma'am," he answered as he removed the bullets from his weapon. He handed her the gun and watched as she held it carefully and squeezed the trigger several times. "My brother can fix it, but he's out of town today. I'll lend you a good weapon so you can be armed. Your weapon has been used quite often, that's why there's play in the trigger. I suppose you practiced a great deal. We have a good selection of weapons to choose from. Our prices range from $2.98 up to $20.00 for our best." She leaned over the counter as she handed the loaner to Jason. Her hand was soft and warm on his. "So, you're Henry's sister?" he asked. "I just came in on the stage yesterday. I was fearful of the trip because I had heard so much about road agents. Our father had been sick for some time and he died last week. I was winding up the sale of his business and our home and preparing to come here. He was a weapons man too. I learned the trade from him and my uncle. Your gun needs a part replaced. Don't worry, if we don't have the part in stock, Henry and the blacksmith can make it." Fifteen minutes later Jason exited the shop smiling.

The sheriff was in the saloon when Jason entered. "Well, you look quite happy so early in the day," said the sheriff with a smile. Jason said, "I just met Henry's sister. She's a pretty girl, and she handles a gun like a man." The sheriff smiled, "She ought to; I taught her; well, my brother and I taught her." Jason was surprised, "She's my niece," the sheriff said. "It was my brother who died last week. I helped convince her to move out here." "I'm happy you did Jason said, "I like that lady." Jason ordered a beer and sat at a table. The sheriff remained at the bar. Just as Jason sat down, a young man of about 19 years of age entered the saloon. He saw the badge on the marshal and walked to his table. He sneered as he said, "I hear you're pretty slick with your gun, Marshal." Jason said, "Don't believe everything you hear, young man." The young man tried to sound tough, "I come here to find out just how slick you are." Jason pointed to the doorway, "I saw you when you came through that door. I figured you for a snot-nosed kid trying to make a name for himself. I have a gun under the table pointed directly at your manhood and I'm itching to pull the trigger if you make the wrong move." The young man removed his hand from the butt of his .44, and held it at his side. The sheriff stepped forward and disarmed him, then said, "I guess you didn't want to sit to pee for the rest of your days, Kid." At that moment Jason withdrew his empty hand from under the table. Some of the men laughed. The sheriff said, "If the marshal didn't shoot you, I would have. Consider yourself lucky, and don't try it again." The young man whined, "I need my gun, Sheriff," The sheriff said, "Sure, Kid, here," as he handed back the gun. The man walked toward the door, then hesitated and turned toward the sheriff, resting his hand on the butt of his pistol. The sheriff said, "Don't plan on anything, Kid. I emptied your pistol. Now, get the hell and gone before I toss your pitiful ass in jail for felony stupidity." The man hurried out.

Jason had lunch at the saloon then returned to the gun shop. "Hello, Janice," he said as he walked to the counter. "Has Henry returned yet?" She smiled, "Not yet, Mr.....er... Jason. We had the right piece in stock for your gun, however, and I fixed it. Try it." He took the weapon and first checked to ensure it was empty before squeezing the trigger several times. "There's no play in it now…wonderful." He reached into his pocket and asked, "How much is it?" She replied, "It's 18 cents. I know it sounds expensive, but that's because it is so difficult to find the proper parts and metals." Jason was more interested in her voice than in the price. He handed her the money then said, "There's a dance Saturday night. Would it be all right if I…? I mean, if you accompanied me there?" She averted her eyes and said, "We hardly know each other. I'll ask Henry and give you my answer tomorrow."

# MIX OF STORIES

Jason left the shop with a smile on his face until he looked up to see the young man who accosted him earlier. Jason continued loading his pistol. The young man had a loaded .44 aimed at him. "I'll wait until you holster your piece Marshal, then we can start off even." Jason holstered his weapon. "Looks like I get another chance at the slick marshal," the man said as he smiled. Jason asked, "Where do we send the body? Can I at least have your last name, for the record, you know" The young man shook his head and said, "My name is Bill Henderson, but you won't be writin' up no death certificate for me." Jason smiled, "We'll put on your grave marker, 'He didn't like the law.'" The young man said, "I'm going to kill you whether you draw or not, marshal. One, two, three..." One shot was heard, a gun thumped into the dirt street, and the young man fell to a sitting position, then rolled to his side. He was dead. Janice came to the door of the gun shop, put her hand to her mouth and shut the door.

A crowd of people had seen and heard what happened. No one was taking Jason's side. He had done what he could to avoid bloodshed, but the young man was hell-bent to try him. The people saw it as a gun-bully killing a young kid. Janice opened the shop door again. Jason turned to face her. His voice was almost pleading. "I tried to stop him, Janice. I didn't want to kill him." Someone in the crowd yelled, "You didn't have to kill him." Jason answered, "When someone is hell-bent on killing, you don't just wound him. By feeling sorry, you put your life on the line, then and for later. If you can take the time, just look at the door behind me. You'll see where his bullet hit." "Murderer," someone shouted. "Are you going to put his body on display next to the other two you killed?" Jason knew that to argue was futile. He went to his office, then opened the door as someone shouted, "The bank's been robbed." Someone else shouted, "Murder!" Jason hurried to the bank and pushed the people aside to enter. The bank owner told him that three horses ridden by two men had been tied up outside the bank. "Those two men robbed the bank and left one horse still tied to the rail when they rode away." Jason saddled up and rode after them. He lost the trail about two miles out of town, and then he backtracked. The tracks took off to the right of the road. He turned his horse. Ahead of him was a grove of trees and a shack that was built in a hollow, invisible from the road. It was open ground from the road to the shack, however. He reined his horse to the left and made a wide arc to get behind that grove of trees, and then he tied his horse to a tree and sat on the ground with his back to a tree. There were still 100-feet of clearing between him and the shack. Someone was inside and two horses were tied up in back of the shack. Jason waited.

A small canoe of a moon rose as the sun set. He needed darkness to sneak up on the men. He was prepared to make his move when the back door opened and two men walked to their horses. They unsaddled and tethered them, then returned to the house. Jason made his move to the front door. He turned the knob slowly, swung the door open and shouted, "Raise your hands." He saw the money bag on the table and two piles of money. One of the men reached for his gun. Jason shot him in the arm. He had no trouble getting the men to jail.

The sheriff questioned the men. They were brothers. Their name was Henderson, the same as the young man who was shot earlier. When the facts were brought out, it was learned that the men had sent young Henderson to engage the marshal, just keep him busy, kill him if he had to, while they robbed the bank, then they would ride to him with his horse for their getaway. But when the kid didn't show up, they were dividing the money two ways. Jason was sickened by the confession. One of the men was the kid's father, the other was his uncle. Jason went to the saloon. He was hungry. He had no lunch or supper. As he crossed the street several people thanked him. One called him a hero. He walked on. The sheriff was in the saloon. He asked Jason, "Well, what is it, are you a hero or villain this hour?" Jason shrugged his shoulders and answered, "Don't rightly know." The sheriff put his hand on Jason's shoulder and said, "I spoke with my niece and gave my consent for her to go with you to the dance." Jason grimaced and said, "I'm not sure I'll be going." The sheriff laughed. "We still have two days to go."

MIX OF STORIES

# TOM BAKER

Tom Baker was 17. His father was sending him to college in Yuma because his school teacher said she was not authorized to teach college courses. When the time came, Tom rode his horse into Overton, leaving it at the livery stable. Tom's father was in a wheelchair since he was gored by a bull two years earlier, so the ranch wrangler would pick up the horse in the morning. Tom had a room at the Overton Hotel until the morning, and then he would board the stagecoach for Yuma. It was now six in the evening. Tom went to the restaurant and sat at the only empty table. As he sat, five men entered the room, and sat at his table. "You don't mind, do you kid? "Tom answered, "No." The man said he would buy Tom's supper as appreciation for allowing them to sit at his table. "Sure," Tom answered. The men ate a small meal and drank their coffee. They paid the bill and to Tom's surprise, dropped money on the table for him. It amounted to $14.00. He pocketed the money and was somehow glad that the men had left. There was something about them…

He had just finished his coffee when the sheriff approached him and sat at his table. "Who was sitting here with you?" Jim was puzzled. He answered, "I don't know their names except for Jim. He seemed to be the spokesman." The sheriff then asked, "Where did they go?" The question seemed to be accusatory. "They didn't tell me; why would they?" The sheriff looked angry, "I'll ask the questions. Are they holing up around here?" Tom tried to stand, but was pushed back into his chair. He said, "How would I know their plans? I never saw them before." The sheriff smiled, "You're under arrest." Tom looked at the faces of the sheriff's men and said, "But I didn't do anything." The sheriff then told Tom what his gang did. "They beat your father until he told them where he hid his money. They stole that, and then came here to talk about your next job. Where's that going to be? Empty your pockets." Tom did so. The sheriff smiled. "See this money with ink stains? That came from your father. He said he splattered ink on his money when giving it to the thieves." Tom was surprised. He said, "The men gave me that money." The sheriff nodded, "Of course they did, Kid" Although Tom asked the sheriff to contact his father, no news came from the ranch. He went to trial two days later. Neither his father nor anyone else from the ranch was present until after the trial. Frank, his father's wrangler, was there when Tom was led back to the jail. He whispered to Tom," The sheriff made you out as one of the thieves, or else you'd be free." "They gave me twenty years. I would never have done that to my dad."

In his sixth year at Yuma penitentiary, he saw one of the thieves, who was also a prisoner. The man was surprised to see Tom. He said, "I thought you were a good kid." Tom told him, "I was sent here for the crime you committed against my father; they gave me 20-years." The men spoke for a long time. The man's name was Sam. He promised to do what he could to set it right, but he had only two weeks before going to the gallows. He wrote to the warden and to the Territorial Marshal's Office. The warden did nothing, but the marshal put a deputy on the case, a man named Andy Swenson. He spoke with Tom and agreed that Tom was dealt from a crooked deck. Andy also visited the Baker ranch and reported that Mr. Baker was sick. There was only one person at the restaurant who recalled the incident. The dishwasher knew Tom and knew the men at his table were strangers to him. He also had overheard Jim introducing the others. He said the man's name was Jim. The man Tom recently met, named Sam, had an attempt made on his life. A wire was put around Sam's neck from behind. Tom saw this and punched the would-be killer in the kidney. The man yelped, then he couldn't catch his breath. A guard had also seen the attempted killing. Sam later talked, telling the warden that Tom was innocent of any crime. The would-be assailant owed the real thieves $1,000.00 which they would forgive if he killed Sam. After Andy questioned the man, he took all his information to the Territorial Judge who ordered that Tom be released immediately.

Two hours after Sam went to the gallows Tom was released. He was given his money, but that was not enough to buy a horse. He walked most of the way to his father's ranch. Six years had brought changes to the awkward kid who left when he was 17. He was now 6 feet and 2 inches tall and about 210 pounds, but Frank and the cook recognized him. He asked, "Where's Dad?" Frank grimaced as he asked, "Nobody told you?" "Told me what?" Tom was puzzled, Frank said, "Mr. Baker died two days ago, Tom." "From what?" Frank did not know, and said, "The doc didn't rightly know either." Tom was deeply saddened by this news. "Is my horse in the corral?" Frank said, "We kept her in good shape. Your father wanted it that way." Emma, the cook, said, "We are very sorry about your father." Tom said, "I'm going to California and make a fresh start." Frank asked. "What shall we do with the ranch? You are now the owner." Tom looked surprised, "You mean, Dad didn't change his will.?" Frank said, "No, he never meant to. He somewhat believed the sheriff, but then someone by the name of Andy Swenson spoke to him and said he was trying to free you." Emma asked Tom to come to the kitchen, "I'll fix you a good meal. You look so tired," Tom told her, he was very mixed up right now, and too tired to travel anywhere. "I've just about worn out my boots too. I'll start out after the burial, maybe."

The burial was a sad affair. Tom said his final good- bye and Emma cried into her handkerchief. At the ranch, Tom noticed the absence of his father's coin collection. He asked Frank about it and was told that it was stolen along with $700.00 his father had from the sale of cattle. Tom was remembering that his dad loved his coin collection. "He told me he started collecting during the war. He said he had been offered $1,000.00' for the coins years ago. I'm going to get that coin collection and the money back. I'll leave in the morning. I was told in prison that the gang liked a place in Mexico called Cananea."

He was on his way at sunrise with some of Emma's fried chicken. He felt rested and had practiced his draw and aim until he was satisfied. He bedded down the first night on the north bank of the Rio Grande. In the morning he forded the river and rode south to Cananea. At the cantina he learned that the gang had been there, but returned to the north because the federales were hunting them. Two days later he had tracked the four men to Bisbee. He learned there that the gang was called the Blanding Gang, and they had been there, but had left. Tom went to his hotel room at nine and slept until seven in the morning. He had breakfast at a restaurant near his hotel where he ordered a big meal. As he carried his coffee to a table, he almost dropped it. Seated at a table was the Blanding gang. He pulled a chair over to their table and sat down. The leader smiled. "Who the hell are you?" Tom acted surprised, "You don't remember me? Sam remembered me, but only for a short time before he was hanged. I'm the kid who spent six years in the pen for your crime, and none of you had the guts to tell the truth, to free me." One of the men asked, "So, what do you want from us?" Tom told them he wanted his dad's $700.00 plus the coin collection he loved and worked on for years. The leader said, "Well, we aint got the coins. We sold them to someone named Hastings. He owns a ranch hereabouts. As for the money, yeah, we have more than that, but none of it is for you." Tom mulled this over before saying, "Looks like I'll have to earn it the hard way." The leader then said, "Shouldn't be that hard, kid. We'll be at the saloon later. If you want to, come and take it. We got $1,300.00 for those coins." Tom said, "I'm a peaceful man, but if I get the urge, Molly hide the kitten!"

Tom returned to his own table and finished his meal as though nothing had intervened. In the morning he rode to the Hastings ranch. His knock on the door was answered by an elderly man. Tom introduced himself. Mr. Hastings smiled and led Tom into the house. "So, you're John's boy. I held you in my arms when you were a few days old. Haven't seen you since you started school. Your father and I served together in the war you know. He was a lieutenant first grade; I was a second grade. We were wounded on the same day and for the second time. Come, sit down. I am Bill Hastings How is John?" Now Tom looked sad as he said, "He died recently." Hastings faced away from Tom as he wiped his eyes on his kerchief. "I'm very sorry to hear that." Tom waited a minute before he said, "I actually came here on a delicate matter. Dad's coin collection was stolen." Mr. Hastings looked angry, "So that's where they came from. Those bastards stole them and sold them to me. When you leave, you'll take those coins with you. I will not have stolen goods in my house." Tom shook his head, "No sir. Dad would want you to keep them. Now you don't have stolen goods Dad made you a gift of them." Mr. Hastings again wiped his eyes on his kerchief as he said, "I can't believe that John is gone." They had coffee, and Tom left before it got dark.

Tom arrived back in Bisbee at sundown, dismounted at the saloon and placed his gun belt in his saddlebag. He was thirsty so he ordered a glass of water and a shot of whiskey, then he carried them to the table where the four gang members sat. He pulled up a chair and sat down. "Jim, you and your gang of thieves don't have to worry about owing me my dad's coin collection." Jim smiled and said, "Well, that certainly relieves my mind." Tom told him that he was not quite off the hook yet, "You still owe me the $700.00 you stole from a cripple." In mock pity Jim said, "Oh, we are so sorry about that." One of the thieves stood with his hand on the butt of his pistol. Tom said, "Is this the extent of your bravery? I'm not armed. He stood and showed the men he was unarmed, then downed the last of his drink and went to his hotel room as he placed a hand over his heart to feel his pulse slowing.

Sometime after midnight he heard a noise from the open porch outside his window. He had been lying on the floor expecting something like this. Now he sat up, his back against the wall, in darkness. He watched the window. A shadow appeared. The window opened wide. One leg came into the room followed by a man aiming a gun at the bed. The man fired, so did Tom. The man fell heavily to the floor. Tom searched him and pocketed the $200.00 he found. Later, Tom played the innocent victim when the sheriff questioned him. In the morning he ate breakfast in the restaurant then walked to the saloon. He was not surprised to find three of the gang members seated at a table. Tom carried his beer to the table and sat down. One of the gang said, "One of our friends left town last night." Tom smiled and said, "I know. He gave me $200.00 before he left. That means you owe me only $500.00. He couldn't spend the money in Hell anyway. Oh, it isn't really the money I'm after, It's the principle. My dad worked hard for everything he had and I promised to return what was stolen, and I will." Jim smiled and said, "I have a principle too, what's mine is mine." Tom looked him in the eye and said, "Yes, but even you can't spend that in Hell." Tom stood, prepared to draw his weapon if necessary. No one stood against him. He pointed to the leader named Jim, and said, "You owe me $500.00," as he walked to the door. Jim said, "We're getting tired of you, kid."

Tom left the saloon and went to the general store. He needed a box of ammo. On entering, he noticed cans of food, beans, and peaches. He had heard of peaches, but had never eaten one. He asked the clerk for a can, then hefted it and exclaimed, "What do you know about that?" The clerk asked, "About what?" Tom smiled for the first time in days, "I'm sorry, Miss. I guess I was talking to this can of peaches." She smiled and said, "Oh yes. They were originally made for the army. They're 16 cents per can, but they come with an opener. Did you want one?" He was hungry. He said, "Yes. Hey, why didn't I see you before? You're pretty." The young woman smiled and said, "They're still 16 cents." He smiled with her. She asked if he lived in Bisbee. He told her he lived near Overton. They talked for nearly an hour. Tom was in love. She was a sweet girl from an orphanage. She was working at the store, but a man from the orphanage was collecting most of her salary. She was no more than an indentured servant. She slept in the back of the shop and was given one meal per day. She was locked in the shop through the night. She learned much about Tom also. They made plans for her to come to his ranch for a sort of vacation. Her name was June Kelly. "I have to get back to work before Mr. Cobart finds me lollygagging."

Tom was walking to the livery stable when the sheriff stopped him and told him there was a $600.00 reward for the man he killed in his hotel room, but it would take a few days for the papers to come. Tom felt that a heavy load had been lifted from his mind.

## MIX OF STORIES

His spirits were raised and he felt free. He shared all this with June, and then went to the saloon to sort of celebrate his freedom. A shadow moved across his table as three men approached and sat down. Jim said, "So the sheriff told you about the bounty for Henry?" Tom said, "He sure did. And that means my business with you is done." Jim asked, "You mean, the feud is over?" Tom said, "Yep." Jim smiled and said, "We always liked you, kid. Go home to your ranch and have a happy life." Tom stayed the few days, waiting for his money and talking June into going with him to his ranch. If she didn't like it there, she could leave with $100.00. toward a fresh start. The papers finally came in the mail. Tom and June met the following morning at the general store. He brought a horse for her. After tying her carpetbag behind her saddle, they set off. They were only two miles out of the city when a shot broke the silence. Tom's horse fell dead with a bullet just behind her eye. He jumped from the saddle and led June and her horse behind the protection of some boulders. June asked, "Who would do such a thing?" Tom told her that the feud isn't over yet. He said to be very careful because there are three men out there and they don't care if you're a man or a woman. "They're after the money I have." Another shot kicked up flakes of stone near June. Tom saw the flash from the rifle, but needed a better firing position. He stayed hidden as he climbed higher in the rocks. He saw the flash again, and shot at it. A body fell to the ground as a shot came from another position. He heard the "pop" when a bullet came close to his ear. He went back into the shadows, catching his breath and then climbing higher until he could see the top of the men's heads. A shot sent slivers of stone through the air four feet from him. He saw the smoke and fired at it. A man yelled in pain and surprise, "Son of a…" One of the men was gone from his view. Now he concentrated on the one remaining man, waiting for him to rise up and fire. He aimed his pistol at the spot. He saw the man stir and rise up. He fired twice and waited. "You got me, kid. It aint too bad, but you broke my arm. It hurts like hell. Now what? I can't even hold my pistol." Tom

stepped into the open and answered, "Your brothers are dead. You get on your horse and don't ever let me see you again, because I'll kill you on sight." Jim said, "Gee, and I thought the feud was over." His humor was meant to put Tom off guard, but he walked from behind a boulder holding a pistol in each hand. Tom was alert. He fired twice. Jim looked surprised as he fell dead. Tom and June rode double back to Bisbee because his cousin's horses were nowhere in sight. They set out for his ranch a bit later than expected. June loved the ranch, not only then, but for the next 67-years.

# WWII
## THE PLANE

My company was taken off the front line to a safer area for a 48-hour rest. On the following morning Captain Mike called me to his tent. He said, "Mac, the British have a plane down not far from here. What I could make out from the message is that it contains some new secret, scientific apparatus that must not fall in the Nazi's hands. Go over there and guard that plane. The pilot has already been taken from it. He's in the hospital. Don't you get too close to the plane either." I answered, "Yes sir."

I reached the downed plane within five minutes. It was a one-seater, smaller than I had imagined. It had nosed into the dirt just off a tarred road. I stayed away from the plane as captain Mike had warned. Hell, maybe jarring the plane would cause it to blow up. I could not permit anyone to go near the plane. It looked so out–of-place with its nose in the ground and its tail sticking in the air at 45 degrees. It reminded me of a dead eagle I had seen. I could see almost a mile in any direction, it was all open grassland. Nobody could approach without being seen.

The plane was a dirty orange color. It really stuck out like a wart on my uncle's nose. I wondered how far the Nazis would go to get their hands on this secret plane. I also wondered why the captain would trust me to do this job and others. My drill sergeant back in the states believed I was a screw-up. Maybe that's written somewhere in my records. I thought that my captain was testing me. I straightened up and began pacing back and forth, rifle at the ready. Time passed. No one came near the plane. It was getting dark and I had already missed supper. I was hungry. I hadn't seen a soul in over four hours. Did everyone forget me? Then I saw one of my buddies in the distance and two British officers were walking toward me. My buddy shouted and waved his arm, "Come on, they're holding supper for you." One of the British officers said he would take charge of the plane. He also told me that I was invited to sit in the officer's mess hall. They had a German chef serving them, despite the fact that there was a standing rule of Non-Fraternization with Germans. The officers had already eaten, so I ate alone. I had never seen nor tasted such a wonderful meal complete with several choices of desserts.

# WWII
## THE BRITISH

To prepare for the big push into Germany, my entire division, in fact, the whole $9^{th}$ Army was turned over to the British General, Bernard Montgomery. He was also leading the British and Canadian armies. I never considered myself a hero or even very brave, but I served with heroes and very brave men, English and American. I guess I just tried to keep up with them. I knew men who were wounded, but would say nothing about it to the sergeant for fear of being left behind. Many of us were hit in the legs with chips of concrete when a sniper's bullets hit the sidewalk near us. No one mentioned it. We would see others cleaning up the blood when they thought no one was watching. I was hit in my right hand with a piece of shrapnel from a sniper bullet when we entered Germany. I put three stitches into the wound to stop the bleeding. I couldn't believe how tough the human skin is to get a sewing needle through it. A British soldier then used the kit to sew up a gash in his leg. We used black thread from a German sewing kit. It was all we could find. We didn't report the injuries for fear of being separated from our friends.

One night in a foxhole I offered to rub my buddy's feet. He said he could not feel them. He took off his boot and I could see the blackened toes, and cold, crinkly skin on his foot (trench foot). I carefully tried to rub some life into it, but the skin came off in my hand and rolled up. I told the first sergeant about him despite his protests. He was taken off the front line and driven back to a hospital. As Captain Mike said, "We didn't come here for medals." Those I served with are the true heroes.

# EDWARD MCCARTHY

# THE PEERS

Bob Cassidy was with a group of workers at a restaurant. They were saying farewell to a fellow worker who was retiring. Bob was a minor owner in the company, but was requested to be present. All the workers liked him. During the evening a worker told the group that he had sent his DNA to a company that will tell you your heritage. Well, he discovered he was mostly North American, but 22-percent Italian. He was very surprised. This experience appealed to Bob. He wondered if there were any surprises in store if he sent in his DNA. He started the process. Two weeks later he received a reply from the W-A-I-F LABORATORY (Where Am I from?). The letter stated that his submission was contaminated. It told him what precautions to take when resubmitting. Bob followed the suggestions. Again, his submission was rejected. Bob did a bit of cursing under his breath and tried to forget about it.

Three days later he received a letter from a Judge William Carey. "What the hell did I do now?" he muttered before opening it. The letter was a cordial invitation to dinner at the Judge's home. Bob was at a loss as to why he was invited. He drove to the judge's home and noticed several other cars parked in the judge's yard. Before he could ring the doorbell, a servant opened the door and led Bob to a large room. Bob counted five men in the room. One of the men separated himself from the others and shook his hand, "I am William Cary. I sent you a letter and will soon explain the reason. We must keep this and any future meetings top secret. It may be a matter of life and death for us. Let me tell you why: All the people in this house, excluding me, but including my servant, have an American heritage that goes back only to 1933! No, men, I am not crazy. I was a member of a flight from a planet called Maris-Four. Our ship began to break up high over Nevada. Twenty men made it to an escape module. I found four children in another escape module and joined them to protect them as best I could with all the blankets I could find. The other module broke up thousands of miles over Earth, it bounced off the layer of heavy air, and skipped off into space. My module entered the heavy layer at a better angle and continued to plummet to Earth. The parachutes deployed and we settled to Earth just as the module broke apart. The children lived. I am 162-years old and have many more years to live. You men will not live as long as I because you are three or four generations away from Maris-Four. You are the descendants of those four children. With each passing generation the life span of your descendants will shorten to eventually match that of other

# MIX OF STORIES

Earth people. In time, they will be true Earthlings." The men in the room looked from one to the other. What they heard was unbelievable.

"We Marists also have the special ability to clone, we can look like anyone we wish. I taught the Maris children to clone into Earth beings and to act like Earth beings. They were your original Earth parents and did not exactly look like Earth people. Each of you has sent in your DNA samples to WAIF, and they were all said to be contaminated, right?" The men answered with a nod or a "yes." "The samples you sent in were not contaminated. You sent in a Maris-Four DNA! Resubmit your DNA, but only after telling it to be human." The men looked from one to the others with furrowed brows. The judge walked to the large table and put some water into a glass. "Jim, would you come closer, please?" Jim did so. "Now, tell this water to turn red." The men laughed. "Turn red," Jim said as his brow wrinkled into unvoiced questions. The water did not turn red. "Now, Jim, please be serious and want it to turn red." The men could see that the Judge was serious. Jim said, "Turn red!" The men looked from one stunned face to another as they saw the water turn red. Bob asked, "What does this mean?" The judge looked serious, "It means we have this ability. We can also make it taste like lemonade or whiskey. It really is not lemonade or whiskey; it is merely apparent. Try your powers at home, but not in the presence of another person. What goes on here must stay here. There is a group of people who knows something about us and has already murdered some of us. We call each other Peers, and there are perhaps fewer than 100 of us throughout the world. Non-Peers are true Earth people. Now, let's eat, I'm famished."

When Bob went home that night, he was anxious to learn what powers he had, if any. He turned water red. He tasted wine when drinking water. He went to a large mirror and cloned into several people. He tried to magically clean his dishes, but that didn't work. He couldn't move things with his mind either. He also sent another sample of his DNA for a reading, after telling it to be human. The results came back a week later; he was informed that he was mostly North American, with a smattering of German and French inheritance. He had a lot to mull over.

A few days later, Ann Marsh, who worked in the billing dept. of his company, asked to see him. She was a pretty girl. Bob remembered her from the day he hired her. She had heard about the trouble Bob had in getting a DNA reading. She had sent in two samples and both were said to be contaminated. What did he do to make his DNA acceptable? She had asked. "To be truthful, Ann, I told my sample to be normal just before I mailed it." "Mine was a legitimate question Mr. Cassidy; your answer seems to make a joke of it." She looked like she could burst out crying as she rose from her chair. "Please Ann, believe me. It is no joke. I will prove it to you if you'll allow me, but not here. Will you be my guest for dinner tonight?" "I-I'm not sure if you are toying with me or not." Bob reassured her that he was not toying with her. She took a few seconds before answering, "I...I guess it's ok."

They met in the lobby of the Jefferson Hotel and were ushered to a table. When they ordered, Bob told her how he felt when she was near. "I feel very safe and close and comfortable. I believe you are a Peer. Oh, you don't know what I'm talking about. Allow me to explain" and he did. Ann did not believe him until she turned her glass of water into sherry wine. On the following night he took her to the Judge's house. She was fully convinced after speaking with him. She was also fearful of those who would harm her and other Peers. The judge had explained that when one Peer comes into contact with another, both are overwhelmed with a feeling of safety and comfort. There was more than this type of feeling growing in the minds of Bob and Ann. The judge also told them that another facet of life for Peers was the fact that they could never give away another Peer.

In the afternoon of the following day, Bob received a phone call from Jim. "What's up, Jim?" Jim answered, "I called Phil, you know, the detective Peer we met? Well, he was out on a case. Someone's been following me! I sent my wife and kids to her brother in Virginia, Then, this morning I noticed a dark spot under my car. Someone had cut the brake lines," Bob said, "Take a cab to the Jefferson Hotel. I'll meet you near the bottom of the entrance ramp." After a time, a taxi came down the ramp and stopped. Bob called to Jim, who then entered Bob's car and ducked down. "Were you followed?" Jim whispered, "Yes. They were right behind me, didn't seem to mind if I knew it or not." Bob punched in Phil's number on his cell phone. Phil answered and Bob told him what was going on. Bill whispered, "They're coming down the ramp now." Phil said, "I heard that. Hold on; I'll be right there." The men waited but a short time. Phil arrived

with two uniformed police. Jim pointed to the strange men in a red car. The police told the two men to exit their car, then patted them down and took two weapons from them. They arrested the men and took them away.

Bob had a license to carry a gun because he often carried large sums of company money to the bank. Now he began to carry his .38 revolver every day. Phil called Bob on the following morning and told him not to worry anymore about those two men. "We let them go. Later they went fishing in their boat and it somehow exploded, killing them and another member of the Alien Hunters. The newspaper called the victims members of an off-beat, screwy club." Bob could tell from Phil's language that he knew more about the explosion than he was willing to say.

Bob left the office the following evening and was driving to a restaurant when he spotted a car behind him. It had been behind him for the last few blocks despite the many turns he had taken. Bob drove to a men's-wear store and entered the shop. He went directly to an empty dressing room. He watched himself in the large mirror as he cloned his face into a different one. Then he made himself four inches taller and twenty pounds more muscular. He then cloned his clothing into a police uniform and exited the store. The two men who had followed him were waiting. "You men are loitering," he said in his best policeman voice. He patted down the men and took their semiautomatic weapons, and then he called Phil. "Lieutenant, I've got two men who were following another man. Now they're loitering. Me? I'm Officer Peer, New York City Police Department. OK sir, I'll wait." It took ten minutes, but Phil finally arrived with a uniformed officer who took the two men and their weapons to headquarters Phil said, "I'll call you." Phil phoned Bob the following day and told him that he let the men go free, but when he tried to locate them for a court appearance they had mysteriously disappeared. "They'll bother you no

# MIX OF STORIES

more, my friend." Again, Bob was sure that Phil knew a lot more than he was saying, and he was also sure that the two men were dead.

While making his morning coffee, Bob answered his phone. It was Phil. "What the hell happened now Phil?" "Well, I've been trying to locate Jim for two days. Some kids found a body this morning in a vacant lot in South Brooklyn: it was Jim. He had been beaten badly and shot in the head. There was also a needle puncture in his arm; now the sons of bitches have his DNA to study or else they poisoned him, maybe both. There was no sign of a struggle at the scene. I'm working on it as fast as I can; now we're all in danger. No need to tell you to be careful. I am so tired of being on the defense. Notify Ann, will you?" Bob phoned and told Ann what had happened. She said she was scared, could she stay with him for a while? "OK, be there in ten minutes," she said. He made some coffee and waited. Twenty minutes passed. He punched in her phone number on his cell phone, He heard Ann call for help, and then a male voice said, "Gimme that damn phone." Bob cursed under his breath, then ran for the door.

He arrived at her house in eight minutes. The front door was locked. He went to the back door. It was unlatched. He turned the doorknob quietly and eased himself into the laundry room. He heard male voices, and then he heard Ann's voice answering them. Her voice was high-pitched with fear. Bob held his .38 pointing forward, as he slowly advanced toward her. One of the men questioning Ann saw him and reached for his automatic. Bob shot him dead. Ann's head was covered with a paper bag. The other man who had been questioning Ann stepped behind her and ducked down to use her as a shield. Just then, a third man stepped from another room with his automatic pointing at Bob. He shot Bob in the upper arm. His sleeve was soon covered in blood. He could no longer hold onto his revolver, it clattered to the wood floor. He told himself to stop bleeding and to start healing. He fell to the floor, retrieved his gun, then rolled and was about to pull the trigger, but the man was no longer in the room. The man behind Ann then fired, hitting Bob in the upper thigh. Bob took careful aim and shot the kidnapper in the head. He rose to his feet and told his leg to heal while he limped about in search of the third man, but he was not in the house. As Bob came down the stairs, he heard a shot from outside the front door. He ran to Ann's side and removed the paper bag. Her face was bruised and bloodied, but she was fine otherwise. He told her to heal herself. She said, "I wouldn't have thought of that, things happened so fast." Someone was coming in the back door. Bob aimed his revolver, and then pushed it into his pocket. Lieutenant Phil and several cops came into the room. The uniforms started searching the house. Phil said, "I was driving this way when I got word of shots fired in this area." He then took Bob's gun because it had now been involved in a shooting. "I'll get rid of it" Bob asked "When will this end, Phil?" "It ends now with the last three of the club members." Bob was surprised, "You got the third man.?" "Well, someone did; the guy in the blue suit was on the front porch. He had already been shot in the head." "Phil, the third man wore a white shirt, I didn't shoot him. I'm afraid that our third man shot someone who was unlucky enough to be at the front door as he was escaping. He could be a Fuller Brush salesman for all we know." "We've got a murder charge against him now. We'll get him." Phil sounded hopeful.

Bob slept in Ann's guestroom that night because she was too frightened to be alone, but the night was uneventful. It was two days before Phil called again. He said that the third man was Homer Gatsby, former member of the Klan, and he was also a former member of the state asylum for the insane. "He's spent most of his life in a jail cell or locked up in an asylum. Watch your ass, he's armed." All the Peers were sleep-deprived because of this maniac. They wanted to get on with their lives. Later in the day the judge called Bob to notify him that he was going into retirement. "I can't just stay here for fifty or a hundred years. I have to make myself and my age appear normal. I'll be going to Texas. There I'll have to make up false papers, just as I did to be a judge here. Oh, yes, I was a good judge, as I was a good surgeon in California before this. It was a pleasure to know you. I'll be here for another week or so to clear up my business dealings." Bob was saddened to hear this, but the judge was right. There would be one more meeting at the judge's house before he left. The time came and all the Peers arrived at the house. The judge appeared angry. He said," I just sentenced a man to four years in prison for chasing an unarmed black man. This hero had a knife and a baseball bat, yet he called the black man a coward for not facing him. I have studied anthropology and many other ologies. Such scientists know that all Earth people looked alike early in the history of man. There were no races of people. Because they settled in different places and married within the tribe, each tribe began to look alike, but different from other tribes in distant places, where their DNA was altered in a different manner. These started as little brown men and women with black hair and brown eyes; men about five feet tall; women about four inches shorter. The environment has a large influence on changes in the DNA. When people are isolated for a long period of time, their DNA will not be the same as someone who lived some distance elsewhere. Thus, the four races of man came about because of where they lived, what they ate, etc., not because one was better than another. Each was different from the others, but they remained in the same species, Homo sapiens. They are different because of where and how long they were separated from the others. A much longer period of isolation would cause them to change to a different species, and then they could not interbreed. This same thing occurred to animal, even in viruses... This accounts for the African elephant having large ears, and his Asian brother having small ears. I am sending a sample of those hero's DNA to WAIF Laboratory. These Alien Hunters could be half Negroid or Mongoloid, Mexican or Jewish or whatever. We'll find out. I am sorry to burden you with this very common crime, but it keeps the world's people from becoming civilized." He told the peers that changing water to whiskey was not magic. This applied also to cloning. What occurs is that our wish or command clouds the mind of the observer. You can prove this by photographing the change you have made. The photo will show what is actually there; the camera has no mind to be clouded. The judge said a farewell to their friend Jim. After dinner, the Peers said their farewell to the judge.

It was two am when Bob was awakened by a strange sound from outside his window. His room was on the first floor. He held his new .38 caliber revolver as he strode to the window. Nothing seemed out of place, but he was thirsty. He uncapped a bottle of water and took a drink. He heard a shot and his face was suddenly soaked in water. He ducked to the floor, rolled and came up ready to fire. He saw the broken window and a face; he fired and heard an awful gurgling sound. Bob swiftly put on his pants and ran outside. A man lay on the ground. There was a bullet hole between his eyes. Bob phoned Phil. "Lieutenant, I think we have the third man. I just shot him after he shot at me. Ten minutes? OK, I'll wait. Sorry to wake you up so early."

Phil arrived in fifteen minutes and eyed the dead man. "Yep, that's our boy. I have photos of him in my office. Let's hope that is the end of Alien Hunters or A-H's." Bob and Ann dated for two weeks more before he proposed. Their children will have far more abilities than their parents because both parents are peers.

# EDWARD MCCARTHY

# IT'S RELATIVE

Sheriff Williams saddled his horse and complained to the livery man about getting old. He rode along the stage coach route to learn why the coach was more than an hour late. On his way out of town a wagon approached him. Driving it was Jeb Johnson, beside him was Mrs. Epsen. She was supposed to be on the stage. Jeb Johnson halted his horse and told the sheriff that he found the stage about two miles behind him. The driver of the stage had asked him to drive Mrs. Epsen to the stage depot where her husband was waiting. "Had a dry axle, he said and they couldn't find the bucket of grease. Wanted me to relay that message to the stage office." The sheriff thanked him and rode on. He saw the stage up ahead, but no one was moving. He rode on more carefully when he saw a man on the ground. He knew it was the coach driver. Ten feet off the trail was his shotgun rider; both were dead. The sheriff stood and heard a shot. The bullet had penetrated his heart, but he was yet unaware of it. A feeling of weakness dropped him to his knees. His chest felt warm. Suddenly he toppled over.

Farther up the road Jim Landis heard the shot and spurred forward. He saw the sheriff fall. He also saw a man in the brush and the smoke from his gun. A bullet dug into the soil six inches from his horse's hind leg. "I'm not a part of this!" he shouted. He pulled his gun when another bullet struck a stone near him. Jim fired at the puff of smoke. The shooter stumbled forward and fell on his face. Another shot hit the dirt in front of Jim's horse. His horse bucked. Jim jumped to the road and fired at the man who had stepped into the open. Another shot hit the dirt only six inches from Jim. Another bullet was fired at the shooter. The shooter fell heavily. Jim located the three horses of the dead men and loaded their bodies on them He rode into town towing the horses.

He was looking for the sheriff, but he wasn't in his office. Someone shouted as he pointed to one of the bodies, "That's the sheriff, Mister!" Mayor Johnson took Jim into the sheriff's office and asked, "What's going on?" Jim answered, "Beats me. I was coming to town when someone took a shot at me. I heard a shot earlier that probably killed your sheriff. Well, I killed the shooter, and then someone else shot at me and scared the hell out of my horse. I killed him too. What the hell's going on?" The mayor said that the stage was carrying $27,000 from a bank in Yuma. "I'm afraid we'll have to search you." Jim grimaced, "It's all right. I don't like the distrust, but…" Jim was interrupted by someone shouting, "Hey, Mayor, lookee what we found." The mayor went to the man who was holding a bundle of cash. The man said, "It was in the dead man's saddlebag." The mayor returned to Jim and apologized for distrusting him. "All is forgiven Mr. Mayor. Now I need something to eat and a drink or two, then I have to find a job and a place to sleep." Someone asked, "Who's the lawman, Mayor?" The mayor answered, "He aint no lawman." Someone said, "But he killed two road agents and we need a new sheriff. What do you say?" The mayor was addressing the gathering crowd, then asked Jim if he wanted the job, "At least until the next election anyway." Jim answered, "I'll have to think it over during lunch. "I haven't eaten since yesterday morning." The sheriff said, "You do that, and your lunch and drinks are on me."

    The crowd began to gather outside the saloon as Jim was eating lunch. He was curious. He drank his coffee and a shot of whiskey. He needed a room for the night so he headed for the door, taking notice of the crowd. At the hotel he was given a room free of charge. As he exited the hotel, he noticed the crowd again. He was puzzling this out when the mayor approached him and asked if he had made up his mind about the sheriff's job. "I haven't really been considering it at all. Sure, I need a job, but I worked as a deputy in some towns in Wyoming territory, and the danger wasn't worth the pay." "This is a fairly decent town, Jim. We can pay $60.00 a month. That's $2.00 a day," When it looked like Jim would turn it down, the mayor said, "And half the fines up to $50.00. Wish I could do more." Jim thought for a moment, then said, "OK, Mr. Mayor." With this said, the crowd cheered. Jim asked, "They were waiting for me to accept the job?" "They would be disappointed if you hadn't. By the way, your deputy quit when he learned about the sheriff being killed." Jim asked if he could wire a friend of his "The mayor nodded his head, "Go right ahead, Jim. You have to work with him. The pay is $40.00 a month and a room at the hotel." "I'll wire him today," Jim said.

    Two days later, Zeb rode into town and asked directions to the sheriff's office. After a quick handshake, Jim and Zeb sat and talked for an hour. During the long talk, it was clear to anyone listening that the men had served together in the army during the uprising, and then had joined the Union Army against the Apaches in Texas. Most recently, Zeb was out of work and down to his last two bits when he arrived. "I've got two bits between me and prostitution Jim, and I'm going to spend it all on a meal. Haven't eaten since yesterday morning." Jim asked him to wait, "I'll go with you, and the meal is on me. I certainly don't want you to go into prostitution, you'd starve to death." The men were finishing their meal when a young man approached them and said he wanted to write a piece in the town's paper about the men who killed the sheriff and shot at Jim. The man asked, "Do you have any remorse for killing those men?" Anger took over Jim's face, "I'm going to ignore that question." The young man looked indignant, "But sir, the people have a right to know." Now Jim was angry, "Well, that is a bald-faced lie. What you mean is you have a right to sell what you learned, but nobody has any right to my feelings. I can imagine someone like you asking a distraught mother how she felt when her two young children were murdered. Neither you nor anyone else has a right to her misery being made public. That question was asked of my mother after my two younger brothers were killed in the war. I threw that man out of the house." He was staring at the young man who now rose and walked rapidly out of the saloon. Zeb said, "I recall that day. You were mad as hell."

A stranger approached the table. He said, "I'm Jason Wright. I own the town newspaper. I overheard your talk with that young man and I wish to apologize for my reporter's question. The young man was close to tears when he left. I realize we cannot display your emotions, but Jody is new to the job." Jim shook the man's hand and said, "I shouldn't have been so testy." When Mr. Wright left the saloon, Jim turned to Zeb and said, "Looks like we made a friend." When they returned to the sheriff's office, the elderly widow Campbell was waiting with a child about 6-years-old. Jim asked, "Is this your granddaughter?" The woman shook her head, "No, she lives about two miles from me on Duffy road. She came to my door this morning and told me a terrible thing." She patted the child on the shoulder and said, "Tell the sheriff what you told me, Annie." The child looked up and said, "It was awful dark, and then he lit the lantern in the other room. Granddad told him to go out, but he wouldn't go. Then he hit Granddaddy, and kept hitting him and hitting him. Granddaddy fell down and couldn't get up. The man saw me so I ran into my bed and put the blanket over my head. He came in later, after searching the house, and stealing things. he...he did awful things to me, I shouldn't talk about, 'cause I'm too little to have a baby. He hurt me and made me cry too. He's a bad, bad man." Jim asked, "Do you know what the man looks like?" The girl answered, "Yes, he's my uncle." The widow Campbell said, "That's what she told me. She was bloodied, but I cleaned her up. She's such a sweet thing. I will be glad to care for her until you find someone else Sheriff." Jim asked the if she knew where her uncle lived. "He lives in the third house on the same road, Duffy Road."

Jim rode out and questioned the man. He claimed to have been at home all that night. His wife said the same. Jim was inclined to believe them, but thought it best to leave it up to a jury. The circuit judge would be in town in two days. In Jim's mail was a letter from the U.S. Attorney General. It reminded him that his function was not only to apprehend suspects, but to investigate each case to assure justice for the involved parties, and to lend all assistance to the federal marshals. Included in the envelope were four flyers. Two of them offered rewards of $200.00 each for the two men Jim had killed. He felt rich because he was not a lawman when he killed them. He asked the mayor to apply for the money. When he had the time, Jim double-checked the alibi of Ann's uncle. Nothing had changed. Now and then he spoke with the uncle. His name is John Balen. He and his wife came to Johnsonville about seven years ago from Virginia. He made a living as a cabinet maker back home, but now he made furniture. Jim did not believe he was the sort of man to do what the town now believed he did. There were even rumors of a lynching if he were found guilty.

The courtroom was packed that Thursday morning. Mr. Balen sat up front. He would act in his own defense. No lawyer would accept the case. The trial was expected to be over in a short time because there wasn't but one witness and no evidence to counter the charges. Ann was called to testify as to the events. She was halting in her words. When she saw her uncle John in the room, she smiled and waved to him. The people saw this and whispered throughout the court. The judge was almost gagging in his surprise.

"Ann," he called, "Why did you smile at a man you blamed for killing your granddaddy?" The girl looked surprised. "Why, I never said that." The judge looked surprised, "Didn't you tell the sheriff that your uncle killed your granddaddy?" She answered, "Yes sir." Now the judge looked lost, "Is the man who killed your granddaddy in this courtroom?" Again, she said, "Yes." The judge asked her to point him out. Ann pointed across the room from her uncle John. Jim hurried to stand behind the man. The judge said, "Ann, you said your uncle was the bad man." Ann began to cry. The defendant stood and said, "Your honor, Annie has three uncles. One is back in Virginia; the man she pointed to is her uncle Phil on her father's side. He was released from prison about a week ago. I knew he was bad medicine since he became an adult, but I never thought he was this bad." The judge called out, "Jury, take a few minutes to decide whether John Balen is guilty or innocent." The jury members raised their right hands and all said, "Not guilty."

"I'll be back in three weeks to try Uncle Phil," said the judge. The sheriff whispered to the uncle, "We'll tell the hangman to be ready." Once outside the courtroom Jim and Zeb spoke about how quickly angry people rush to judgement. Jim said, "The child said her uncle did it, and everyone assumed she meant John. Now she'll be growing up in John's house." The men returned to the sheriff's office. On Jim's desk was a note. It read, "I'll be back." It was signed by the bank owner. "Wonder what he wanted?" asked Zeb. Just then the banker walked in and handed him an envelope. Inside was a check for $400.00. Then the banker handed him another envelope. Inside that one was a check for $2,500. This was 10% of the stolen money recovered by Jim. "Hell, I feel like a rich man. Thank you, Mr. Lukas."

When they were alone again Jim wondered just what he would do with the windfall. He snapped his fingers and made up his mind to leave $500.00 with Uncle John for the proper raising of Annie. He would keep the remainder to save for a ranch, sometime....

## EDWARD MCCARTHY

# JACOB

There was a loud, insistent knocking on the door. Mr. and Mrs. Aaron Steiner glanced at each other. Dread was evident on their faces. Mr. Steiner opened the door to two soldiers. He called to his wife and two sons. Then they picked up their luggage and exited the apartment. Mr. Steiner had been warned a day earlier that the Gestapo would "relocate" his family in the morning. There were many neighbors on the street, lined up in rows. They were marched to the railroad depot, a mile distant. Those unfortunate people who could not walk or keep up with the people were beaten and left to die. The people reached the depot and were loaded into cattle cars. Mr. Steiner caught a glimpse of his sister Margo as she boarded a railcar in the distance. Before they boarded, they were made to toss their luggage into another car. This worried Mr. Steiner because the tools of his watchmaking trade were in his baggage plus 8 ounces of gold. A man said. "That's the last you'll see of them."

The cattle cars were built to hold 40 men or 8 horses. Mr. Steiner reckoned there were 74 people in his car. Aaron was Mr. Steiner's eldest son. He was 14, and had been sick for three days. He was curled up on the floor in the corner of the car. After 6 hours the train stopped to make repairs to the track ahead of it. The door was unlocked and slid open. A soldier shouted, "Offload your dead and put them on the platform" Mr. Steiner helped to place the two old women from his car onto the platform, then reached out for the youngster. Shock and grief changed his features. The boy he held was Aaron, his son. Mr. Steiner asked a soldier if his son could be buried in the public cemetery; he could see it only about 100 feet away. The soldier asked his officer and was told that children could be carried to the cemetery, but the adults must remain where they are. Aaron carried his son through the slippery snow and gently lay him on the ground. He kissed his son on the forehead and returned to his car as a soldier called for him to hurry, He had counted 6 other children in the cemetery, and 2 were infants. The tears on his face were freezing to his beard. He also took note of 8 bodies on the platform, 2 of which were old men, and one was a nun. He learned later that all these people were classified as enemies of the state. Someone said that the townspeople would not bury the Jewish children in the cemetery; they would be ditched elsewhere.

## MIX OF STORIES

The track was finally repaired after 2 hours. The people saw soldiers robbing the dead on the platform. They were fingering the clothing because people were known to sew money into their clothing. The train began moving. He heard a shot and later learned that a rabbi was too slow in reentering his car. Through all this grief and hardship Jacob said almost nothing. He was small for his ten years. Although they looked, they did not see Aunt Margo again. They arrived at their destination after many hours. It was a prison camp which already held thousands of Jews, enemies of the third Reich. Every morning at least two dead bodies greeted the prisoners as they stood to be counted. The dead would be carried in wheelbarrows to a ditch outside the camp. The officers thought it was funny to invite a prisoner to view that ditch, then shoot the man in the back of the head. Usually, the body fell into the ditch. Jacob heard of this from his new young friends. He also learned that no one had ever escaped from the compound. One evening Aaron told his son Jacob that his family was originally German, but had moved to Poland when WW l started. "Now we don't know the German language. Your mom and I were thinking of moving to Russia, but the Russians cannot be trusted. They welcomed thousands of Jews, then notified the Gestapo to come and take them away. Hitler has killed many Jews, but he's not the only madman. Stalin is said to have murdered as many millions of Jews and other 'enemies' as Hitler, including many of his own top military men." When Jacob asked, "Why do they hate us, Dad?" Mr. Steiner said, "They don't need a reason Son, except to show their power and prove how much better they are by having 8 men chase 1 Jew to beat him with baseball bats. It's all religious ignorance. Today is June 14, son; It's your eleventh birthday. All I have to give you is all my love and a watch I made, but you must keep it hidden or it will be stolen. I kept it in my boot. You should do the same." Strangers wished Jacob a happy birthday in several languages. Jacob thought over his father's words and asked him, "Are you and Mom going someplace? When you gave me your watch, it sounded so…so final."

During the days and weeks that followed, Jacob noticed that some of his young friends were missing. "We noticed it too," said a friend," Mr. Levi and Steinman are gone too." Jacob told his dad that he looked all around the compound for Aunt Margo, but could not find her. What seemed strange were the sounds of bombs and intermittent gunfire in the distance. His father told him that the Russians and the Americans were closing in on Berlin. If Jacob got out, he was to go to the Americans, not the Russians. Then he told of a camp secret: There was a tunnel being dug under the floor of building no.6. He told Jacob to find out the day of escape and to be there. On the following morning his mom and dad hugged him and held him close for a long time. Then they said their goodbyes. It was time for his parents to be transferred to another camp, usually a death camp. After they were taken away Jacob remained in one spot outside his building, hardly moving in his grief. He didn't care about the escape tunnel or about eating the slop he was given. He drank some water that night before going to sleep. Many people coped with their grief in different ways. Jacob was learning. He was told that there were 3 types of camps, holding camps, work camps, and death camps. The one he was in was a holding camp. He also learned that Hitler was searching for the cheapest way to murder Jews. Bullets were too expensive. Carbon monoxide was tried. The back of a modified ambulance was filled with people and the small children were held above the occupant's heads. Exhaust fumes were piped into the back of the ambulance as it was driven to a bulldozed ditch, it emptied the dead into it. That method, however, was too expensive and the Reich was short of gas and oil.

Jacob learned the escape plans and was there at the proper time. The men looked at him with some fear, but what could they say? He got in line behind the second man. When he reached the end of the tunnel the man behind him lifted him up to the surface. The men had to stoop over to travel in the tunnel. Jacob could walk almost erect all the way. It was a wonderful feeling to be free, to breathe free air. He had been scared in the tunnel. Now he was in a wooded area. It was not long before he heard the sirens and whistles. A little later he heard rifle fire. It sounded far away. There was only a quarter moon, which helped him to see. He headed west toward the American lines. A half hour later he arrived at a village. He saw a café and headed for the alley where the garbage cans were. He ate his fill and was surprised at all the leftover food. He then fell asleep in the alley until awakened by people talking on the street. He listened, and heard that the Americans were not too far away to the west. He was aware that the sun rises in the east, so as he walked, he kept the early sun at his back. He was becoming proficient in several languages also.

The only traffic on the street was military. Some German soldiers gave him a ride for 4 miles. He pretended to be mute and a bit addled. These soldiers wore the same uniform as those in the camp, but the men were much nicer. He was homesick. When he was alone, he took the watch from his boot and looked at it as his eyes filled with tears that rolled down his cheeks. His blond hair looked like a dirty mop, his clothing was dirty and smelled of rotting food. Another stench reached his nostrils. It came from a dead and bloated donkey. He would have cut off a chunk of the hind quarter, but he had no knife.

He had holes in his boots and his socks, and he was looking for cardboard or something to put into his boots. He found a hunting knife on the sidewalk where a sporting goods store had been. He found the scabbard later. He tucked them under his belt. It was not long before he came upon a dead cow. He cut a large piece of it, but could not carry it because he was so weak. A woman had been watching him. She helped him carry the meat to her apartment, telling him, "It's all right. I have some clothing that will fit you. The white-haired lady told him she was a teacher. She had been married and had a child, but her husband and child were killed in an air raid. She still had the boy's clothing, "First, you must take a shower and give me your filthy clothes so I can wash them. Then you can try on my son's clothing and boots." In the meantime, she was slicing the meat and boiling it.

The clothing and boots fit him perfectly. The good lady said nothing when she saw how thin his arm was, but he knew that she came close to tears. He remained with the woman for two days. Now he felt like he had been renewed. He did not know why, but his trek to the west was not over yet. One morning he kissed the woman goodbye and continued his slow trek. He could hear rifle fire, and wondered if he knew the Jew who was being shot. Suddenly, bullets smashed into the brick wall behind him and destroyed a street sign he stood under. He could hear a voice in a strange language shouting, "Stop the goddamn firing, it's only a kid."

## MIX OF STORIES

A tall sergeant approached him and spoke, but neither understood the other's language. Jacob knew instinctively that he was among friends. The tall sergeant was Terry Murphy of the 75th Combat Infantry Div. They were in the city of Dortmund, Germany. As Terry's squad moved up, Jacob stayed with them. Terry said, "Hey, you can't go where we are going. There's a war going on." Jacob followed the company though the skirmishes and the days that followed, then the war ended. Terry had no idea of how Jacob could have done it, how he ate, etc. Any other kid would be too scared to follow his company. Terry found him on the side of the road with an open wound in his arm. A medic treated and bandaged it.

Terry didn't know what to do with the kid. He sneaked him food and a blanket. Then it was time for Terry to be discharged. He somehow got a ride for Jake, as he called him. When they arrived in Le Havre, Terry headed for the card tables. He knew there was a lot of cheating, but he could stay out of those games. He was an honest man. He was very good at poker too. At night the two friends talked; Jacob told of cutting off a dead dog's hind quarters and sharing it with seven homeless people who lived under a bridge. He told of eating grass and becoming sick. Sometimes he slept in barns and milked the cows. He drank the milk and ate some of the oats he could find. He found preserved food and peaches in a basement, and ate it for days. He also told of the disappearance of Aunt Margo and his parents, and the death of his brother, Aaron. Luckily there was a man who spoke Polish in Terry's company. Someone said," He's an orphan." Terry added, "He's our orphan. We have to take care of him."

Terry tried to locate Jake's parents and his aunt through official channels but with so little information to go on, there was little that could be done. There was no hope for locating them, especially because the SS had speeded up the murder of Jews as the Americans approached. Terry learned that his ship was in port, The USS N.Y U. Victory. Terry's men fixed up a barracks bag so that Terry could fit Jake inside it and carry it on his shoulder up the ramp. This went off perfectly. Terry busied himself at the card table all the way to New York. Aboard the Victory ship were men who had fought in Africa. One of them had sneaked a monkey aboard. Whenever a player tossed a lit cigarette on deck, the monkey pounced on it, brushed off the embers and then field-stripped the cigarette. It was fun to watch.

The men had been told in Le Havre that customs would confiscate all weapons and any amount of French or German money in excess of $30.00. This was baloney. It was said so that the people with excess money would gamble it and sell their guns and souvenirs. And they did. Terry had won thousands of American dollars and was going to hide it from customs agents. However, when they arrived in New York, Terry noticed a long table, but no agents. The men were off-loaded without a customs agent in sight. He and Jake hailed a cab. Terry wanted to show Jake the Empire State Building, then they were driven to the battery where Jake could see the Statue of Liberty, then they rode the subway to Brooklyn and his home. When they arrived, Terry's mother made him feel unwelcome when she eyed him and spoke about how needy they were. Terry handed her most of his $3,000. In winnings. He cautioned, "Mom, he speaks English a little. He's a bright kid, and wait until he tells you his story." His mother hugged Jake and kissed his forehead. She said, "You poor kid."

Terry had been a private detective before entering the army. When he visited the agency, he was welcomed back. Four firms that had used the agency's service had left them when Terry entered the army, but would return when Terry was rehired. Carl Matthews, the agency owner, offered Terry a partnership if he would return. Terry accepted the offer. The agency had not been doing well, but Terry was a good salesman. He bought a bicycle for Jake. The boy rode it all through the neighborhood. When he passed the grocery store one day, he saw a woman who looked familiar. She was carrying packages. This memory gnawed at him for hours. Then he remembered where he had seen her. She looked like his aunt Margo, or at least she walked like her. He told Terry that although he was sure that his aunt was dead, He wanted to check it out. Terry could not walk far because he had been shot in the leg, and it would give out. He and Jake took a taxi to a car dealer where Terry bought a used car, which was needed for his work. Then he and Jake went to the house where Jake had seen the woman entering. Jake knocked on the door.

His face looked grim, but he was hopeful. The door opened slowly. A woman asked, "May I help you?" Jake blurted out, "Aunt Margo?" The woman gasped, "Aaron?" "No, I'm Jacob." The woman looked over Jake's shoulder and asked, "Your mom and dad?" Jacob looked sad, "I'm afraid they are gone, Aaron too." A male figure appeared behind the woman. He asked, "Vas ist los?" The woman answered, "The boy is my nephew, Aaron's son." She asked her guests to come inside. Terry and Jake sat on the sofa. Jake spoke for a time, telling all that had happened to him and his family. Then Aunt Margo told her story: Her husband had been a guard at the prison camp. A day after she arrived there, he noticed her, and it was love at first sight. He didn't care that she was Jewish. He spoke with her whenever he was sure it would not be noticed by another guard. He made plans for her escape. Mrs. Levin died during the night and was placed outside the building, as ordered. Hans, her husband, changed the name on the tag tied around Mrs. Levin's neck. The body was buried. Then he sneaked Margo out of the compound in civilian clothes. He too left with her that night. As far as anyone knew, Margo was dead and the guard and Mrs. Levin were AWOL. They made their way south, with the use of false papers. No one questioned them. They were not safe until they crossed the border and were in Switzerland. They were then sent to England, where they were married. Then they were shipped to New York. "Jacob, you have a new uncle now".

Terry and Jacob had some decisions to make. Margo and Hans would be happy to care for Jacob. Hans was an engineer, and he already had a good job. But first, Jacob must see a rabbi. He had a lot to catch up on. Terry reluctantly agreed because he didn't know the Jewish dietary laws and holy days, He told Jake, "Hell, I'm not even a good Christian." Jake told Terry, "We can do a lot of things together, if you want, like fishing or going to the movies. You won't forget me, will you, Terry? There were tears in his eyes.

## MIX OF STORIES

Author's note: JACOB is a composite of the children I noted in Germany during WWII and the Cold War that followed. I saw the homeless and starving children so willing to work hard for food. I learned why cigarettes were so important to the economy of France and Germany also. Cigarettes were trade items, valued for the vegetables and meat they could buy. A carton sold for $20.00 in France and western Germany, but it was worth $200.00 in Berlin. GI's bought a carton for 50 cents. The people may have had money, but it had very little or no value. The children I noted looked like children I had played with in my youth.

EDWARD MCCARTHY

# FALLEN ANGEL?

He was reluctant at first. He demanded more liquor before accompanying me to my studio. I was in the process of completing a painting I had begun two years earlier, a painting of Jesus and His apostles in their meeting after the resurrection. I had already painted Jesus and most of his apostles; now I plied Mr. Korman with liquor to have him pose without shaking. He would be the last apostle, Judas. I had searched for two years for someone so distrustful and wary to be my Judas. I first saw Mr. Korman when he was being released from the city jail. I determined to find him at a later time. I saw him later as he exited a bar on Main Street. At my studio Mr. Korman seemed to know what was expected of him. I learned that he had held a job with a large corporation, but walked out of his office one day some years ago, giving no explanation. He was now deep into drugs and alcohol, stealing what he could to purchase his needed coke and whatever liquor he could drink. He had spent several periods in jail for theft too. Although he was a most obscene and truly ugly person, he was a perfect specimen for my Judas. I had already painted the other eleven apostles with various expressions of sadness, but Judas was to be outstanding in his furtive and guilty countenance.

I tried to remember where I had seen him before. Perhaps it was when he worked for that large corporation? Maybe I passed him on the street or had seen him lying in a doorway? I noticed his furtive look as he scanned my studio (for something to steal?). When he asked me, "Where is the mantle clock you had years ago?" I first thought he had asked because of intentions to steal it, but then it struck me, he must have been here before. Suddenly I remembered where I had seen him before. Yes, of course, he had been right here in my studio two years ago, I had painted this man as Jesus.

# HOME INVASION

Roxanne and Martin Corwin had been married but two weeks. They were still furnishing their house, and Roxanne was going through a catalog for furniture. She heard a noise at the front door; someone was turning the doorknob, and not too silently. She rose to answer the door for the first visitor in her new house. Suddenly, the door splintered and fell to the floor with a thunderous sound. Roxanne was very frightened. The larger of the two masked men grabbed her arm and told her to open the safe. He led her to the secret safe, which was behind a picture of an Irish castle. "Open it!" he demanded loudly. She heard her husband shout as he came from the bedroom, "What the hell is going on?" The man holding her arm turned the gun on her husband and fired. She watched fearfully as her husband fell to the floor. At first, she was so frightened she could not recall the combination to the safe. After fumbling, she told the man she could not remember it. The man stuck the cold muzzle of his gun into her neck. The touch of the cold steel urged her to remember. She tried again. This time the safe was unlocked. The man reached his hand into the safe and scooped out the paper money. He then put his gun to her head again. She grabbed at his arm, scratching it, but he fired anyway She fell to the floor and the two robbers quickly left.

She and her husband regained consciousness at about the same time. He ran to her as he held his stomach, which was bleeding. Roxanne's head was also bleeding. She was holding a handkerchief over the gash in her temple. He asked her to call 9-1-1, but she merely stared into the distance. He dialed the number just before he passed out. Police Sergeant Bill Hardy was at their house in less than seven minutes. Mrs. Corwin was of no help in telling what had happened. They were transported to the hospital in an ambulance. Mr. Corwin was under the knife for more than three hours. Her head was treated and bandaged, but her problem could not be repaired with a scalpel. Her memory was gone. The doctor said this was not too uncommon, and usually the memory would return in a short time. Mrs. Corwin was sent to a nursing home until her husband was released from the hospital and could care for her at home. He was released a week later. He explained to her at home that the bullet nicked a bit of his intestine and he would be on a liquid diet for a while, He had to be aware of any infection, however. She listened, but was devoid of all emotion. She did not know who she was and who he was. He was a stranger, and pictures of their honeymoon made no difference. "Just give me time. I'm sure I'll get my memory back. Every now and then I get little glimpses of someone's earlier life, but was it mine? I don't know," she said.

Mr. Corwin's brother had their door replaced and he had cleaned up their house of all the splintered wood. Sgt. Hardy questioned him about the break-in, but he didn't even know where the safe was until he closed it and replaced the picture on the wall. Sgt. Hardy had also sent fingernail scrapings to the lab and they now had a DNA profile, but no match could be found on their files or those of the FBI. A few days later, Mrs. Corwin said "I'm beginning to get some clearer pictures of my life. At least, I recognize you as my husband. I couldn't do that before. I think that is a good sign. Martin hugged her, but did not linger. That night after they went to bed, she asked, "Are you wearing shorts?" He answered, sleepily, "uh-huh. She said, "Well, take them off. It's been a long time, Honey."

At the breakfast table in the morning, they talked about the case for the first time. She remembered the man who forced her to open the safe. He was white. She knew this because she could see his arm when she scratched him. He was about 6 feet 2 inches tall and weighed about 210 pounds. The other one did not speak and was about 5 feet 4 inches tall. "It would not surprise me if that was a woman." She pointed out that the sergeant was checking with the neighbors concerning Martin's brother, but the sergeant had never mentioned the people who built the safe and those who put it into the wall. "The thieves knew where the 'secret' safe was." Mr. Corwin phoned Sergeant Hardy and informed him of what Roxanne had said. The sergeant was relieved that Roxanne was doing so well.

The sergeant got nowhere with the people who had built the safe or those who installed it. The man who did that work was a Mr. Ferguson. He was 62 years old. Roxanne looked up the name in the phonebook, and then parked near his house so she could observe who came and went. She parked across the street. She thought that Mr. Ferguson could have told someone about the safe. She was about to leave when she saw a tall man exit the house. "That's him," she told herself. She returned home and discussed this with her husband. He chided her for taking such a chance. Just then there was a knock on the front door. It was suddenly pushed open by that same tall man, but now he was holding a gun pointed at Martin. "If you two don't keep your traps shut, I'll be back to shut them for good, better yet, maybe I should do both of you now." Sergeant Hardy was suddenly behind the thief. He ordered him to drop his gun or risk a bullet in the spine. The man dropped his weapon. Sergeant Hardy explained to Roxanne. "We saw you pull up by the Ferguson house. We were in an apartment across the street. You didn't know it, but we watched Ferguson watching you. Then he followed you home. We followed him. That's how we got here so fast. His girlfriend gave him up. She was the other robber. The man has a long list of felonies in other states he's also wanted for. Now as for you, Mrs. Corwin, you scared the hell out of us by trying to solve a crime by yourself. Please, leave the police work to the police. By the way, we have four police openings in our department. Why not take the test?"

MIX OF STORIES

# MRS. BANNER

Memory is a little understood aspect of one's life. Every now and again I am reminded of a little old woman named Mrs. Banner; it could be when I see a woman with white hair, or a wrinkled face. These things remind me of the woman I knew when I was a kid of about ten, back in the 1930's. Often, when I was playing in my front yard, she would beckon me to come to her fence. She would then ask if I would "run" to the store for her. Never did anyone ask me to "walk" to the store. It was always run, and always for a nickel. I could go to the movie house for a dime, so it was always necessary to run to the store twice to earn that movie money.

I remember a time when I had to add three cents of my own money so Mrs. Banner could get a full three pounds of potatoes at Russo's Vegetable Market. When I returned to her, she didn't have the three cents to repay me. She didn't even have the nickel that was owed me for running to the store. That was OK though. I earned a quarter that week and took my brother to the movie. Mrs. Banner paid me what she owed in the following week. That's when she proved she wasn't a liar or a thief. I didn't know anything else about her but those proven facts. I continued running to the store for her. She owed me a nickel another time, and that grew to another nickel, movie money. She promised to pay me the following week. I trusted the woman because I knew she was honest. Then I didn't see Mrs. Banner for days. When I saw her daughter hanging a Death Wreath on her front door, I knew what had happened. I cried when my grandmother died, but I didn't have any such feeling for Mrs. Banner. Instead of feeling pity for the poor soul, I had feelings of guilt because whenever I thought of poor Mrs. Banner it was, "She died owing me two nickels." Does that make me a terrible person?

# EDWARD MCCARTHY

# CHICKENS AND EGGS

Pat Collins rode into Silverton on his black mare. In his right hand were the reins of another mare; in the saddle was a man, a dead man. All the residents were aware of Pat's job. He was a bounty hunter since two men had killed his wife two years earlier. Within two months Pat captured both men, and a jury found them guilty. The judge gave them each 20 years to mull over their sins. Pat was a fair man. The town's folks knew that. As much as they disliked bounty hunters, Pat remained a good man to know, and a friend. He stopped at the sheriff's office and took a receipt for Henry Patson's carcass. There was a $300 reward offered for this killer of a child. The sheriff looked at the body. "Wouldn't come peacefully, would he? I'm glad I warned you about him." Pat nodded, "Yeah, me too. He put his .44 on the floor like I ordered, but when he rose, he held a boot gun. I just had no choice." The sheriff said, "That's how I'll write it up, Pat. By the way, you have some mail at the post office and here's a wire that came in yesterday." Pat read the wire aloud. "Where the hell are you?" It was from the warden of the territorial prison at Yuma, Arizona.

Pat walked to the general store. The post office was there. He was given his letter. It was also from the warden. "Pat, there's a prisoner here that wants to see you. It sounds important. He will be hanged in two weeks, so don't dally. You know the man. You brought him in. His name is Henry Egan." The letter was a week old, so Pat still had a week. He stayed the night at the hotel, and then boarded the stage in the morning. The day and a half trip was uneventful. He rented a horse and arrived at the prison late in the afternoon. The Warden met him at the main gate and took him to his office. He ordered a guard to bring Egan to his office. In the meantime, he and Pat sat and drank some whiskey. When Egan arrived, Egan asked to speak with Pat alone. The warden mulled this over, and then said, "Make it quick." Egan wanted a promise from Pat. "First, this is all secret. Second, swear to do as I ask." Pat said, "I can't do that Egan. I can keep a secret, but I can't swear to something I don't know. Let's just forget it." Egan became agitated, "No, no, I just want you to promise to give my money to my wife. I drew a map to the money, and you can have half of it." Pat asked if it was stolen. "No sir, I saved it when I was working as a cattle buyer." Pat said, "OK, I promise." Egan handed Pat a folded paper which Pat pocketed before the warden returned. Pat was convinced that Egan's money was stolen, and not saved as he said.

65

## MIX OF STORIES

He mulled this over on the long trip back to Silverton. He ate a sandwich and drank a glass of beer at the saloon before going to his hotel room. It was 4:00 pm. He lay on the bed because he was still tired from the long trip, and fell asleep until the next morning. He stayed in town that night also, then rode his horse toward Egan's money. Pat had the eerie feeling that someone was dogging his trail, but he saw and heard nothing strange. In the afternoon he spotted a lone Apache on a horse. Pat hid behind trees and was not spotted. Later he camped by a stream and filled his canteens. He fed and hobbled his mare than he ate. That strange, wary feeling struck him again. He listened intently. There were no strange sounds. He went to sleep. He was awake at sunup. His horse had been feeding on the lush grass in this small area. He searched and found her hundreds of yards distant. He fetched her, and was on his way in minutes. Pat was not careless as far as his mare was concerned, and for good reason. Two years earlier he was involved in a shootout with two kidnappers he had cornered. He killed them, but had taken a bullet in his right thigh and another in his left arm. He could not mount his mare. He stuck his arm through the stirrup and held on as his mare walked slowly on the back trail, dragging him. Some horses would be so frightened by this behavior they would run and jump in efforts to dislodge the threatening figure, but not his mare. She just kept moving, and when his arm slipped out of the stirrup, she halted until Pat got another grip. It seemed an endless distance to Pat but the mare arrived at a prospector's shack and stopped at the stunned man's door. It took weeks, but Pat was finally fit enough to ride again. He split a $4,000 reward with the prospector and promised to put his mare on lush pasture for weeks.

Pat finally arrived at the treasure spot. He was to locate a shack which held the money, some $30,000 under its floorboards, but there was no shack in sight. To his left he spotted a cloud of dust coming his way. He laid his horse down and hid behind her. It was not Indians raising the dust; it was union cavalry. There was a lieutenant in charge of ten troops and one sergeant. They stopped at Pat's camp. The patrol was hunting down 4 or 5 Apaches who got drunk and burned a rancher's wagon. "No, I haven't seen them," Pat said. "By the way, have you seen a shack in this general area? I believe a Mr. Egan owned it." The lieutenant stood in his stirrups and said, "Yes, I recall the shack," and then pointed. "It's was over there, but it was burned down. Mr. Egan had rather a bad reputation, you know. He was hanged yesterday."

When the soldiers were gone, Pat went to the place the lieutenant had pointed out. The shack was gone, but the foundation and the floor were still there. He pulled up the floor boards on the south-west corner, reached down and scooped up a canvas bag. It had $30,000 in it. He heard the rifle shot. He then saw where the bullet had gouged up a puff of powdery sand. He ducked behind the foundation and studied the area. There was only one outcropping of rock for the shooter to hide behind. He kept his eyes on it as he wondered if those elusive Apaches had found him. It wasn't long before the troopers came racing back. "Did you fire that shot?" the lieutenant asked. "No, I think the shooter is behind that mound of stones." The lieutenant dispatched two men to bring back the man who fired the shot. They did so, but it wasn't a man they brought back; it was a woman. When the lieutenant saw the woman, he told his sergeant to get the men mounted. None of this was his business, he told Pat. The woman said she was Mrs. Egan and he was trespassing on her property and she wanted that package he found under the floor.

"This package is going to be returned to the bank it was stolen from, but I'll share the $3,000 reward for its return," Pat said. She seemed agreeable. Her agreeable disposition didn't last long.

That night, Pat emptied his weapon and left it in the open when he went to sleep. The woman sneaked over and grabbed his gun. She kicked Pat to awaken him. He said, "You are a bitch!" This angered her, "Don't talk to me that way. I've got the gun!" Pat said, "Yeah, but you don't have any bullets in it." She pulled the trigger six times, but the hammer fell on empty chambers. She suddenly slumped to the ground, but didn't rise after Pat reclaimed his weapon. She appeared to have fainted, but was dead. Pat placed his arm under her back and promptly withdrew it. His hand had hit the shaft of an arrow which had broken off when she struck the ground. His hand was now bloody. He lay flat on the ground as his eyes searched the area. As he reloaded his revolver, he saw the Apache, and fired. He peered at where the figure had been. Again, the Indian became visible. Pat fired again. The Apache stumbled into the open and fell. Pat waited, maybe this Indian wasn't alone. Finally, he checked the man. He was dead. Pat mounted his mare and rode some distance before bedding down again.

In the morning he rode back and buried the two bodies, then dragged weeds over his footprints and the graves. He arrived in Moorsville at two in the afternoon. Egan's wife was dead, but his children could still share in the $3,000 reward for returning the bank money. He turned the bank's money over to a federal marshal who was visiting Moorsville, and then he rode to the Egan ranch. When he knocked on the door, a woman answered. Two small children clung to her leg as she spoke with Pat. "Are you the children's caretaker?" he asked. "No, I'm Mrs. Egan, their mother. Why do you ask?" Pat was shaken, "Well, I...Well, you look so young, that's why," he lied. "I have something on the stove. Will this take long?" He quickly answered, "No ma'am, I'm looking for work." She said, "Oh, I can't hire anyone. Try in town." Pat said, "Thank you, Ma'am." The visit was so short because Pat didn't know what to say after learning that she was the real Mrs. Egan. He returned to the sheriff's office and asked enough questions to satisfy him that she was indeed the real one. The sheriff told him that his $3,000 reward would be at the bank tomorrow. Pat asked how Mrs. Egan had been making out. "Barely," the sheriff said. "She takes in laundry, sells some eggs and cakes and pies to the restaurant, and she does some sewing on the side. Her husband was a good-for-nothing criminal. He was finally hung." Pat said, "Pretty busy lady, eh." The sheriff nodded, "Always busy, if you ask me."

Pat made a decision. He would put Mrs. Egan in the chicken and egg business. For this he was directed to a Jesse Ralls, a carpenter. He was told that Mrs. Egan already had about 20 or 25 hens. "I want you to buy another 100 hens and half a dozen roosters plus lumber and chicken fencing and a nice size incubator, and set it up on Mrs. Egan's property. She's going into the chicken and egg business, Mr. Ralls. She won't have to work half as much in the future, because her kids can help her. She'll also share in the reward too. Maybe it will make up a little for her lousy husband." Mrs. Egan was very grateful. She began making eyes at Pat, but he had a wanted poster that would take him into Utah.

**MIX OF STORIES**

# JODY AND ASA

It was April 1865. Aunt Clara would call it the cleaning time, "A time when God cleansed the earth and His people." It was also the month that ended the Civil War. Jody York found himself with his good friend, a soldier and full-blooded Sioux called Asa Red Bull. These two men had joined the rebel cause back in 1861 and served together for almost four-years. Now they were somewhere in Pennsylvania. The war was lost, and union soldiers were scouring the countryside for rebels to imprison them. They hid out at the Wellington Farm that first night of freedom from military duty. Many men of their unit had already been caught, or had given up, or were killed trying to evade capture. On the second day of freedom from military service, they found two cavalry horses that blundered into the barn where they were hiding. The horses were thin, starving, and thirsty. Jody rode one into town, only two miles away. There he bought oats for the horses and food for himself and Asa. He filled two canteens with water, drank a cup of coffee at Hal's Café, and then rode back to his friend. They had coffee and two cans of beans that night. In the morning Asa waited on the south side of town while Jody bought more food. In the gun shop he bought two Harrington and Richardson revolvers and two belts with holsters and ammunition. He shared all of these with Asa when they met outside of town. They rode west, stopping often to rest the horses and allow them to graze. They buried their uniforms after buying new 50-cent shirts, $2.00 trousers and $5.00 hats. Now they could more easily pass as ranch hands. Asa asked, "You aren't rich I know, but where did you get all the money you've been spending?" Jodie said, "You know I sold my cattle and horses, but I was also paid $100.00 for taking the place of a man who was conscripted, but had just married. I needed the money; he didn't want to go in the army. Hell, I didn't have any chance to spend much of it all the time we were in the army." Asa wanted to know if the money was crooked. "No, it's honest money; A person is allowed to find a replacement if conscripted. It's legal, honest."

They camped that night at Rafe Sander's well. Jody told how it got its name. "The man had dug it back in the forties on a bet. He won the thousand bucks when he struck water. Old Rafe died about five years back." In the morning they filled their canteens after drinking all they could. They had a dry ride ahead of them. Their destination was Wyoming Territory where Jody had a ranch. The two men had met about five years earlier when Asa found Jody unconscious after being knocked from his horse by a bullet that hit his upper arm. A stranger was going through Jody's pockets. When the thief saw Asa, he fired at him. Asa shot him in the chest, then put Jody on his own horse, took him home, and treated his wound. They became good friends and Asa helped with the chores around Jody's ranch until they went into the army.

The men didn't see familiar ground until they reached Nebraska and the Platte River. Following this took them into Casper, Wyoming Territory. They replenished their food supply then took the north trail. Asa had agreed to work Jody's ranch with him to put it back in order. Another day in the saddle took them to the ranch. As they dismounted, a man exited Jody's house and asked what they wanted. Jody was building anger. That was his house! Asa recognized this and elbowed him before he could answer. Asa said. "We're looking for work and we'd like to fill our canteens at the well." The man answered, "You can fill your canteens at the well, but Mr. Garway aint hiring right now." They thanked the stranger, filled their canteens, and rode off a mile or so before they camped for the night. Asa said, "I've seen that man in South Fork. He's a gambler and a killer. I stopped you from talking back at your house because I recognized someone who was standing at the front window with a carbine aimed at us. He works for Ned Garway, a lawyer and land grabber." Jody said, "I left enough money with Uncle Jim to pay my land taxes, so that can't be the reason he's grabbing my ranch." Asa said, "Whatever the reason, you can bet he's standing on legal grounds, so what do we do now?" Jody said, "We sleep."

After a cup of coffee in the morning they rode to Uncle Jim's ranch, just a half-mile away. Uncle Jim was about fifty-years old, slightly lamed in one leg from a bear attack, but a good man with a gun. He answered the knock on his door then hugged Jody and was introduced to Asa. Jim said, "I'm glad to see you're not an Indian hater, Jody." "Well, how could I be? Aunt Clara is part Arapaho. Where is she?" "She passed about a year ago from the fever. I wrote you, but then someone said you were killed in Virginia." "No, I was shot in Virginia, but the good doctor took out the bullet before it poisoned me." "You and Asa are welcome to whatever I have. You can stay here as long as we can stand the close quarters." They told the story of the theft of Jody's ranch. Jim said, "That Garway is a fast worker. The man you talked with is called Apache. He's a cold-blooded killer, but Garway makes sure that everything is legal. I think he's got the sheriff buffaloed too. Don't you have your deed to the property?" "It's in my house, hidden behind a fireplace brick, but it only proves that I once owned the ranch. It looks like Garway wasted no time to take my property. He probably saw me selling my cattle and horses."

Jim said. "Let me get in touch with Judge Worth. He's nearing retirement, but maybe he can help." He left at sunup. Two days later Jim returned from his trip wearing a federal marshal's badge. When he entered the house, he removed it from his vest and handed it to Jody. He said, "I told the judge what was going on and that you would be a better marshal than me, so he changed the name on the paper to yours. He knows a lot about you and he was a good friend of your parents too. I think he did this to help you get your ranch back, but he said he also needs a marshal." "That's OK with me," said Jody. "Now tell Asa why everybody calls you Uncle Jim." Jim smiled, "Oh, this happened about fourteen years ago. I took in two runaway kids, the sheriff said would be only for two days, no more. Well, it was two weeks later when the parents came and picked them up. The children were calling me Uncle Jim by then. The sheriff and just about the entire town then started calling me Uncle Jim as a joke. I guess it stuck." Jody said, "My dad built most of my ranch house with his own hands; no smart-ass lawyer is going to grab it from me without a fight. I'll get it back if I have to fight Mr. Smart-ass with fists or guns." Uncle Jim said, "No sense in feeling sorry for yourself, Jody." "Well, I'll go along with that too," chimed in Asa. "I agree. Three out of three aint bad," said Jody.

They rode into South Fork in the morning and went to Garway's Saloon. Jody ordered three beers. The three men then sat at a table near the back wall. They were making plans for visiting the sheriff and eating lunch at Garway's Restaurant when Garway, Apache, and two other men entered the saloon and walked to the bar. Garway ordered whiskey all around, then turned his back on the bar and looked around his saloon. He saw the three men and walked to their table. He warmly greeted Uncle Jim, who then introduced his two friends. Then Uncle Jim pointed to Jody and told the lawyer that it was Jody's ranch that Garway was trying to steal. "You knew that Jody sold his cattle and horses because he went into military service, didn't you, Garway?" "I knew nothing of the sort. He abandoned his property and I filed on it. It's all legal. I guess I was there at the opportune moment. The ranch is mine." Garway was becoming angry. "If the man wants it back, he just has to come and get it…. any time." Just then, the man standing at the bar next to Apache drew his weapon and fired at Jim, knocking him to the floor. Asa and Jody then drew and fired. Two of the attorney's men fell to the floor. Apache seemed to be having trouble drawing his weapon although anger showed in his face. Jody aimed his weapon at him and told him to calm down. "Draw that weapon and die." Apache preferred not to die. He and the attorney put their hands in the air. Jody told Garway that he was a federal marshal. "Now that you know it, it's a federal crime to fire at me or my men." Garway and friends left the saloon. Uncle Jim needed medical attention, so he and his friends left too. They rode the short distance to Jim's ranch where Jody set to work on patching Jim's arm. The bullet had gouged a rut in Jim's upper arm that looked like a burn from a red-hot poker. He winced in pain now and then. Less than half an hour later the sheriff rode up alone. "Hear you've been in a shooting scrape at the saloon, left two dead men for me to scrape up too. Nobody tells me anything; now I hear that Jody York's a federal marshal." "They drew first." Jody told him. They shot an unarmed man too. Uncle Jim's sidearm is at the gunsmith's and has been for days. Check on it if you want." The sheriff shook his head, "No, I'll chalk this up as self-defense, but keep clear of that son of a bitch, Garway. He's got a lot of power because he can afford to hire killers. He's mad as hell now."

For a week there were men all over Jody's ranch. One by one the number reduced as Garway felt safer. Uncle Jim knew this because he had been watching Jody's house from a safe distance each day. He was waiting for an opportunity to get into the house and take Jody's deed to him. A few days later he had his chance. A rider came racing to the ranch one day. Garway opened the door and spoke with him. The man was gesturing with his arms. Jim waited. Garway armed himself with a sidearm and rifle then he and the man raced toward South Fork. As soon as they were out of sight Jim ran to the house, knocked on the door loudly, then entered the house when no one answered the knock. He found the loose brick on the fireplace, reached in his hand and withdrew Jody's proof of ownership. He returned to his own ranch and handed the paper over to Jody as he explained where he had been every afternoon when he disappeared. "You shouldn't have taken such a chance, not at your age," joked Asa. "My age? You whippersnapper! I was the fastest when I was your age. My age hasn't slowed me... much. That damn bear did." Jim smiled. Jody said, "This deed proves only that I once owned that property. It doesn't prove present ownership." Asa said, "Yeah, but you have your papers showing you went into military service and didn't abandon your ranch. You went on a business trip, so to speak. Uncle Jim paid your taxes too. Even if you were conscripted you wouldn't be abandoning your home," "Looks like I'll be going back to Judge Worth," said Uncle Jim. "We could all go," said Jody. Uncle Jim answered. "No, I wouldn't want to leave my ranch unprotected. And you two men are better at that than I am." Jim was miles along the north trail when Jody and Asa awoke in the morning. Uncle Jim and Judge Worth conducted their business at the Buffalo Saloon. The judge strongly advised against doing anything until copies were made of all necessary papers and one copy of each was hidden in a safe place. "Copies?" How can anyone make copies?" "They do it every day in photography," the judge explained. "Why didn't I think of that?"

Judge Worth said he would ride down to South Fork on Friday and would meet with Jody at the town courthouse at 11:00 am. "I won't put up with any nonsense from a slick attorney who is misusing his talent and knowledge of the law to steal land from the public. I'm aiming to get Garway disbarred for life." Uncle Jim was back at his ranch the following day. He told the men his news. Jody and Asa rode the stage coach south to Casper. They had copies made of the necessary papers for a sum of $1.75. They drank two shots of liquor while waiting for the return stage coach and were back in two days. Jody and the judge kept their appointment on Friday at the South Fork courthouse. The clerk appeared to be all thumbs as he searched folders or wrote. The judge warned him to stop stalling. The clerk whispered something to another clerk who left the office in a hurry. They finished their business before Garway could interfere. As they walked across the street to the saloon, they passed Garway and Apache. Asa drank his beer at the corner of the bar. Jody and the judge sat at a table. Garway and Apache strode in. Garway walked to Jody's table. "I know you, York, but I don't know the galoot with you. If he's your lawyer, you'd best get one that's a bit younger and up to date on the new territory laws." Judge Worth was very calm as he advised Garway that he was the territorial judge and had written some of those new territorial laws. "Can we ask the owner if we can borrow a room? I'm having a hard time hearing you because of my elderly ears?" Garway said, "I'm the owner. Sure, step into my office." motioning to an office door.

Once inside, the judge quickly stepped behind the desk, rapped on it with his sidearm and claimed an open court session. "Please remove your hats." The two men refused. "That calls for a $50.00 fine. The men removed their hats. "Mr. York, is it true that you did not abandon your ranch, that you entered military service and were denied entrance to your ranch house upon your return?" "That's true, your honor. These two men stole my property and lied about me abandoning it." The judge faced Garway and said, "Mr. Garway, do you have anything to say in your defense?" Garway answered, "Not here, not now. If he wants the ranch, he can come and get it." "That sounds like a threat, Mr. Garway. I'm fining you one hundred dollars. Since there is no defense, I declare the property in question is owned by Mr. Jody York. Pay your fine before you leave this office." Just then Asa came into the room with a drawn gun. "Pay your fine now or spend sixty days in jail," the judge added. Garway tossed the money on the desk. The judge pocketed it.

On the ride home to Jim's ranch, Judge Worth warned the men that Garway was a very dangerous man. "This isn't over yet." They saw the smoke as they topped a hill. They raced to Jim's house. It was too late. They could only watch it burn. Uncle Jim came from the barn limping, and his face was black and blue from a beating he had taken. "Wasn't much of a house, but it was home," Jim said. "You better check your own house, Jody." They overlooked Jody's house from a hill. In the yard were seven-armed men. There would be more inside. Judge Worth said, "They're in violation of my court order." Asa smiled and said, "You're welcome to ride down there and tell them, if you're of a mind, Judge." "I'll leave that to you gun slingers. Must be a dozen or more gunnies down there. Let's get back to town. I haven't sat a saddle for so long since I broke horses for old man Taylor back in the thirties." They drank at Garway's saloon, ate at Garway's restaurant and slept at Garway's hotel that night. In the morning they again ate at Garway's restaurant, and then walked to the sheriff's office to ask for a posse to evict Garway. He was also in violation of a court order. No one knew where the sheriff was. He wasn't in his office or at the barber shop. In the middle of the street stood Apache. The judge whispered one word, "showdown," then walked away from Jody and Asa. In the shadows, Garway was lurking with his rifle. Apache grabbed at his holster. Jody beat him to the draw and dropped him with one shot. Garway was reloading his rife after missing with his first shot. Asa saw him and fired. The bullet struck Garway in the throat. Some of Garway's gunnies ran from the saloon. Jody yelled, "Calm down, folks. There's no one left to pay you." Then he added. "For your dirty deeds…where the hell did I read that?" The men turned about and reentered the saloon.

A short time later, Jody sat at HIS ranch, drinking coffee from HIS mug. The judge had returned to Buffalo on the north stage after selling his horse. Jody now offered Uncle Jim and Asa a third share in his property. Jim said, "I've been without friends for a long time. Now I've got the best."

# LE GUERRE FINI
**WWII**

      I was stuck in a hospital in France, the result of a shrapnel wound from three mortar shells. It was May 8th, 1945. The skin graft on my leg was healing well and I just wanted to get out. I had been cooped up inside that hospital ward since April 10. I borrowed a uniform and climbed over the back fence, leg cast, crutches, and all. I walked around the village of Chalons sur Marne for a while. When I was tired, I returned to the hospital.

      I was almost to the back gate when a woman on the second floor of a house opened the shutters on her window and shouted to me, "Le guerre fini." I believed she had cursed me so I yelled back, "Same to you! When I made my way back to my large ward. I told the men that I didn't know why a woman cursed me. "What does le guerre fini mean?" Just then a soldier from Louisiana (he spoke French) entered the room. He asked, "What was that you said?" I repeated, "I was walking back to the hospital when some lady yelled it at me, "Le guerre fini." What does it mean?" The GI answered, "The war is over, that's what it means," then he left the ward in search of a radio. Indeed, it was not an empty rumor. We had had many of them.

### EDWARD MCCARTHY

# THE BAILIFF

The stage was late, not just an hour or so, but four hours late. The sheriff guessed that either Apaches or gunmen had held it up. Linc and the judge were on that stage. There would be four trials tomorrow if the schedule were kept. Sheriff Downey gathered a posse of four men, and headed south on the stage road. After passing a two-mile marker they found the stage as well as Linc, the judge, and a Mrs. Carlisle. The stage was rigged for four-up but one of the horses had injured a leg and was removed from her harness. The harness was now rigged for three horses. The driver and passengers had all helped in the rerigging and were about to board the stage when the posse arrived. The stage proceeded north, followed by the posse. Judge Matthews looked at his watch when they arrived in Willow Lea "That's a wasted four hours and twenty five minutes," he said. Linc answered, "Well, maybe not quite wasted, we learned how to re-rig a four- up to a three-up."

After Sheriff Downey gave the judge his worksheet containing the names and offenses of the prisoners, the judge and Linc went to the Willow Lea Saloon. They ate dinner and had a few drinks. Then a stranger approached their table with a proposition. He placed a fat envelope on the table and said, "This can be yours if you find George Gibson not guilty." The judge answered, "Really? Linc, place this man under arrest." Linc stood, revolver in hand and said, "Bribery is a prison offense mister. Put your hands behind your back." The man said, "Look in my shirt pocket, right side." "U.S. Marshal's badge." The man said, "My name is George Jenkins, I had to check you out. Look in the envelope it's only cut up paper, no money. If you took the bribe, you two would now be under arrest." The men sat and relaxed. "Let me explain why I did that. The mayor of this dinky town, Fred Hoskins, is in league with the land agent. That land agent has raised the mortgage percentage on all properties claiming the north wants reparation for the war the north won. That is a lie. Mayor Hoskins and the land agent are sharing that excess percentage, and when someone is forced to sell out, he will offer less than half of the property's value. Four families have already sold out and headed west to California, but none of them have arrived there. A family west of here found the wagon with the name Carl Jenkins burned into a wooden floorboard. The Jenkins family left here two months ago. Carl and Emma never got to Carl's brother in California. I'm gathering evidence against the Hoskin s' gang and others, so if you come up with anything, please let me

## MIX OF STORIES

know." "You bet we will," said Linc. Then he turned to the judge and said, "Looks like these families are paid for their property and when they leave here, they are robbed and probably killed on the trail, including children and pets." "If we find that to be true, George Gibson will hang high. The judge offered, "You can look into it if you wish." Linc answered, "OK, I may do just that." Linc believed that if those people were killed, the killing site wouldn't be very far from town.

One morning he rode the west trail. When he was about three miles from town, he noticed the dense brush on the north side of the road. He stopped and studied the area. He walked into the brush and found footprints of three different sizes and several cigarette butts. He continued searching the area for graves, but found none. He saw a shack about one-half mile away and rode to it. He noticed boot tracks leading to the door, three in all, and different sizes. Linc pushed the door open. Inside were a stove, water pump, a cot and boxes to store food. There was nothing there of a personal nature, nothing to pin down the killers, but he was sure that the graves would be found nearby. He walked to the side of the shack and found two mounds of dirt about two-feet by six-feet long. He was puzzled because more than three people were missing. Then he found where wagons had been burned, all but the metal and wheels which were tossed into a pile. There were five wheels, enough for one wagon, including the spare.

Linc and the judge discussed these findings that evening. Three wagons had headed west. The Jenkins family wagon was found intact and Linc found the ashes of another. They could only surmise that one family of the three had gotten away safely or was buried elsewhere. Judge Matthews checked at the land office and learned that Mayor Hoskins owned the property where the graves were. It was not for sale. That afternoon a stranger approached the judge in the restaurant. He wanted to know if the judge was looking for a ranch. He had a small, 160-acre ranch for sale. The judge asked the man to sit down, and then he asked if the man was selling out because he couldn't pay the mortgage. The man said, "Yes, I was born in that house. When my dad died, he left me in deep debt which I had to clear up, but that left me owing the bank a great deal. The banker was a good man. He lowered my mortgage to $18.10 a month. Now that Hoskins bought that mortgage, I'm about to lose the property." "How much do you owe on the mortgage?" "I believe its $600." Aaron thought for a moment, then said "All right. I'll lend you the money, and you can pay me a small monthly amount, but our contract will stipulate that if I believe I am being taken advantage of, I will claim that property. Is this all right with you?" The man almost cried. "Wait 'til I tell my wife." Linc later said, "I never knew you had money available to lend out." "Oh yes," the judge replied, "My family is in the oil business; ever hear of Matthews' Coal Oil Company?" Linc answered, "Everybody's heard of them." "That's my dad's company." "So, now you're going to lend money to those who can't pay their mortgage?" Aaron believed that his actions should put Hoskins out of business."

By the end of the week seven families had received loans from the judge. Hoskins heard about what the judge was doing. He confronted the judge and Linc at the saloon one evening. "You're eating into my business, Judge." Aaron said, "It is perfectly legal for friends to lend money to friends, Mr. Hoskins." Hoskins was angry. He said,

"Seems like you got a hell of a lot of friends who owe me money." "That may be, Mr. Hoskins, but you can't spend that money in prison." Hoskins looked puzzled, "What the hell are you talking about?" Aaron answered in anger, "I'm referring to those bodies you buried at your shack." Hoskins asked what the hell he was talking about. Aaron answered, "The sheriff's men will be there in the morning to dig them up and give them a proper burial. Then he slapped his hand over his mouth, acting as though he had let the cat out of the bag. Hoskins turned and walked out of the saloon. The judge left the saloon and waved to the sheriff, a signal that Hoskins was on his way to the burial site. The sheriff, marshal, and three deputies would wait in ambush and watch as Hoskins and his men dug up the bodies. When it was over, it was learned that there were three bodies in each grave. One grave also held the body of the family dog.

Hoskins, Gibson, and two other men went to the gallows. A day after the hanging a letter was received by the sheriff, who hurried to the judge with it. The letter was from Henry Sable who lived in California. It read: "A friend sent me a copy of your local Bugle. I'm so glad that I did not take the west road when I left there. I first went south to my brother. Our families then came west together. We love it here. I'm enlarging my ranch house. Yep, Ellen is pregnant again. It makes me sick to think that if I had driven west that day, me, Ellen, my daughter, and her dog would be dead. I never did trust Hoskins, didn't vote for him either. Visit us when you can. I hope the other missing families made it to California. I knew some of them."

MIX OF STORIES

# SLIM

It was April of 1872 when Slim arrived in Rosedale, Arizona Territory. The first place for any-one to visit was, of course, the saloon. This is where a person could get the lay of the land or information on jobs, etc. The saloon was the primary center for information, food, drink, women and gambling. Hank Basset was at the bar when Slim entered. He recognized Hank and approached him. The two men had fought side by side in a terrible war only seven years previously. When the war ended, Slim and Hank were lying in a hospital along with four other southern soldiers. Word had spread about yanks searching for rebels to put them in prison camps. They were checking jails and hospitals, and so far, had rounded up seven men. Slim and Hank were the only men who could walk. Both men had been wounded, one in the leg, the other in his shoulder, but they could walk, or run if needed. They knew they had to get out of Virginia and go to a place where they would not be treated as criminals for fighting in a war.

The men left the hospital and were forced by circumstances to become criminals. They stole clothing, boots, and later found two army horses abandoned by their riders, complete with saddles and carbines. They rode west and were making good time until Slim was shot in the thigh by a sheriff who thought he was an escaped prisoner. Seeing Slim close-up changed the sheriff's mind. He apologized and promised to get Slim healed so he could continue his journey west. He was an honest man. He took Slim into his home where his wife cared for him. The sheriff and his good wife were in their sixties, but were spry for their age. Hank continued west. "You stay here in Oklahoma and I'll see you again in Rosedale, Arizona. It isn't that far from here. You take care of yourself, Pard," Hank had said before he left. Slim was ready to leave after a week spent mostly in bed and on crutches. He was still limping, but had that traveling itch. The sheriff talked him into staying and taking a job as his deputy. "You'll need some traveling money." And he did. The sheriff told him that he had been looking for an honest man for two weeks. "I found that man in a stranger." The pay was forty dollars a month, plus a small amount from fines. He could stay at the sheriff's house, too. He was very handy at repairing roof leaks, mending the chicken coop, etc. Slim was weary of traveling. It would be good to settle down for a while. He agreed to stay and did for seven years. He explained all this to his friend Hank when he arrived in Arizona.

"So, what happened while you were a deputy? Did you have to kill anyone?" Another man at the bar stepped forward and said, "I lived there at the time. Slim was the best lawman that town ever had. You should have seen him take on the town bully who toted two pistols and even had the sheriff buffaloed. Nobody ever saw a faster draw. That bully kept egging Slim until there was no way to avoid a gunfight. He had his guns only half way out of the holsters when Slim fired. The people cheered Slim for doing that. Everyone was scared of that bully, but not him." Hank asked, "Is that true, Slim?" Slim mumbled, "I reckon." "Just be glad you're not a deputy here," The man said. "Why?" "This town's been taken over by the sheriff. Now the mayor and the council can't get him out. There have been three murders here in the last three days and I'd bet my last dollar the sheriff was mixed in them." "Well, Hank, I'm just looking for a job before my money runs out. I don't want to get mixed up in dirty politics. That's not my business." Hank said, "I went to war and served with you, Pard. It's not going to be easy for you to stay out of it. I know you." Slim asked, "Who is the sheriff?" Hank answered, "It's a man named Jimmy Crispo." The man who just walked into the saloon was standing behind Hank. He said, "Someone looking for me?" Slim answered, "No. Sheriff, I'm looking for work, and my friend thought maybe you would know of a job." The sheriff looked him up and down before uttering, "No. I don't know of any jobs." Hank then said, "Come to think of it, check with my boss, He may need another teamster. Can you handle a four-up, a six-up?" Slim nodded his head, "I could do that since I was twelve. I don't have anything else going. I'll try it." In the morning Slim was offered a job, but it was part-time. He would ride shotgun on the stage and maybe take some trips to Tucson for supplies occasionally. The stage came down the street as they spoke. "Here's your first job. Take this shotgun and be on this stage when it pulls out." Slim climbed aboard and sat to the driver's left side. The following afternoon he arrived back in town on another stage. He worked most of that week, making two trips to Tucson for supplies and the mail. Mr. Richter was pleased with his work and gave him the Tucson supply trip because the man who had it previously played sick too often and took three days to complete the ride instead of two, as Slim was doing. After two weeks on the job, he was earning a good salary. Everything seemed right with the world. Then one morning he was given the job as shotgun again. This time there would be twelve thousand dollars aboard, a transfer from the Rosedale town bank to one in Tucson.

Later that afternoon two young men carted Slim's unconscious and wounded body to town in their wagon. Beside him was the dead driver. A passenger had driven the stage back, but had left Slim on the side of the road believing he was dead. Hank saw Slim in the wagon, asked a few questions, and then rode at a gallop to where the men had found Slim. Hank found hoof prints of three horses at the site. One of the horse's shoes showed a nick on the leading edge. Hank told this news to Slim when he awoke two days later. Slim had a bullet hole in his upper left arm and another one in his back. The bullets went clean through him without damaging a bone or an organ. "I followed the horse with a nick in its shoe until I lost it on some hard and rocky ground," said Hank. Slim's back healed rapidly. His left arm gave him trouble, however. He told Hank," You don't realize how much you use your arm until it gets hurt." He was laid up for three days. On the fourth morning he was ready for work although Doctor Harrington was against it. Slim reported to his boss, who was currently speaking with the sheriff. "Hi, Sheriff," Slim said. "Do you have any questions for me?" The sheriff said nothing, but gave Slim a sidelong glance, as though he had been annoyed by the interruption. "It was a simple question, Sheriff. I thought you'd be investigating the shooting, but I suppose you already know all about it." Sheriff Crispo sneered, "And I'm not about to let you know what I know."

Slim merely shook his head and smiled as he walked away, his brow wrinkled in puzzlement as he walked to the saloon. Hank was at the bar. He was surprised to see Slim on his feet so soon. They sat at a table. Hank asked about the robbery. Slim explained that the stage was stopped by a pile of branches on the road. As soon as the stage stopped, the driver was shot in the back of the head. That was followed by two more shots that hit Slim in the back and in the arm, one from behind and one from in front of him. He could not recall anything after that. "I guess all we can count on is that horseshoe with a nick on the leading edge that you found." Slim acquired the habit of looking at the ground under horses in search of that hoof print. Three days later he saw it under the deputy sheriff's horse. One of the passengers in that fateful coach had told people that there were three men who robbed the coach. Two had a slight build, one was heavy-set. Slim kept a watch on the law man, hoping to locate those two men with a slight build. The deputy was tall and weighed about 200-pounds.

The route for the stage was changed to avoid places where gunmen could hide, but it was impossible to find a perfectly safe route. The teamsters would have to be extra careful whenever approaching a questionable area. Slim had driven the new route several times without incident. The two slightly built men he looked for were believed to be the sheriff and Tom Riley. These men were often seen together at the saloon and at the sheriff's office. One morning Slim was on the return trip from Yuma when he spotted three riders ahead of the coach heading toward a part of the road that ran between high brush and trees. Slim had to do something. He halted the coach and watched the riders go beyond a rise. He then turned the horses and drove the team down the original route. He arrived at the stage depot in time for lunch. The $14,000 he carried was safe. He ate lunch at Helen's Café with his friend Hank. After coffee they went to the saloon and sat at a table. Hank went to the bar for a bottle and two glasses just as the sheriff, his deputy and Tom Riley walked in. The sheriff walked to Slim's table and asked, "Why did you change your route today?" "How do you know I did that?" The sheriff sneered, "I'm asking the questions!" Slim was slowly angering, "That's for me to know, Sheriff. You have no right to know, but I took the route I believed was safest. I think I avoided a holdup, too." "Very wise of you," The sheriff said as he walked back to the bar.

Slim asked Hank if the sheriff was out of town in the morning. Hank said, "Yeah, he was gone with his two lovelies for more than an hour. They returned just about the time you drove in." "I saw them on the road ahead of me. I think he and his men were setting up another robbery so I changed the route. Maybe he guessed what I had done. Anyhow, he came back empty handed. He's as mad as a scorched dog right now. Hank said, I've got to take some cash, all in coins, on my trip tomorrow. Can you ride-shot gun with me?" "I can ask the boss," said Slim. "What time do you leave?" "Seven." The boss approved of this change, mostly to give more protection to the bank's money. Slim and

Hank met in the morning. There were no passengers, but the coach carried mail, and money from the bank. They climbed aboard and left the depot. Hank was armed with a .44; Slim had a shotgun and a .45. They were very wary and watchful. Hank told of how he once worked as a teamster for a mine owner. His job was to drive wagons of ore. No one tried to rob him then. It was a boring job, but it paid well and was relatively safe. Slim broke into the reverie and said, "That spot up ahead is where I saw our three lovelies going yesterday. It would be just like them to return to the same spot to plan on killing us. Stop the coach. I feel like a target. I'll ride inside. Don't worry I'll be ready. You duck down behind the footboard and drive through that area, and don't dawdle. Hit 'em up!"

When they neared the spot, Hank ducked down and drove fast through the danger spot. They heard the bullets as they sank into the wood of the coach. Slim called for Hank to stop the coach. Three men were standing in the road behind them. Hank emptied his gun at them. One of the robbers fell on the road. The other two clambered aboard their horses. They rode toward the coach. Hank reloaded and took more careful aim. Slim knocked one from his saddle. He took careful aim at the last man and pulled the trigger. The sheriff grabbed at his chest and toppled from his saddle. The three bodies were placed inside the coach. Within a few hours they were back in town When they told their story, someone searched the sheriff's office and found some bank papers in a drawer, papers the sheriff shouldn't have had, but were stolen from past coach robberies. Most of the stolen money from past robberies was also found in the sheriff's safe also. The town celebrated two heroes that day. They were back to work the following morning.

# EASY

Ed added some wood to the campfire and poured himself a cup of coffee. He looked at the man called Easy and said, "Tell Jack how you came by your name." Easy took a deep breath, "It all had to do with my dad. He never went to school. He liked the name Ezekiel, from the Bible, but he couldn't spell it, neither could the sawbones who delivered me. He was just a barber really. Dad spelled my name E-A-S-Y and that's how it was written down in the family Bible." The men talked for a half-hour or so, and then went to sleep on the ground. Ed and Jack were driving 22 horses to Ed's small ranch, but they would gladly share their food with Easy, whom they recently met. In the morning Easy chose to remain with the two men and to help drive the horses the remaining 15-miles. They took their time and arrived just before noon. They were welcomed by an elderly Indian woman. She was glad to see them because their presence helped to keep the wolves away. Easy was asked to stay for the night and Anna, the Indian woman, would make him a good meal and some trail food from the antelope hanging in the shed.

Ed and Jack were roused from a deep sleep by three shots outside the house. They put their pants on, grabbed their rifles and ran outside. They saw Easy reloading his .45. "What the hell are you doing, target practice?" asked Jack. There was some annoyance in his voice. Easy said, "I heard a noise and came outside to see a whole pack of wolves attacking your horses." The men approached the corral and saw the scratch and bite marks on the hind legs of a horse. Easy said, "They were not there when we arrived. I knew they were wolf bites and scratches. Anna had a right to be scared and I knew they'd be back." Three dead wolves lay on the ground inside the corral. "Most of them got away before I could reload. They will be back so be on guard," warned Easy. "You're a right handy man to have around. How about sticking around for a while?" asked Ed. "Be happy to oblige," said Easy.

Easy stayed for three weeks and was not sure of how to tell his friends he was leaving. He and Anna were decorating their Christmas tree with strung popcorn and rock candy while Ed and Jack joked about him being as happy as a twelve-year-old. Ed called out, "You're supposed to tie the rock- candy on the tree, Easy." Anna spoke up. "I make extra sugar candy. Is all right for Easy to eat it." Easy joked, "Thank you, Anna, for sticking up for me." She answered, "You good man."

## EDWARD MCCARTHY

It was three days before Christmas, and supplies were low. Ed asked Easy to accompany him into town. They left early in the morning for groceries and repairs on Ed's .45. When they reached town, Easy went into the saloon while Ed took his .45 to the gun shop. Easy ordered a beer and selected a table. He sat nursing his drink as he waited for Ed to join him. A man approached and said, "I'll be damned, it's you." Then he called to two friends who just entered, "Hey look who's here, our cousin Easy." Easy did not like or trust these men since they had tried to recruit him into their crooked schemes. He told the men to just forget him; he was staying with the owners of the bar-E J ranch, and to make sure they stayed clear of that property. The three men had another drink at the bar, and then left without a word or a wave of the hand to Easy. It was another fifteen minutes before Ed returned from the gun shop and entered the saloon. He had one drink, then said, "The wagon's loaded and my gun is fixed. We'd best get back. Looks like a storm's fixing to hit soon." They put a tight tarp over the supplies before they left.

As they approached the house, they could see Anna. She ran toward them. She was yelling something. Ed stopped the wagon. Anna caught her breath and blurted out, "One, two, three men come to ranch. They kill jack, shoot Anna. They take one, two, three horses and run away." The men ran to the house. Jack lay on the floor. There were two bullet holes in his back. Anna sat in a chair as the men attended to her wounded shoulder. "This is all my fault," said Easy. Those men are my cousins. I told them to stay clear of this ranch, not knowing they needed fresh horses." Anna said, "I no blame you; you good man." Ed added, "No, you can't blame yourself for this. You weren't tainted by the same bad seed as those cousins of yours," Easy was quite saddened by Jack's murder. "I was planning on heading west tomorrow. I wish I had left earlier. I'll head out in the morning, but I'll be trailing those killers." Ed said, "You're welcome here any time, and for as long as you'll stay." Easy said he would be leaving at sun-up. Anna told him she would fix food for the trail.

The rain let up just before dawn. Easy had his horse saddled. The house was quiet and dark. Easy mounted his horse and headed west. Ed was peering through the window and didn't leave until Easy was out of sight. The rising sun felt warm on Easy's back, but it would soon get overbearing for him and his horse. He looked for signs of water, such as a line of trees. Near sunset, he saw a line of trees, and there was a stream. He camped there for two days, regaining his strength. Easy arrived in Westridge, near the California border. He was tired so he holed up at the hotel until six that evening. His first stop was the restaurant, and later he sat at a table at Wilson's Saloon. He was not thinking straight and he felt weak and confused lately. He had seen the doctor's sign a few doors from the saloon. He made a visit to Dr. Anderson. The doctor probed and thumped and all the while said, "Uh-huh."

"What's the bad news, Doc?" Dr. Anderson replied, "It aint all that bad. You need some rest, two-weeks I'd say." Easy asked, "Why?" The doctor placed his hand on Easy's arm and said, "You say you came here from the east? I'd say it rained a little before you came here, and you camped by a stream." Easy said, "Yes, that's all true." The doctor continued. "Well, that water runs only after a rain, and it's laced with poison called arsenic. It affects your memory and your muscle coordination. I'd say to drink a lot of water, flush it out of your system. In the meantime, get that rest I spoke of. That'll be two dollars." Easy returned to the saloon muttering, "water? Rest? Arsenic? I'll stay here another day. I have the money, but I'm not giving up the chase." He began asking questions as soon as he was on the trail, "Have you seen three men who ride together, one is taller than the others?" Finally, a man said, "Yeah, three men stopped for water at my ranch and asked how far it was to Santa Rosa. I told them about 20-miles. It's just over the California border. They said they were promised jobs there. That was yesterday mister." Easy asked, "What kind of work is there in Santa Rosa?" The man said, "Hell, I don't know, ranching, maybe mining. They're opening and closing gold and silver mines around here every day." Easy shook his head, "The boys I'm looking for wouldn't do any hard work like mining or ranching. They'd prefer to rob the ranchers and miners." The man said, "Well then, they'd work for Charley Sikes. He runs the town, owns most of it. The damn sheriff is in with him too. If you're thinking of going there, take my advice and hide your money in your sock." Easy practiced his quick-draw and accuracy that afternoon. He was very good. Two days later he was feeling a little better. He rode into Santa Rosa and ate lunch at the Sikes Saloon. He had noticed the Sikes Gun Shop and tool shop, even the Sikes Lady's Wear Shoppe.

After lunch, he nursed a beer. One of his cousins took one step into the saloon, saw Easy, turned, and exited. Easy's right hand raised and lowered his .45 inside the oiled holster. Then he doubted what he was doing there He decided that he just could not kill his cousins, not like this. He cursed silently. They had been friends for so many years. Hell, maybe they would go away or get killed, or go to prison. His anger lessened in time. He took a deep breath and then sighed, feeling the tension leaving his body as though dropping a heavy weight. Murdering his cousins just wasn't for him. He made up his mind to return to his friends' ranch. He was told by the barman that there was a way station for the stagecoach line about half-way back to Ed's ranch. He stayed in Santa Rosa that night, but was mounted with an extra canteen of water at sunup when he rode east. He was on the trail for about an hour when someone took a shot at him from a rocky ridge. The bullet kicked up dirt in front of his horse. He fell and thumped his head on the ground. When he awoke, he shouted, "You shouldn't have done that, boys. I had already given up the chase. You killed my good friend back at the ranch, and all for nothing, now you made it personal." One of the cousins shouted, "You had $200.00 in your pocket, you can't say that's nothing." How much you got in your pocket, Easy? Just hand it over and go on your way," shouted another man. Easy was in a rocky area and could not spot his cousins, but he was becoming angry again, He shouted, "Ok, come and find out, unless you're still too yellow." Time seemed to slow down. Every sound had significance. A shot hit four feet from him. Then the birds sang again. Fifteen minutes passed. The birds became silent again. Easy knew someone was approaching. He quickly changed his position. A cousin came into view and aimed his gun at where Easy had been. Easy shot him dead, He shouted for the other two to halt. They continued to approach him. One drew his weapon and aimed. Easy shot him dead then aimed at the last man who dropped his rifle. "I quit," the man yelled. "Bury your brothers, and don't ever let me see you again," warned Easy. Even though he was still a bit groggy, he did not like to remain with or near his cousin. He mounted his mare and rode east, back to his friends with three of the stolen horses in tow. He knew that Anna's cooking would soon get him back in shape.

# DR BEACH
## WWII

My mom, Carolyn McCarthy, came from Ireland during the 1920's. She had sailed those thousands of miles in steerage. It was not long before she was working as a telephone operator until she got a job as a nurse for a Dr. Beach in Brooklyn, N.Y. He attended my birth in 1926. Mom always spoke of him as a very good man.

Eighteen years later I was wounded in Germany. I waited two days at a large medical tent, and then was flown to the 239th General Hospital in Chalons sur Marne, France. I spent 62-days there on a regimen of penicillin every three hours, and had two operations for a skin graft. The doctor did a fine job. The scar is hardly noticeable. That doctor's name was Beach. I later learned that he was the son of that same Dr. Beach in Brooklyn that my mom had worked for. That's some coinkidink.

EDWARD MCCARTHY

# McNULTY'S DOG

Come get your dog, McNulty and take him out of here.
Your precious Irish Setter just drank up all the beer.
He's eaten all the pretzels, the cake's still on his face.
He also drank my glass of wine. He's a damn disgrace

My little Spitz is pregnant and many neighbors called
to tell me of the others your little angel balled.
Remember widow Murphy? She said he wore a fur.
She never could see close-up, and what he did to her

could not be said politely or in normal tones
He had her fooled for days. She cries, "He never phones."
She walks down the avenue asking about her "gent".
"A chest full of hair," she says, "a speech impediment."

"I know that he is very odd, yet he knew his place.
Who else would sit so patiently as he licked my face?
He was too short and penny-cheap for my expensive taste.
and if he comes a- groveling, I'll tell him he's a waste."

Come get your mutt, McNulty, and take him far away.
I never want to see him another blessed day.
You know your Irish Setter is a great disgrace
And wipe that nasty grin off your ugly face

# LAND GRABBER

The campfire was still glowing when Jim Wilson awoke. It was dark. He sat up and tossed some small bits of wood on the embers, then rose and shook off the cold. When he looked into the coffee pot, it was nearly full. He placed it back on the rock to warm it a bit. He was thirsty. "Warm is good enough," he said aloud as he felt the coffee warming his innards. He looked up into the blackness and said, "Thank you, Lord." Card Nelson awoke. "Why do you say that?" he asked. "Oh, I guess it's because my dad was a sometimes preacher, and he said it doesn't hurt to thank the lord." Randy Welsh was also awakened. "What the hell are you two gabbing about?" It's hours before sunup." "Have some coffee, Randy; there's still more in the pot." said Jim. The three men were close in age. They had met only two days previously, but were already close friends because of their similar recent experiences. Jim had merely walked out of a northern prison camp when the gate guard was busy with a woman. Randy and Card had dug under a fence at a different prison camp. They told how they froze when two yanks spotted them. However, the yanks turned their backs on the two escapees and walked away. On the road, they met two yanks who were drunk. They recognized each other. The yanks told them to stay away from towns and to head west to the streets of gold. The three men had suffered similar privations. They drank what coffee was left, then returned to their blankets. They remained asleep even after sunrise. The men were emaciated and weakened from the paltry food rations at the camps.

They reckoned they were somewhere in Ohio, and decided to head for a town despite the good yanks' warning. They counted their combined treasury. It totaled $2.83. When they reached the town of Salisbury they went into the saloon. The barman said, "It's hard times, boys. Hasn't been any work here for months. Them that's got a job live here. No one's goin' to hire a saddle tramp, and you boys don't even have a saddle." They wasted no time in leaving. Later, on the road, they came to an overturned wagon. As they studied on it, the driver came from hiding behind some bushes. He was wielding a shotgun. "We don't mean you any harm, mister. We came to help if we can. If not, we'll be on our way," said Card. "Well, I see that you men don't even carry firearms. Something frightened my mare as I came around the turn. I think that's what happened. It frightened her and she turned too quickly. I own the Bar-Oh ranch. I call it that because I had to borrow the money to get started. My name is Frank Wilman."

"How is the ranch doing now, Mr. Wilman?" Jim asked. "It's doing fine now. I paid off that loan years ago. "You men set my wagon aright and come with me. I can repay you with a meal, at least." The men climbed aboard and were at the ranch in a short time. They were surprised at the cleanliness of the ranch, and were impressed by the large size of the main house. They were discussing this when Mr. Wilman came to them and said, "What the hell are you plotting now?" Then he noticed the expression of fear on the men's faces. "Oh, I'm sorry, I was just joshing you. Hell, you could have done me in anytime in the past half hour. I can use men I can trust. I expect many horses to be delivered today, and I need them saddle broke. Can any of you do that?" All three men answered' "Yes." Mr. Wilman offered to pay a dollar a head plus a horse of their own choosing when they were through. "Fair enough?" The men answered with a nod. Jim was smiling. "Best offer we've heard all day," he said. The men laughed. Then Mr. Wilman invited them to the table for dinner. They ate so much that the cook had to return to the kitchen twice for more food for the famished men. Mr. Wilman enjoyed watching them eat.

That night in the bunkhouse, the men spoke of their good luck in meeting Mr. Wilman. If driven to it, they could have dispatched him and stolen his horse and rig, but they were not that sort of people. Then the talk turned to retirement. Card told of Mr. Wilman's advanced years, but he was still working the ranch. He recalled when his dad was sixty; he was all stove up from breaking horses and all his bones in his youth. When he needed help, no one came. The reverend Jensen brought him a meal once in a while. "Dad worked with a buffalo skinner for a time until Indians caught up with them. We found them a week later." They spoke of hard times and families with many children. Large families seemed to pleasure the religionists, but many of those children died of bullets and disease unlike children in small families. There were eleven children in Card's family. Randy came from a family of eight children, and Jim claimed nine. It was hoped also that children would help the parents when they got old. As a rule, however, most children left home with resentment for their parents, leaving the girls to stay and assist the parents in their old age. Jim told them what Mr. Wilman had told him. He said that Mr. Wilman had left Connecticut and went to Ohio. He won much money at the gaming tables and bought this ranch. He bought so many cattle and horses that he was forced to borrow money, but it paid off. He fattened those cattle and broke those horses, and made a fortune. He sent for his wife and infant son, but they never arrived. The coach they rode in was overturned and both were killed. The accident was blamed on a snake in the road.

At the end of the month, the horses had been broken to saddle. Mr. Wilman was good to his word. He paid off the men, gave each a horse, saddle and tack, then told them he could hire back two of the men. Randy Welsh picked up straws, but Jim said, "I always wanted to see California, so never mind drawing straws. Jim had a stake of $43.00. His friends chipped in another $5.00 each, and Mr. Wilman gave him a blanket, gun belt and a .45 caliber revolver, plus $7.00 more. He said, "A man should have some walking-around money." Jim put $50.00 of his money into his sock, just in case. If anyone asked, he would say that he was going west because his uncle had a job for him. In a fair fight with fists or guns, Jim could easily hold his own. He was put to the test on his first night on the road. He was gathering twigs for a campfire when he saw a shadowy figure dart from one tree to another. He heard dry twigs and leaves rustling. He hid behind a great oak and instinctively drew his weapon and ducked down. A figure darted again. Another shadow moved behind a tree. Jim shouted, "Can I help you gentlemen?"

The response was immediate. Two bullets struck the tree and showered bits of bark onto Jim's shoulder, but Jim had seen the muzzle flash from one of the shooters. He fired at it and heard the loud, "Uh, dammit!" then a shot came from the left front. Jim changed his position and fired. He heard the man fall. Jim ran to the spot. The man was dead. A voice some distance behind him said, "Drop the gun mister and I'll leave." Jim could not see the man. He picked up a stone and tossed it to his left. "Now, that was pretty stupid, Mister. You're done for now." The man stood, but Jim could not see him. He fired at the voice. The man fell to the ground. Jim waited. When he believed it safe, he looked about him, and then searched the men. They had $14.00 among them. He pocketed the money, took their guns and ammo, found their horses and cut them loose, then he rode another ten miles before making camp on the side of a river. The sound of the river lulled him to sleep.

In the morning he followed the river to a town and railroad depot. After loading his horse in a cattle car, he sat in the coach section of the train. The conductor punched his ticket and bragged about the speed of the train. "Fifty miles an hour is a good speed, and this train goes that fast once in a while. I've heard that people may go insane at 100 miles an hour." The young man who had sold Jim two sandwiches said, "That's nonsense, some birds fly at that speed and you will not find one in a looney bin." That called for a loud laugh from all the travelers. The trip was too fast. Jim had just gotten used to the hard seat and two nights of sleeping on a wooden plank placed across two seats. He enjoyed the view from the window and he could buy coffee and sandwiches at each stop, even a wedge of pie at one stop. He had viewed herds of buffalos and antelopes from the train windows. He was told that the men in the car behind him were shooting buffalo. He remembered smiling when he saw a house with clothing on the line and children playing in the front yard. He had even seen four Indians waving at the train.

The train arrived at Andover, Arizona Territory. The conductor advised the passengers that the train was not continuing until the army cleared away the Indians who were tearing up track. Jim collected his horse and rode to the nearest saloon in search of a job. His attention was drawn to two men because he had seen one of them pointing to him a few minutes earlier. He drew a deep breath, sensing trouble. Surprisingly, the men left the saloon while Jim was eating lunch. When he walked to the front door, sandwich in hand, he saw the men. They were leading his horse away. "Hey!" Jim shouted. The men's heads jerked about. "We were just admiring your horse, mister," Jim said, with a little anger, "You can just as well admire it where you found it. Put the horse back." The men merely stood looking at him. "Now!" shouted Jim. The men hurriedly led the horse back and tied it to the hitch rail. Jim ate the last of his sandwich as he watched the men walk down the street and into a saddle shop. Jim mounted his mare and rode in the opposite direction. He then stopped and tied his mare outside THE OFFICE, another saloon. He ordered a whiskey as he sat at an empty table. As he reached for his drink, a stranger sat down opposite him. "What can I do for you?" Jim asked. The man said, "I saw what you did to the Mason brothers, my friend. They are very dangerous people. They may want to get even. Be careful if you spend any time in this town." Jim said, "I don't expect to stay. There are no jobs here." The stranger smiled and said, "I need a deputy. I'm the sheriff." He showed his badge. Jim asked. "What aren't you telling me, Sheriff?" The sheriff told Jim about his deputy being shot two nights ago and his suspicion that the Mason brothers were the shooters. 'Shot him in the back, too." Jim said, "Sounds like a dangerous job." The sheriff nodded his head and said, "Yeah, but you had the guts to face down those two dangerous men, so you must be fast with a gun." Jim smiled, "Flattery will get you nowhere, but I'll take the job. I need the money." "My name is John Matthews: Call me John." "Mine is Jim Wilson. Maybe it'll be good to settle down for a change. It seems I've been on the road forever. I need the rest. I don't even know the date, John." John said, "It's September the fourteenth." "Hell, you say. I missed my 25$^{th}$ birthday last month."

    The sheriff swore him in and assigned Jim to patrol the town after dark. "Get a drink if you want. I'm grabbing some shuteye while I can. I've been up for thirty-seven hours. I'm fifty-two and I feel it more than you would." Jim walked about the town, familiarizing himself with the shops and the people. He passed the Mason brothers as they entered the HAPPY TIDINGS saloon. He felt dirty and crawly just from seeing them. After a week, Jim started feeling better. He weighed himself on a penny weighing machine. He was back to 175 pounds. The numbered stick showed he was six-feet, and two inches tall. His only friends in town so far were the sheriff and June and Ginger McGuire. The women owned the millinery shop. He had met them when they were locked out of their shop and Jim sent the town locksmith to open their door and allow them to work. They had broken off the key in their lock. While Jim was trying to date Ginger, the Mason brothers were across the street, pointing and tittering like the fools they were. When Jim glared at them, they left. The trouble with the brothers would soon come to a head.

    For two days the sheriff and deputy went about the town and surrounding area collecting taxes on property, horses and cattle. They had collected $18,000. When finished, they rode back toward town, talking about a good meal and some needed sleep under a roof. They could see the taller buildings in town through the trees when a gruff voice ordered them to stop and drop the money bag. Jim slowly reached for his gun when a voice behind him said, "Keep your hands up." When Jim hesitated, the man shouted, "Now!" Jim immediately knew that voice. When the men had the money, one said, "Now, skedaddle!" The thieves rode off in the opposite direction. The sheriff and Jim took their horses into the trees and tied them where they wouldn't be seen. They returned to the trees closest to the road and waited. It was about 15-minutes later when they heard voices on the road. At the proper time, the sheriff shouted, "Stop, you idiots, and put your hands up." One of the unmasked Mason brothers reached for his gun. The sheriff shot him. Then the other one drew his gun. Before he could raise it, Jim shot the thief in the shoulder. The sheriff remarked, "I'm glad to see you don't enjoy killing." Jim replied, "Did all that in the big war, John."

## MIX OF STORIES

When the Masons went to trial, half the town's people filed charges against them. they were hanged that night. Sheriff Matthews was also shot that night. He was shot twice in the back as he checked doors on the closed shops. Jim was soon at his side and saw it was serious. Before the sheriff blacked out, he told Jim that he had a good idea who shot him. Jim called on two men he could trust to take the sheriff out of town to the Farley ranch, and to tell people the sheriff died. They agreed. Doctor Winston removed the bullets from the sheriff and said that with good nursing, he would make it. Mr. Farley and his daughter were given this chore. They would gladly do it for the sheriff. Jim wired his two friends back in Ohio that he needed help if it wouldn't interrupt their lives. The reply was, "Be there in 2-days. Mr. Wilman doesn't need us until spring." Jim met the train two days later. Their first stop was the saloon. They sat at a table and talked in low tones. It wasn't long before a husky, middle aged buffalo hunter entered, walked to the bar and shouted, "Whiskey!"

"Pipe down," the barman said. "I heard you. You don't have to shout and annoy the other customers." "Whiskey," the man shouted in defiance. The barman poured the man a drink, but before he could withdraw his hand, the annoying man sank his knife into the bar a mere inch from the man's hand. Jim strode to the bar. He grabbed the knife and pulled it sideways until it snapped off the tip. The buffalo skinner raised his arm to strike Jim, but he was slow. Jim hit the man's arm with the side of his hand. Everyone could hear the snap of bone. The very surprised skinner winced in pain as he grabbed at his arm. "I can't work with a broke arm." "The barman can't work with your knife in his hand either. Straighten up or get the hell out of town." The buffalo skinner asked, "Who the hell are you?" "I am your worst boogie-man if you don't straighten up. I'm the sheriff, who are you?" "Clyde." "Clyde what?" Clyde whined, "Clyde Mason. Can I go now? I gotta get my arm fixed up. These two men behind me can answer your questions. They're my brothers." Jim asked if they were related to the men who were hanged. "Yeah," one of them answered, "they were our nephews. Clyde was their pa." When the men had left, the barman warned Jim that these men will try to avenge that hanging, and now that broken arm too. He added that the men had been in trouble all their lives, "So my grandma tells me." Card was leading the way as he and his friends were leaving the saloon. He suddenly stretched out his arms, halting his friends, and asked the barman if he had a side door. "I smell danger out there. I think the uncles are in hiding, waiting for us to go out." The barman pointed to the alley door. The men turned and exited through the alley all the way back to the sheriff's office. Jim asked, "What the hell was that all about?" Randy spoke up and told how Card was their scout in the army, and he was able to smell yanks and snipers in hiding. Our company skirted around them. "That's what it's about." Jim recalled a Sioux scout in his company who also claimed to smell the enemy. Randy later saw two of the Masons come from hiding across the street. They were toting their buffalo rifles, and indeed had been waiting for the men to exit the saloon by the front doorway.

In the morning, Jim barely noticed Mr. Watkins as the man boarded the northbound stage. Jim and his friends were going to the restaurant. About a half hour later as they finished their meal, the Masons walked in. Jim's hand slipped down to rest on the butt of his .45. He noticed the sweat on the men's faces. He also noticed their horses. They looked soaped up and were reeking of sweat. "They must have been in a hell of a hurry," Jim said. A little later, a man came into Jim's office to tell him that he had passed the stage on his way to town. He said that everyone was dead, the driver, Frank Watkins, and Mrs. Lila Gibbons, the Barber's wife. Jim and his friends rode out to find the stage. It was about seven miles from town. They checked the area, but found nothing of value. Mrs. Gibbons' purse lay on the floor of the coach; its contents had been spilled out. Mr. Watkins had been robbed too. His pockets were turned out. Card drove the team of four back to town. When he returned, Jim visited the barbershop to inform Mr. Gibbons of his wife's death. "It's bad, Noah," he said. "I didn't want her to go." Noah said, "But she tied a red ribbon around her money for good luck, and told me not to worry."

The sun was setting behind the western mountains when Jim and his friends decided to go to the saloon. What drew their attention as they entered were the loud voices of the Masons. The men tried to ignore the din, but had to shout to be heard. Jim finally had enough. "Quiet down!" he shouted. The Masons stopped bullying the barman as they turned to face Jim. Clyde sneered, "Looks like the sheriff and his posse want some peace. Let's go visit Maggie and her girls." "Wait up," shouted the barman. "You owe me three thirty for those last drinks." Clyde tossed a five-dollar bill on the bar and sneered, "Keep the change." When Clyde had reached for his money, some bills were tied with a red ribbon, which he tossed to the floor. "You don't care how you spend Lila's money, do you?" Jim asked. "Who the hell is Lila?"

"Lila Gibbons, the helpless lady you killed this morning and whose money you are now spending. So that is why you and your horses were so sweaty this morning. Drop your gun belts or draw. You are under arrest. Card, collect their weapons." Only two minutes later the Masons were in jail. In the morning mail were posters on the Masons, offering a total of $2,000.00, dead or alive. Jim told the men they would get the reward "because a lawman cannot claim it here." He showed the men several more posters and said he knew where some of the wanted men were. "Are you in?" The men glanced at each other and said, "You bet." The Masons were tried two days later and sentenced to 20-years each. They were hauled away by Marshal Durant.

The next day was Sunday. Jim and his men passed the church on their way out of town. Jim saw a buggy with a sign in the rear. It read, "Just Married" Jim asked a young man, "Who's getting hitched?" "You know, the lady who runs that millinery shop, Ginger. She's marrying the preacher." Jim was quite surprised, but he had been so busy lately, he had not kept up with town affairs, even with the woman he intended to visit more often, but his courting was too slow. Farther out of town the men could see a line shack in the distance. They hobbled their horses and sneaked up on the shack. A man came from the shack and walked into some brush. A few minutes later, he returned to the shack. "That's Frank Hogan, inside is his partner. They're worth $1,400.00 each. Let's wait until they're sleeping. Then we can take them more easily." "How did you get your name, Card?" Randy asked. "My pa was a gambler. Someone bet him 20 to 1 that he wouldn't get the card he needed during a poker game. Pa lost the bet. When I was born, he named me card then bragged that he did get the card he needed. "Are your parents still alive?" "No, Pa was shot in a saloon, and Ma died of the grippe." The men soon settled down and slept. Jim awoke at 2:00 am and awakened Randy and Card. They sneaked up to the shack and burst through the door. It was a rather easy arrest. Card later murmured something about getting enough money and then buying a ranch. The men agreed on $10,000.00. They were still discussing this later in Jim's office. The mayor had made him Sheriff. Card said something humorous. Jim laughed, but it was cut short when a bullet came through a door glass and struck him in the shoulder. Card ran out the back door to circle around and get behind the shooter on the other side of the street. He soon walked in through the front door shaking his head. Jim was stemming the blood from his shoulder with a kerchief. The men helped him to the doctor's office. Card said that all he could find was a cartridge from a buffalo gun. Jim asked the men to ask around town. "Maybe someone saw something."

They returned in an hour. "You wouldn't believe it. The barman was taking out his garbage when he saw Clyde Mason walking toward this office with his buffalo gun." Jim asked Card to send a wire to the state prison and ask if Clyde Mason is a prisoner there. An answer came in short time. Clyde Mason had escaped prison and was seen heading toward Andover. That evening, Card and Randy were on the other side of the street, watching the alleys, but Clyde wouldn't be there this night. He was at the back door of the sheriff's office. Jim heard a slight scratching at his back door. He saw the knob turn slowly. He ducked down at the side of his desk. Suddenly, the door burst open. Jim could feel the swish of cool air as he fired two bullets into Clyde Mason's belly. Mason fell, firing a bullet into the floor as he died. "Tomorrow we should know if there is another reward for Clyde," said Jim.

The telegrapher delivered the answer on the following morning. An additional reward was offered for Clyde, dead or alive. The men were elated. "We can buy a ranch now." said Randy. Card was wiping his eyes. I never owned property before; I'm going to be a rancher. Jim told of where there were many wild horses. "We can break them and make a fortune. Card said, "Here we go, from lawmen to breaking horses again. Let's go have a drink. Sheriff Mathews should be healed up in a day or two, I hope."

EDWARD MCCARTHY

# THE BAILIFF
## RAPE

Territorial judge Wm. Matthews and his bailiff, Linc Chambers arrived in town to conduct trials for six county prisoners and two city prisoners. Trials would be held at the county court house. Hal Stahl was held on a rape charge involving his own wife. The defense claimed that the Bible made women for the pleasure of men, as Eve was made for Adam. Judge Matthews became angry. He said, "Many claim that our laws were taken from religion. That is not true. Our laws are separated from those of religion. We do not stone people. We do not tell children to honor parents who lead them into sins and crimes. Religion has its place in the church, not in the streets or the court rooms. Now, do your duty as lawyers, not as spreaders of the faith. I want the evidence and witnesses." The defense attorney was justly chastised. He sat.

"We have a witness, your honor," said the prosecutor. Mrs. Wilson took the oath and told of hearing her neighbor screaming. She could see into the neighbor's kitchen. She saw Mrs. Stahl being beaten by her husband who punched her until she was unconscious, and then he raped her. "Her face was all bloodied, and she couldn't walk a straight line. He punched her in the back, and she fell down. Then he was choking her on the floor. I couldn't look any more." "I'm giving Mr. Stahl two years in prison for battery and rape of a defenseless woman. If the cowardly cur ever repeats this crime in my jurisdiction, I will sentence him to hang. I hope no one else attempts to misuse religion in my court to make women second-class citizens." Judge Matthews tended to the remaining cases then he and Linc walked to the saloon for lunch. They were drinking their second cup of coffee when a man approached and said, "There's a child out in the alley of the restaurant, and he was eating garbage." "You should tell the sheriff," said the judge. "He's gone out of town, Judge. I told the kid not to eat garbage, but he ran away, then he came back later. He said he was six-years-old and hungry." "I'll look into it," promised Linc. When he went to the alley the child was there. "Aren't you thirsty?" Linc asked in a friendly voice. The child was prepared to run, but Linc's quiet voice seemed to calm him. "Yes, I am," answered the boy. "Come with me. We'll get some water or milk. I'm a bit thirsty too," said Linc. The child asked, "Are you going to put me in jail?" Linc smiled and said," No." The child reached up and took Linc's hand as they walked to the restaurant. Linc asked the child where he lived. "One mile out on the south road. That's what my dad always said." "Where are your mom and dad now?" The boy looked worried, "They're home, but they won't wake up. Two bad men hit them and made them bleed and I couldn't wake them up." Linc took the boy, Carl, to his home, and told him to wait outside. He knocked on the door. There was no response. He entered the house and was shocked by the terrible odor of death. He saw a man lying on the floor. When he approached, he saw a woman lying by the fireplace. They were dead. The rooms were in a mess after being ransacked by the killers.

On the way back to town Carl asked, "Can you fix it, Linc?" The sheriff had just returned. Linc brought the man up to date. "Those two killers could still be in town. They had not seen Carl because he had been hidden under the bed. He's the only one who can identify those men." "That's a terrible burden on a six-year old," the sheriff said. "He's our only witness. Don't let that fact get out, Sheriff." "I know better than that." Linc asked where he could leave the kid. "I can't be taking him from town to town. "Linc, this aint Chicago or Boston. We aint got those kinds of places. We're lucky to have a schoolhouse and a teacher. Maybe you'll find such a place in one of the towns on your circuit." Linc shook his head, "No, they're no bigger than this town, but maybe..." Linc wasn't very hopeful.

During the next two weeks they worked in nine towns. Linc and the judge were now on a first name friendship. They discussed how unfair it was to the child to be pulling up stakes every day or so and moving from one dusty town to another. Carl couldn't even attend school. "I'm becoming very fond of Carl too. It won't be the same when I can't see that six-year old flopping around on your horse, or asking me how I know a bull from a cow," said the judge. Linc smiled and said, "Well, he can tell anyone now, how to tell the difference, so he's learning, but maybe the wrong things" "Sounds to me like he's listening to the wrong people, Linc."

Bill Tarman had a terrible reputation in Red Bluff and anywhere else he was known. When the judge tried him, Carl was in the care of Mrs. Hornstock. but he disobeyed her orders and went to visit where Linc and the judge worked. He was waiting outside the saloon, where trials were held in Red Bluff, when Tarman was marched back to his jail cell. Linc came out presently and took Carl's hand in his as they crossed the street. "Did you punish that bad man?" Carl was pointing at Bill Tarman. "We surely did. He was given six months in jail." Carl jerked free of Linc's hand in obvious anger and shouted, "Six months? Is that all you get for murdering a mom and dad?" Linc knelt down to be eye-to-eye with Carl. "What are you saying?" Carl was close to tears, "Those bastards killed my mom and dad and all they get is six-months? He held onto my mom while the other bastard man hit her with his gun, then they both beat my dad, and he was fighting and yelling at them. Boy, my dad could fight."

Linc could see the tears building in Carl's eyes. He said, gently, "We didn't know Tarman was one of those bad men. He was tried today for hitting an old man." "Are you going to fix it, Linc?" "I certainly will." Linc went to the jail and faced the prisoner. "Where is your partner?" Tarman answered, "I aint got no partner." "You had one when you killed a married couple and stole their money." "I don't know what you're getting at, what couple?" "Paul and Josephine Phelps, up in Red Ford. They had a little ranch and Mr. Phelps collected $700.00 that morning for selling some cattle and horses. They were needy people and you left their family with nothing. The owner even foreclosed on the house and stock for what was owed on their mortgage." "Well, I didn't kill no one," Tarman asked. "Are you saying your partner killed them?" "Well, it wasn't me, had to be him." Linc asked, "Who is him?" "Jess Williams. We split the blanket after that job 'cause he said no killing, then he killed." Linc wanted to know where Williams could be found." "He hangs out at the Trails End saloon in Phoenix. That's where I met him. Linc sent a wire to the sheriff of Phoenix, who promised to search for the man. The upshot of the case came a month later in Red Ford. The kid identified both men and told the court in his own words, what the men had done. Several members of the jury dabbed at their eyes as the facts became known. The jury reached a decision at the end of the testimony. The men were found guilty. The jury requested the death penalty, and the judge complied.

After the trial Linc took Carl aside and said, "There are certain things set aside for only adults, like getting married, wearing a gun, and cussing. I remember what you called those men. By doing that you jumped from a child to an adult. We can't allow that." "Yeah," Carl answered, "but I didn't wear no gun or get married. I only cussed. I promise I won't do it again until I'm old. OK, Linc? Does that fix it?" Linc smiled as he said, "OK, you fixed it."

MIX OF STORIES

# WWII
## PRISONERS

It was during what someone called "The mopping up phase" when my company was fighting in, and capturing 2 and 3 villages per day. My job was usually as first scout or forward radio man. On this particular day I was the radio man, carrying a 45-pound radio on my back. Captain Mike told me to protect the radio by going inside the first house in the village. The sounds of battle started as I reached the front gate to the house. I ducked lower just as a sniper's bullet clipped the nearby hedge and shredded leaves fell on my shoulder. I stayed low and entered the house, someone's home. I noticed photos on the mantle, pictures of a mother, child and grandmother. I noticed the little souvenirs from various German cities, pictures on the wall depicting relatives. There were no swastikas or pictures of Hitler hanging anywhere. Why, these people were just like my folks back home in Brooklyn, N.Y. Just then a German soldier entered the kitchen. He scared hell out of me, but I had the drop on him. I believe he thought it was the place to surrender? He removed his helmet and dropped his rifle outside. Within 15-minutes there were 23 prisoners in that small kitchen. I was going to use them to get me safely out of the house because snipers had the front and back doors covered. Yes, I tried both doors. I planned on getting among the prisoners as they walked out of the house. The snipers wouldn't shoot their own men, would they?

Then, two G.I.'s entered the kitchen. One of them told the prisoners to toss their wallets on the floor. "Whoa," I told the G.I, "We're not here to rob these people, and I don't need your kind of help. Start moving." I didn't want to say out loud that the prisoners could easily jump us and kill us. The GI's moved out the door. My company was returning. The battle was over. I could hear my friends on the street. I let the prisoners go through the doorway and I got at the end of the parade, safely. When I left them, I shouted, "Good luck, soldaten."

# EDWARD MCCARTHY

# WWII
## THE ROAD

    This story is true and lacking in the embellishments of ego and added memories. I was with my infantry company about a half block from the autobahn highway somewhere in Western Germany in early 1945. We were dog tired after taking two villages that day. I was new to G Company and knew some, but not all, of the men in my squad and platoon. I didn't know the young man who chose me to accompany him on a patrol near enemy lines. We were to try and locate enemy headquarters. Our captain knew we were close. As it turned out, we were but one city block distant.

    The night was moonless. There were no street lights, house lights, traffic or people. We had to keep our eyes on the ground so we would not get lost, trip, or step on a mine. There was to be no talking because sounds carry farther at night, especially if the air is moist. It was slow going. We had traveled only about one block when out of the darkness came a gruff shout, "Halt," in a German accent! It sent a wave of shivers up my spine. We froze. I turned to head back to safety, but my partner grabbed my arm and prevented me from leaving, and then he spoke to the guard in perfect German. I asked what he said. He whispered, "I didn't lie, I told him we are on patrol, looking for headquarters. He told me where it is." I turned to head back, but he grabbed my arm again. Then my partner talked again to the guard. This time it was a longer talk and I wanted to get the hell out of there. The guard laughed. We turned and retraced our steps back to our quarters. I asked him "What did you say to make that guard laugh?" My partner said, "I told him a joke about Hitler." Now I was impressed. "My name is Ed," I said, "What's yours?" Without hesitation, he said "Just call me Jew- boy; that's what everyone else calls me." I said, "maybe so, but not me."

MIX OF STORIES

# SURVIVOR'S GUILT
## WWII

We were racing across a plowed field toward a farm house about 1,000-yards distant. Our goal was the wooded area beyond the field. It was April 10, 1945. My company was at the western edge of Dortmund, Germany. Hank was in the lead. I was second, and a tall man was third. The remainder of our company waited to see if we made it safely. Actually, we didn't. The lead man reached the house and was protected from the mortar shells that exploded only 15-feet away. I had a piece torn from my leg plus several holes I later found in my field jacket. One hole was in my upper pocket. A piece of shrapnel had entered one side of it and exited the other side, neatly cutting a pack of cigarettes in half.

Immediately after the first shell exploded, I turned to the man behind me. He was holding in his intestines which protruded from a gaping tear in his stomach. I ran back to him and half carried him to the house as two more mortar rounds exploded. Once inside, the man fell to the floor. I searched for a sheet to wrap his open wound in, but the rooms were bare except for two elderly women and an old man. The wounded man died before the aid men arrived. I spent two months in a French hospital and while I was there President Roosevelt died and the war ended. I often think of that soldier who died. I felt guilty because I couldn't help him, and I never even knew his name. I later asked a doctor at the V.A. hospital if a sheet wrapped around him would have helped. He said there was nothing I could have done to help him. Wrapping his wound in a sheet could have made his recovery much more difficult.

My company was surprised when I rejoined it two months later. The men and the captain had believed I was that dead soldier. I often think of that soldier, especially around military holidays. R.I.P., my friend. Keep the light on.

EDWARD MCCARTHY

# JED AND RAUL

Jed Wilson was a patient at a field hospital somewhere in western Virginia. He had recently undergone surgery to remove shrapnel from his thigh. Doctor Benson told him he would be walking fine in about two weeks. It was only two days later when he noticed union troops walking about the area, and no one was shooting at them. They were not carrying arms. The truth soon spread that the war was over, and the north had won. Another rumor had it that more union troops would be moving into the area to help move the patients to hospitals and prison camps. Every tent was alive with talk of these rumors and of escape.

Those who were well enough to walk were making plans to steal food soon and evade capture. Jed made up his mind to leave immediately instead of soon. Raul Hastings was in a cot closest to Jed. He too had been wounded in the thigh. Raul was a year younger than Jed and was Jed's closest companion. He sat up and said in a near whisper. "I'm going tonight. By the time these boys decide to go it'll be too late and they won't get twenty feet from the compound." That night the two friends broke into the field kitchen and stole enough food for a few days. There were too many union guards around the horses, so they started walking, well, limping, on the edge of the road to the west. In an hour or so, they caught up with another escapee they knew as Tom Delancy. The man was so weak he could hardly sit the horse he had stolen. He had undergone operations for removal of bullets from his chest and the men could see his blood-soaked shirt. Raul attempted to convince Tom to give himself up, but Tom would not listen. Tom almost fell from the horse when Jed recommended picking up the pace.

They slept in a deserted barn that night. Jed had some stolen bandages and pads under his shirt, so he changed his own bandages and assisted Raul and Tom in changing theirs. All three were in terrible pain from the exertions of the day, but they eventually fell asleep from exhaustion. In the morning, they ate some food and started out again. Sleep had not done Tom much good. He told the men to leave him because he did not want the responsibility for their capture. Jed told Tom where a friendly family lived south of their position and gave Tom directions. Tom thanked him and said, "If I get caught, I will not give you away." Tom rode south and Jed and Raul continued west. They traveled a great deal faster without Tom, yet they wished him the best. They could have gone with Tom, but they wanted to go west, out of the reach of union troops.

The two men walked the best they could despite their serious wounds. One day blended into the next, for they walked day and night when they felt well enough. Sometimes they were lucky to find a wagon going their way. Nobody turned them away. They were out of food given to them by a grateful family when they reached a town named Darby, about 600-miles from the hospital compound, they reckoned. They were hungry, almost broke, dog-tired, and footsore. A sign boasted a population of 104, but it was an old sign. They counted their money; Jed had $1.23; Raul had $2.04. Their first stop was McNulty's Saloon. If anyone in the town knew of a job, it was the bartender. He also knew everyone's business. However, nobody was looking for ranch hands. In fact, the mines were laying off men during this slack time, but they could be rehired tomorrow. A man overheard this, approached them and said, "I'm the mayor of Darby. I heard you asking about a job. I have a job open in the sheriff's office if you want to work." "We're willing to take any job. What happened to your sheriff?" asked Jed. "We knew he would leave as soon as a job came open in the mines. It pays more money. He quit last week and went to Colorado. Nobody else wants the job because the mines pay more, when they're open. Raul asked, "So, what's the deal? And don't worry about us taking a job in the mine. We don't like confined spaces."

"The town can pay $40 a month for sheriff and $30 for a deputy, plus one quarter of all fines. I know, it isn't much, but it's better than nothing." The two men exchanged glances, and Jed nodded his head, "You'll find badges, guns and holsters in the sheriff's office across the street," said the mayor. Who will be the sheriff?" Raúl pointed to Jed and said, "He's the older one, so I'll be the deputy. What is your name, Mayor?" "My name is John Gillespy. I will notify the federal marshal that we have a sheriff so we won't have to depend on him coming here so often. What happened to your weapons?" Jed lied, "We were so broke we had to sell them and our horses and saddles too." "Go see the undertaker. Tell him I said to give you two horses, saddles and tack. We can't have lawmen without horses. Come see me later to fill out some papers." The two men found guns and belts in the sheriff's office. Raul asked, "Why would the undertaker have horses he could give away?" Jed answered, "Because he claimed them from men who died here, and owed him money, I guess."

"Good guess," Raul said. "Well, he could have been a horse thief." They pinned on their badges and walked to the undertaker's office. The sign read "Henry Peary, Mortician, and Undertaker." They spoke with the man and were led to the back door. "Once you pick your horses, remember to get them out on the grass as soon as you can. I was going to take them out, along with the other two this afternoon. They need good green grass to be strong." "We'll surely do that, Henry; maybe this afternoon and tomorrow," said Jed. When they returned to the sheriff's office, Raul said, "Hey, there's a room back here with two beds. Do you realize what we have accomplished in one day? I can hardly believe it."

Early in the morning, the men walked up and down the streets of Darby, checking into each of the small shops to introduce themselves and hear any complaints from the owners. Neither Jed nor Raul had worked as sheriff before. Jed was very handy with a side arm. Raul said he would practice. On their way back to their office, they stopped a fistfight and fined the men $4.00 each. With their share, they could buy breakfast at Big Bertha's. Each time new wanted posters came in, the men studied the faces. They needed this money, but could not accept rewards, as police officers, (a local rule), so they worked out a plan to have a friend receive the reward and split it with them. That afternoon a stranger arrived on the stage and went into the saloon. Jed recognized him as Robert Stewart, a wanted man. The man took a room at the Jasper House. Jed returned to his office to see what the man was wanted for. The man was a wife-beater. The police didn't want him, but his wife had put up the reward of $400.00.

Jed spoke with Roy Simmons, a cowpoke who was usually broke. Roy was willing to participate for a third of the bounty. It was 6:00 pm when the sheriff and Roy went to the saloon where Stewart was. Roy did exactly as he was told. He walked to the other side of the man. As soon as Jed reached the man, Roy grabbed the man's right arm and shouted, "I got him!" Jed stuck his gun in the man's middle and put him under arrest. Roy followed him to the sheriff's office and asked for his money. "I don't have any money here. I have to wire for it. The money should be here tomorrow." When Raul returned from his rounds, he was told he was a little richer, but he would have to wait until the money arrived. The money did not arrive on the following day. Raul asked if Jed had notified the wife. "I wired her yesterday," answered Jed. The money arrived the following morning with a stranger who had a note signed by Jenny Stewart giving the bearer permission to take custody of her husband. Jed released the prisoner and asked for the reward. The man asked, "Oh yeah, how much was that?" "It was $400." The mail arrived on the noon stage. A letter from Jenny Stewart apologized for the lateness of the money, but she had to borrow it. Included was a banknote for the $400.00. When Raul read it, he said, "Good God! Who the hell did I give Stewart to?" Jed said in jest, "Don't be so…so unreligious!" "I'm not," said Raul. "You just said God's name in vain." Raul answered, "No. I didn't. I said God's title, not His name." Jed wondered what they should do now. Raul answered, "For one thing, we have $400.00 for eats and a drink, or two." Jed said that Stewart had a good head start of several hours."

Two days later Mrs. Stewart walked into the sheriff's office and introduced herself. She and Jed spoke for several minutes. She was a pretty woman, no older than 23 years. She wanted to know if Jed was looking for her husband. He explained that he had no men or money to pay someone to go out and search the area for a man who could already be in Mexico. She told Jed how mean her husband was and how he put her in the hospital three times in two years. "He beat me so badly I could not walk for two weeks." Jed was angered, "I'll remember how mean he was to you if I see him again, and here's the money you sent me," She would later tell her friends that Jed was a sort of quiet person. He was one who didn't show his feelings outwardly. Nothing seemed to excite or depress him. He stood about 6-feet 2-inches tall, had even features and blue eyes, and was about 24-years old. She would describe Raul, whom she met later, as a tad shorter than Jed, but no less handsome. He has brown eyes, is about 23-years old, and is much more outgoing. "Ma'am, I will certainly remember how he treated you if I catch him, but we just can't leave the town without a lawman while we traipse around the countryside." Jed told her again. "What should I do, Sheriff?" Jed said, "Stay at the hotel tonight and take the stage back home tomorrow. I don't think he'll be back this way soon. By the way, who was the man who took him out of jail?" "That was his brother, Ray. I think he is worse than my husband. It is rumored that he has killed four men. He's very good with his gun."

    Jed and Raul accompanied Mrs. Stewart to the stage the following day. Jed sighed with relief as the stage disappeared from view. He told Raul all that had transpired in his office. It was not more than two-hours later when the stage returned. The driver was very excited. He told Jed that two men held up the stage. They took nothing. They merely opened the door and shot Mrs. Stewart point blank. He did not think she would live out the day. She was taken to the doctor's house. Within ten-minutes, Jed and Raul were backtracking the stage. A short distance from town, the tracks in the soil told their story. It was just as the driver had said. They followed the tracks of two horses, but soon lost them among the rocks. Later they found a cold campfire and several cigarette butts. They checked the surrounding area thoroughly, but found nothing, then hurried back to town to check on Mrs. Stewart.

    At the doctor's office, they were told it was touch and go. The biggest worry was infection. Dr. Hastings had removed the bullet from her abdomen and repaired the damage, but regardless of how good a job was done, infection could still kill her. "Her functions are fine," he said. "Let's hope they remain that way. She will remain here until she can travel, so I can keep an eye on her condition. You can look in on her if you want. She's a pretty thing, isn't she?" Jed was not thinking of her at the moment. He was wondering aloud why Jenny's husband had hung around Darby for so long and why he came to Darby in the first place. He asked Raul to look into it. Raul was very good at getting information from people, including reluctant people. That evening Raul told Jed, "Mr. Stewart came here to collect a debt from Pete Masters. Pete told me he paid back $300.00 to him yesterday at his ranch and still owes him $700.00 He also said that Stewart bragged about punching his wife in the stomach because she was pregnant. She lost the baby." "That son of a bitch," is all that Jed could say. Raul followed with "I could put a bullet in his head without remorse. What a bastard!" Jed winked at Raul, "Maybe we will get to that, pard." Later that day the doctor told Jed and Raul that Mrs. Stewart went into shock, then into a coma. "It doesn't look good for the poor lady." To everyone's surprise, Mrs. Stewart awoke two days later, hungry and feeling well. She was brought up-to-date by Jed and Raul, but was not out of jeopardy yet, as Doctor Hastings said. "She's lost weight, I had to feed her through a tube, but it was all liquid, not much substance. She probably won't want puree for a while. She will remain here for at least another week to regain her strength." In the evening, Pete came to Jed's table in the saloon and told him that Stewart knew his wife was at the doctor's house. "I didn't tell him. He already knew it. I spoke with his brother just ten-minutes ago as I was riding into town. I wish you had shot that bastard."

An elderly man suddenly rushed to the table, He said, "Been a shooting at the doctor's house just now, Sheriff." Jed ran to the doctor's house with gun in hand hoping against the odds, that Jenny was safe. Dr. Hastings was at the front door. "Everyone's safe, Sheriff, Jenny saw him coming into the house with gun drawn. She shot him in the neck." Jed turned the dead man onto his back. The man was a stranger. Jed said to Raul, who had just arrived, "The bastard paid someone to kill Jenny, I mean Mrs. Stewart." "Looks that way from here, Jed." "That son of a bitch is waiting somewhere to hear that his wife is dead. I'd give an arm and a leg to know where." As Jed was speaking, the doctor made a sudden rush to the side of Mrs. Stewart, who had fainted. Jed asked, "Where did she get the gun?" Raul said, "I gave it to her for protection. We couldn't be here all the time. She said she could handle one, and she sure did," "Now, if we were proper heroes, we'd be riding hell-bent out on the prairie, looking for two killers, but we would be leaving the town unprotected," added Raul. "Hell, Raul, we're only cops, not magicians." Raul said, "I found out why some lawmen are called cops. The name came from the copper buttons on city police uniforms in England. Someone at the saloon was explaining it just the other day. We can't be cops, though, because we can't even afford copper buttons." In the morning, Jed rode to Pete's ranch to scout for signs of the killers. He located two campsites overlooking the ranch, but they were cold. He spoke to Pete and was told he had not seen the Stewarts lately. Jed returned to town and lay in a bunk to catch up on lost sleep. He awoke late in the afternoon and had dinner at McNulty's Saloon, then headed back to Pete's ranch. He found a high spot overlooking the ranch and the two cold campsites just as the sun was fading. Suddenly, a light flashed in the distance, and was snuffed out. A little time later, a light flared again. This time the light was closer to the ranch house. Jed said one word aloud. "Cigarettes." Now, Jed watched the house more closely. Minutes slipped by, then the windows in the house spilled light onto the sandy soil as Pete lit some oil lamps. Jed saw the front door open and a lantern brightened the figures of three men on the porch. They reentered the house.

Jed rode down the hill and tied his horse a safe distance from the house. He then took his time to approach the house in silence. He stopped behind the well, checked his gun and returned it to its holster. He approached the kitchen window and looked inside. Three men sat at a table as they drank coffee. The Stewarts were angry. Pete rose from the table and opened a cupboard door. He drew out all the paper money from the sugar bowl and returned to the table. The money totaled $230.00. Pete withdrew $30.00 of it and pushed it into his shirt pocket as he said, "I'll need this for monthly bills." Roy Stewart withdrew the money from Pete's pocket. When Pete protested, Roy shot him. The men then rose and walked to the front door. They opened it and a yellowish light spilled onto the front porch, silhouetting them.

Jed could see them clearly. He shouted for them to put their hands in the air. Instead, they fired shots at the voice. Jed was behind a corner of the house. The men could not see him although some bullets came close. He took a chance to look and fire, dropping one of the men with a lucky shot. When he looked again, Pete was standing unsteadily at the door. He had a pistol in his hand. For a fraction of a second, Jed did not know where Pete would aim his .45. Pete fired and the other Stewart fell to the floor. Pete slumped to a sitting position, unable to rise. Jed checked the men on the floor. They were dead. He went to Pete who told him how sorry he was, but he could not tell Jed that the Stewarts were camping near his ranch. They threatened to kill him and his daughter. Jed retrieved all of Pete's money and stuffed it into Pete's shirt pocket. "Pete opened his eyes and said, "You got them." Jed answered, "Well, that's something I have to talk to you about in case you want to share in the reward. Can you ride?" Jed took him to the doctor's house to get treatment for his arm, and he wanted to tell Mrs. Stewart she needed to worry no longer about her husband.

Raul met them at the door, "Hi, partner, where have you been?" "Well, I've been out cleaning up the territory, making us heroes, and earning some money." "You found them?" "Pete found them and turned them over to me. He gets the reward, he's the hero, but we'll be a little richer too." He smiled. Raul said, "Jenny told me she has been too scared to divorce her husband. She said she would now. Where's the bastard, in jail?" "The bastard is dead, Raul. Is there something between you and Jenny?" "There may very well be." As it turned out, however, Mrs. Stewart learned of her husband's hidden holdings. He owned a ranch, and was a partner in a bank and a carting company. She was intent on returning to her hometown to manage HER businesses. In the morning, Mrs. Stewart was packed and awaiting the stage with Raul. Jed saw them and approached. "Don't worry, I'm not leaving," said Raul as he assisted Mrs. Stewart into the coach. "Jenny has finally found something she really loves, and it's not here in Darby." "Easy come, easy go, Raul. Let's go get a drink."

On their return to the office, they found a stranger sitting outside and waiting. He did look a bit familiar, but the men did not know why. He was wearing a federal marshal's badge. He said, "I see that you two galoots made it safely." Jed asked, "What the hell does that mean, Marshal?" He wore a puzzled expression. "I mean that you two are escapees from the government troops. Well…I see the anger creeping up in your faces. Maybe I should introduce myself. I'm Tom Delancy." "Now I see," Jed said with relief. "We were so worried you weren't going to make it. Gosh, you look great." "I feel great too, because of your help. I don't think I could have made it alone. Those people you sent me to practically brought me back to life." "So, now you're a marshal too." "My family has friends in congress. They gave me this job to keep me out of a northern prison. I'll make sure you guys are safe too. I saw you walking. Neither one of you was limping or bent in pain. I prayed for you back there in Virginia when I thought the blue coats would get you. You see, my dad was a marshal in this area until he was shot dead, and he was a good one. I have to live up to that reputation. The North found it very costly to feed and care for so many prisoners. Did you hear that the Commandant of Anderson, Georgia Prison Camp was hanged? Yep, they got him for murdering hundreds of Southern prisoners of war. His name was Henry Wirz. They're releasing some prisoners now. I doubt that anyone even cares about you two. Come on, let's go to the saloon. I want to buy my pals a drink, maybe two. I can afford it. I make two bucks a day."

## EDWARD MCCARTHY

# WWII
### RADIO MAN

      During combat in WWII my infantry company communicated via walkie-talkies and the larger back-pack radio which could enable us to talk to tankers. If we needed planes, we contacted tankers who would then relay our need. As radio man I was up front, behind the second scout. When I didn't have that duty, I was the lead scout. We were capturing town after town in February, March and April, 1945, as many as three per day. I was the radio man when we walked into a village that had a large tree in the center of the road which split the road just before the tarred street began. The Germans began firing just as I reached the tree. A machine gun opened fire. I was behind the tree, still on my feet. My company was hunkered down in the ditches on both sides of the road. I was relaying information to the captain as to where the enemy was. "There's a machine-gun positioned to your left front, Mike." Actually, Mike was the code used for the company captain. Then I heard something odd to my right. It sounded like someone firing a .22 rifle. I looked around then heard it again and several more times. I was standing behind that large tree that split the road. Presently a lieutenant came running to my position. "Who the hell is firing a .22?" I asked. The lieutenant smiled, "If you heard that sound, you're very lucky." I must have looked puzzled. He explained. "That is the sound of bullets breaking the sound barrier as they pass by your ear. Now, will you get the hell down?" "Yes sir," I said as I hunkered down, He said, "You have to keep that radio safe, Mr. Lucky. I want you to run forward and get into that house." "Run forward, sir?" He knew I was slowed down by carrying the 45-pound radio on my back. Now I was beginning to feel like a member of Colonel Custer's 7$^{th}$ cavalry. "Run forward, sir?"

      "Go," he urged. I reached the relative safety of the house. Then the lieutenant sent a sergeant with a machine gun into the house because it had not been cleared. The sergeant was shot in the thigh as he dove into the doorway. I went to the kitchen to get him a drink of water so he could take his "shock" pill. While there I glanced out the kitchen window, a large square of glass 4 by 4 feet that overlooked a back yard. The window exploded in my face, thanks to a shell from a German tank. I was pushed back against the kitchen table by the force of the blast. My face stung. My eyes were closed. I was afraid to open them and find them and my face filled with slivers of glass. I finally opened my eyes, but very slowly. They were clear. I gingerly patted my face. There was no glass sticking in it thank God. I shook my uniform to get the bits of glass and brick dust off my shoulders. Yes, I was Mr. Lucky that day. A German tank had fired its 88mm and the shell hit just outside and under that window. The tank was low on fuel, so it remained in its hiding place. Later, my sergeant yelled, "C'mon Mac, we have at least one more town to take today, maybe two. How the hell did you get so dusty, you've been safe and under cover for the last twenty minutes?"

EDWARD MCCARTHY

# THE LIPSTICK MURDERS

Joan Kahn was only twelve when her violated body was found across the border from her home state, Florida. This gave the FBI sufficient cause to enter the case. A deer hunter found her in a wooded area in Nov.2016. He was thoroughly investigated by the agency and cleared of any suspicion. There were three convicted child molesters within five city blocks of the Kahn family. One was in the hospital suffering with complications of AIDS. The remaining two were questioned and investigated. There was not a shred of evidence against either of them to sustain an arrest. In Jan. 2000 the body of nine-year-old Pamela Ranes was found in a different wooded area, but only a mile distant from where Joan's body was found. Both cases were similar in that lipstick was prominent, not only on the children's lips, but on their foreheads as well, as though a word were written there and deliberately smeared with the sweeping palm of the killer's hand. The word could not be made out. It appeared to be a five or six-letter word, but we had no hint of the letters following the "W," perhaps witch, or whore? So far, we had questioned 114 people and we were nowhere.

I was close to retirement after 24 years with the bureau. My boss joked, "It should be an easy case for you, Jack. I know you want to retire, but do me the favor of taking this last case, will you?" Actually, cases were getting tougher, maybe it was my age or the bullet wound in my leg or the one in my back or the thousands of nights of surveillance, anyhow, I agreed. I had a girlfriend, but at 45, it's not the same as at 25. I look healthy enough in my mirror. I am 6 feet tall; I weigh 175 and I still have my hair, although it's getting grey. I am telling you this so you can get a better idea of how it all went down.

I checked with the police of several surrounding states and SURPRISE! There were 6 similar crimes to the one I worked on. The lipstick was the prominent feature. Detective Andrews in Alabama was positive about the first letter on the dead child's forehead. He said it was a "W" and four or five smeared letters followed that. He sent a photo. As soon as I saw it on my computer, I agreed. There were now at least eight children needing closure. I swore to get the one responsible even if I had to work on the case after I retired. I visited each of the sites where bodies had been found. There was no dried blood found on the ground at any of them. This meant they were not the actual sites of the molestation or murder. They had been killed elsewhere and dropped off in wooded areas.

Mr. and Mrs. Hutchinson lived in one such area. They recalled their dog ignoring their calls one night. When the dog returned, she led Mr. Hutchinson to the body of Katy Wilson. He knew immediately that she was dead. No, he did not touch the body or remove anything. He ran back to his house and immediately phoned the police. As he was calling, he heard a car's tires spinning on sand, and then a loud squeal as the tires gripped the asphalt road. The driver then sped away. He showed me the spot where the car had been two nights ago. The soil was scraped up so badly, there was not a clue as to the car's make or shape or anything else. The area had been trampled badly by police and reporters. There were many footprints from the car to where the body had lain, but which one belonged to the killer? I went back and forth over those prints, looking for the oldest. I found an old print half covered by another, then I found an entire print at about where the driver's door had been. They were size 11. I had a mold made of the print. OK, so all I knew of the killer was that he's a male and maybe he wears size 11 shoes, oh yeah, and he seems to get around quite a lot, Georgia, Florida, Alabama and Mississippi, anyway.

I re-interviewed all the witnesses and suspects and others involved in the case. Mrs. LeBron uncovered the body of seven-year-old Janice White. She told me that she had placed a wash bucket over a footprint that was not there the day before the body was found. She had not told anyone about it simply because she forgot it. I went to the site and the bucket was still there. I carefully lifted it. The print was still there. It was beautiful! It matched perfectly the mold from the other site. No one else knew about this, but it was not doing me much good regardless. It took me two months to re-interview those people. Only four of them wore similar size shoes. Only two wore size 11, a Chester Warner and a William Hanks. Chester was a truck driver. William was an elementary school teacher. They were questioned because they had been close to the scene of the murder on the day of the crime. William Hanks was at work, however, on all the important dates. Chester Warner was his own boss. He brought in his manifests for the past year. They showed that he was not near any murder site even years after the murders. He owned his rig, and I knew he could log in Georgia, but go to another place. Chester could be our boy. I requested surveillance, but my boss turned me down. The budget could not afford it. He said he was sorry, and I knew he meant it. The guy had two youngsters of his own.

On Monday, Warner picked up a load in Jacksonville and headed north on Rte. 95. I followed for a while, but I turned back and interviewed his neighbors and friends. They told the same story. He was a nice person, a good friend to everyone. He did not drink or smoke. He never acted mean to anyone, and he had two young daughters who lived with his sister in New Jersey ever since his wife left him for another man. When Chester had learned of this affair, he beat the other man badly enough to put him in the hospital for four days. The man did not sign a complaint for the police. The wife was declared an unfit mother, but Chester could not care for the children either because of his work. He was, however, supporting the children, and very well. Chester did not fit the profile of a child molester or killer.

# EDWARD MCCARTHY

Sgt. Fredricks phoned me from Athens, Georgia. He related an incident that occurred Monday evening. Two young girls, Eileen and Janice Hopkins, were returning from a grocery store when a man stopped them and asked directions to Oak Street. The girls were afraid of him. The man tried to hold one of them, but she pulled away and the two girls ran just as a neighbor came from the grocery store. The bad man ran away, toward a parked truck, the girls had said. The girls did not see if the man entered the truck or ran past it. "I phoned Mr. Hemstead, the neighbor who had scared the man away," said Sgt. Fredricks. "The one he scared away has brown hair, and may be six-feet tall and skinny." I thanked the Sgt. and hung up the phone, realizing I did not have any possible suspects that looked like that. I was thrown for a loop. I decided to call that witness, Mr. Hemstead. I asked if he had gotten a good look at that truck that was parked. "Well, you couldn't miss it. It was a semi. We don't see many of those just parked at a curb. The whole side of the truck was a sign. It read something about local and distant hauling, and a name under that. I don't recall the name though. I think it began with a C." I asked, "Could it have been Chester?" "It sure was. It was Chester Warner. I hope you catch that bastard."

I tailed Warner the next day. He drove from his house about two miles and parked in a Walmart parking lot. A car soon pulled up to the truck. A thin six-footer exited the car and sat in the shotgun seat of Warner's truck. I ordered both men to put their hands up, and then I called for backup. The tall, thin man was Will Warner, Chester's brother. The police car arrived and I explained the situation to the locals. I asked them to transport Will Warner to jail. I had Chester put into my car where I questioned him. I again questioned him at police headquarters. Chester told me that some of his customers did not trust Will. They thought he was weird. He usually picked him up if there was a lot to be moved or if the items were heavy. "I don't want people to see him get into my truck; it's as simple as that." "Well, no. It is not that simple. I have his description from Athens, Georgia, and you drove him there that night. I checked. It seems that when you go out of town, you eat dinner, and Will usually takes off to a bar for a drink, right, doesn't he?" "Yes, but I never saw him drunk though." "Maybe he doesn't go to a bar. Have you ever thought of that, Mr. Warner?" "No, I had no reason to question it. He said it helped him sleep. Do you really think he killed those children I read about?" "I'm sure he did, Mr. Warner."

"Well…I…I guess I have to tell you…" "Tell me what? What is it?" "I found some lipstick doo-dads in his drawer about a year ago. At the time, he said they belonged to his girlfriend. Then there was one night I went to a bar with him. He had one drink then disappeared. When I went back to the motel, he was sound asleep and he had…he had lipstick on his hand. I never saw any on his lips. I thought for a time he could be a cross-dresser, but I never found any women's clothing. I guess that means something. If he's guilty of those terrible crimes, he's no longer my brother."

At this time an officer poked his head into the interrogation room and motioned me to him. He whispered; "Will Warner got away. He somehow got loose from the back-seat restraints and wrecked the police car; Officer Gillian is in the hospital now. Warner had a razor blade. Gillian took 17 stitches in his arm and Warner has disappeared." When

## MIX OF STORIES

I told this to Chester, he cried, "I promised our mother that I'd take care of my little brother. I didn't do such a good job." "It wasn't your fault. It wasn't anyone's fault." I told him. I let Chester go, but I tailed him. He went directly home. I watched the house until I could not stay awake. The next morning, I was back. As soon as I parked the car the dispatcher called me. "Chester Warner just called and said his brother was in his house, then he yelled and the line went dead." I was running toward the house before the dispatcher was finished talking. The front door was open. I ran into the living room. Chester was lying on the floor. He was shaking his head. I whispered, "Where's your brother?" "He's gone. Ran out the back door just as you came in. Oh, I never saw him so scared." I asked, "Are you OK?" "Yeah, I'm OK. He's no longer my brother." He was feeling his cheek as he said, "A brother wouldn't do this. Will was awful dirty and unshaven. I guess he's been living like a wild animal." A neighbor, Mrs. Levi, said she saw Will running from the house. Then she said, "I'd never trust him around my children. Whenever I saw him, I called my children to come into the house. Never trusted him." I drove east slowly along the road Will was said to have taken. I ran out of houses and was facing a wooded area that seemed to be miles long and wide. It would take too many local police and far too long to search that area. I drove home.

My alarm clock read 3:00 am when a sound awakened me. I grabbed my 9 mm and listened. Someone was in the house, but downstairs. I heard a noise again, then silence. I moved to look in the hallway. A shot startled me. I jumped and ducked. Another shot struck the bedroom door and the wall behind it. I aimed toward where I saw the muzzle flash, and then heard a sound like someone jumping from the carport roof onto the ground. I ran to the window in the other room and aimed at the figure, but it turned a corner and was gone. Two police officers soon answered the shots and said they would keep an eye on the house until morning I did learn something from this experience. The older you get, the longer it takes to recover. I was still breathing hard 5 minutes later and it took two hours for me to fall asleep again.

A burglary report came in that morning from Judson Terrace. A .9mm pistol was taken along with food and heavy clothing. No one saw the thief. Now the guy had two guns? I wore my bullet vest from that day on. I wanted a party on my next birthday, not a eulogy. The son of a bitch was armed with two guns. I carried mine too. Most of the day I was on the phone or the computer, trying to track down Will. This case started as a child molestation and murder case; now it was personal. There was another burglary this day, but police caught the young girl. She had burgled at least seven houses over a two-month period. Women's Lib!

Just as I put my jacket on to go to lunch, the phone rang. It was Chester. He told me that Will had called him and wanted me to meet with him at 9:00 this night at the corner of Justin and Anne Streets. This was a place of boarded up stores, very desolate and very dark. I warned Chester that Will may be seeking revenge so, "Go to a motel for the night. Be safe." He agreed to do that. I was at the location at 8:30, hidden in the shadow of a doorway. I was hoping something would happen when I heard footsteps approaching from the west. I had my gun in my hand and I felt my jacket pocket for the two full magazines of ammo. The footsteps came my way and passed me, then continued until I could no longer hear them. Then I heard more footsteps from the west. They approached my position. Then I heard footsteps from the east approaching. They did not pass me. They halted about twenty-feet from me, on my left and right. I couldn't see who they were, maybe local cops? Suddenly, the truth hit me.

    A voice said, "You're getting too close to the truth. We didn't want to do this; you had all the information, yet couldn't put it together. We knew you would do it eventually." It was Chester Warner's voice. I stuck out my head and a bullet struck the block wall near me. I pulled back into the darkness of the doorway. "We got here before you did and we've been watching your every move. I told you that story about a phone call because I knew you would come here. Now you have to die. I am fully aware that we are sick, but where can we go for help where they won't kill us for what we've already done? We don't want to go to prison. We know what happens to child molesters there. The lipstick? Yeah, we get a kick out of using it. The lipstick on the forehead? That was Will's idea. He signed our last name on the forehead as a joke, and I smeared it. It became our logo. Now we have to kill you." He fired again. I saw the muzzle flash and fired at it. I heard Chester yell, and then Will stepped out where I could get a shot. He fired just as I did. He nicked my left arm, but I dropped him. Police cars appeared at both ends of the street. I placed my weapon on the ground just as Chester raised up to fire at one of the officers. He missed, but the officer did not. Chester was dead. Will died at the hospital after giving us all the information we needed for our records. I had a bloody groove in my left arm. At the hospital, I was wondering how my girlfriend would treat a wounded "hero" and just how long I could make that last. I never thought I'd have to use my weapon again, but there won't be any remorse for these two child killers.

MIX OF STORIES

# THE SADDLE MAKER

The reporter wrote on the front page of the Winslow Clarion, "The dumbest thief in 100-years robbed the Winslow Bank of $40,000 on July 7th 1876, but left his wallet containing his identification and business cards on the floor near the safe. The thief was Mr. Sean Murphy who only recently owned a saddle shop on Main Street. Immediately after the theft Mr. Murphy was nowhere to be found." The truth of the matter was quite different. Sean was an honest, professional saddle maker with several years' experience since the age of twelve when he first began helping his father in the shop. He also had begun saving what he could, and had close to $12,000 saved at the same bank he is claimed to have robbed. His father had died five-years earlier when Sean was 19-years old. Sean had saved another $400.00 and went to the bank to add $300.00 of it to his account. This amount brought his savings total to $12,000.00. He believed this was sufficient money to build a new shop and supply it with the necessary hides and equipment. He was now on the train going west. His ticket was made for exiting in Cheyenne, Wyoming.

Sean was stunned by what he read. Someone had left a newspaper on an empty seat. Sean sat and recalled what he could. He remembered handing his money to the teller, Mr. Jerome Stevens. He recalled removing the money from his wallet and pocketing $100.00 of it. He then placed his wallet on the teller's counter. After he boarded the train, he recalled reproaching himself for forgetting his wallet at the bank. Luckily, there was no money in it. Sean sat there and read with great surprise what a stupid fellow he was. He read his own description, light brown hair, white, male, American, 6-feet and 1-inch tall, about 185 pounds. While he read the paper, a young man sat beside him and handed him a false mustache and beard along with a phial of spirit gum. Sean asked the man, "Why are you doing this?" "I've been watching you for several hundred miles and I don't see anything so stupid about you. That was my paper you were reading. I read it earlier and recognized you right off. Don't misunderstand me now; I just thought you needed... well, a friend." "I didn't do that robbery. It had to be that teller who took my wallet and planted it by the emptied safe. I had $12,000 in that bank. It's gone too, but maybe I was stupid to leave my wallet behind. I didn't see it on the counter when I was leaving. By the way, I'm Sean Murphy." "As if I didn't know who you were. I'm Jack Hall. What can you do now?" "I can telegraph the sheriff in Winslow and tell him who really stole the money." "No, you can't. He'll know where you are and have you picked up." "I'll telegraph a friend of mine in Winslow and have him tell the sheriff who stole the money. He won't give me away. I'll have him send the answer to Jack Hall. OK?" "OK by me,"

When the men got off the train, Sean sent his message. An answer didn't come until three hours later. It read, "Jerry Stevens, the teller, quit his job yesterday and disappeared. I told the sheriff about Stevens. The police are looking for him now because someone else told the sheriff that he was the robber. The reward for you has been withdrawn. Stevens may be headed your way. His father lives somewhere around Golden. Good Luck." It wasn't many more miles to Golden. Sean and Jack left the train when they arrived there. For a while they met every train going west in their search for Stevens. "We may as well give up the search. We can't spend our lives watching for him. You are either master of your fate or Stevens is," said Sean. "Oh, now you're a poet." "Nothing seems to work out the way you want," Sean said. "I'm strapping on my .45. Heck, I can hit a 4-inch circle once out of 4-tries, but don't tell anyone that." The sheriff met them when they checked at the train depot for the last time. "Are you men looking for someone in particular?" "Yes, sir," lied Sean. "We're looking for a friend, but we didn't know exactly when he would arrive." "Where do you men work?" "We're not working right now. We just arrived here ourselves, but we are saddle makers when we work." "Really," The sheriff was genuinely surprised and mentioned their youth. "I've been working on saddles for eleven years," Sean said. "I was surprised especially because we lost our saddle maker in a holdup the other day. He was killed by two drunks who tried to hold up the Nugget Saloon. They were tried and hung yesterday," the sheriff said. "We heard about the man's death, but we don't have enough money to buy the man's stock. That's one of the reasons I'm waiting for my friend," Sean lied. "Go talk with the man's daughter. She may make you a deal. You'll never know unless you try." He gave the men directions to the woman's house.

Sean bought two horses and the men then rode to Miss Adams' house. Sean knocked on the door and waited. It wasn't long before Miss Adams opened the door. "I'm sorry to intrude on your sadness, Miss Adams, but we wish to speak to you about your dad's saddle shop and the equipment. I'm a saddle maker and..." "It's all right," she interrupted. "If you're interested in it, take it. I never want to see it again. His business caused his death. He went to collect a debt and two drunks killed him. Just take it all." She closed the door. Sean stood in shock, but then Miss Adams returned with the key to the shop. She pressed it into Sean's hand. Her face was still wet with tears. She could not speak. The men rode to Fremont Street and went into the shop. "This is beautiful," Sean said. "There's even a bedroom here. Heck, we can sleep inside. This shop is complete. There are hides enough for several saddles. It looks like we're in business." Jack told Sean that he would look about town and try to find a job he could do." "What do you do?" asked Sean. "I thought you'd guessed that by now. I'm an actor." "I'll be darned. Well, in the meantime you're welcome to sleep here. That'll save you some money. You've helped me a lot. It's the least I can do for you. We'll get you a bed as soon as we get some money ahead. It looks like Mr. Adams knew the saddle business." He ran his hand along one of the unfinished saddles. "I like the way he worked his leather. It's a shame the poor man's dead. I think we would have liked him. Heck, I like his daughter already. I'll have to pay that lady something when I sell the saddles already in the shop. I can finish off one of them tomorrow. I wouldn't feel right if I didn't pay her for the tools and leather her dad left here too." "You are an honest man, aren't you? I like that." Sean lit the oil lamps and got to work on one of the half-finished saddles. "I don't usually work in dim light, but we need the money and I'm sure that Miss Adams can use some too. It really feels good to handle a hammer and leather again."

"I took the extra blanket, Sean. I'm tired and I'll be getting to bed on one of these benches. See you in the morning. Gee, it's nice to sleep indoors again." Sean was up and working at first light. In the past days he had grown a mustache and beard. He put the finishing touches on one saddle and a sale sign for $30.00 before putting it in the shop window. It was there for only two hours before a young man bought it. Sean set $25.00 aside for Miss Adams. He kept the rest for rent and food. The two men attended the burial ceremony for Mr. Adams. When the prayers ended, Miss Adams approached Sean and apologized for her unmannerly behavior when they first met. Sean handed her the $25.00. She accepted it readily. "Did your dad have any savings, Miss. Adams? Oh, I'm not asking because I'm nosy. I'm just a bit worried about your welfare."

"Please, call me Marie. No, I checked at the bank. He had no savings at all. I am afraid of losing my house. I still owe $1,700 on the mortgage. But I'm sure I can pay the $22.00 monthly mortgage payments even if I have to take in laundering or sewing." "I'm sorry, Marie, I can't help you any more at this time, but I'll have another saddle finished in two days. "She said, "You're an honest man, Sean. In my grief I told you to take everything. I didn't expect to share in your luck. My dad would have liked you. And thank you for attending today. I'm going to miss him for a long time to come." Sean took out a bank loan for $200. He would soon need more leather and perhaps some silver too. Jack was helping out in the shop and was promised a job in a day or two. Sean had been in Golden for about a month when a stranger entered his shop asking for a comfortable saddle for a long trip to Montana. When Sean looked at the man, he recognized him immediately. He was Jerome Stevens, the teller from Winslow, the real thief. The man did not recognize Sean because of the beard and mustache. Sean said, "It may take as long as two weeks. Tell me where you are staying so I can notify you when it's ready" The man answered, "You can deliver it to the Downey Ranch. I'm there with my father."

Sean needed some time to think. He didn't know what to do, but now he knew where the thief lived, how does he let the sheriff know without getting thrown in jail? He couldn't even have Jack or Marie tell the law man. He discussed the dilemma with Jack, who suggested writing a letter to the sheriff, unsigned of course. That is just what he did. He waited for night then slipped the letter under the door of the jail house. Sean and Jack heard nothing about an arrest. Jack said, "The guy probably gave a fake address." A week and a half later the man walked into the shop again and asked if his saddle was ready. Again, Sean was very surprised to see him. His mind was in a flurry of possible actions to take. He settled down and drew his .45 against the man. He told the man to walk in front of him to the sheriff, who was very surprised and shook Sean's hand then asked if he wanted to be a deputy. "No thanks, Sheriff, I'll stick to making saddles." "Well, good. You'll be safer there, and that's better for Marie." Sean was surprised, "For Marie?" The sheriff said, "She's in love with you, you know." "How do you know that?" "Oh, you didn't know? we've been friends for many years."

Two days later the sheriff came to Sean's shop and handed him a fat envelope. Sean tore it open and counted out $16,000. He asked, "Wha…Where did this come from?" The sheriff smiled. "It's yours, Sean. We recovered the entire $40,000, well, most of it. The man's father made up the difference. There's your reward of $4,000 plus your own $12,000. Here, sign this receipt for the bank, Sean." Sean was surprised, "You know who I am?" The sheriff grinned, "I've known since you arrived. They rescinded the reward for you and concentrated on the real thief after his girlfriend snitched on him." "Gosh, I don't know how to thank you, Sheriff." The sheriff nodded his head, "Being good to my good friend is payment enough. If I were 30 years younger; make that 40 years younger, you'd have a tussle on your hands for that lady." Sean visited Marie and was invited into her house. He asked how much she owed on her mortgage. "Why would you want to know that?" She asked. "Because I want to pay it off. I don't want my wife owing money on the house we live in." "Gee, you're so much like my dad." She said then she kissed him.

# THE INNOVATOR

It was sundown in Jason's Ford, a small town in the southwest. The only sounds came from the piano in the saloon and the laughter of its customers. A lone rider rode past the saloon and stopped at Willet's Pay Stable. He asked for a double ration of oats for his mare and to put her into the pasture tomorrow. "It's a buck and a quarter daily for boarding. Now I need your name," said the stable man. "It's Will Baker." The men shook hands; Will paid the man and then walked the short distance to the saloon. The nagging ache in his right thigh caused him to be thankful for the short walk. It had sounded like many more people, but there were only nine customers and four of them were quietly playing cards in the corner. The laughter he heard had come from two men and two saloon girls drinking at the bar. Will walked to the far end of the bar and ordered a whiskey. The barman served his drink then said, "The men at the end of the bar said to give you another drink on them." "Well, OK. I wanted just one, but I'll drink another. Tell them thanks." Then he paid $2.00 for a room.

He walked toward the stairs, nodding and smiling at the two men who bought him a drink. "Have another drink, Mister," someone said. "No thanks. Two is my limit, and I need sleep more than whiskey," he answered. The stranger demanded, "If I say drink, you drink, Mister!" Will was on the stairs. He stopped and turned toward the men, letting out a long sigh. The barman whispered something in the stranger's ear. The man's face drained of color. He said, "Sorry Mister, maybe another time?" Will continued to his room. As he topped the stairs, he overheard his name repeated downstairs. The topic of conversation in the saloon was Will Baker, bounty hunter. They spoke of his buffalo hunting days, the years he spent in the cavalry as a captain, and his latest years as a bounty hunter who prided himself on bringing in his man alive. So now he was in Jason's Ford, which meant he was on the prowl. The men were guessing who Will was after. "It aint me," said Willard, "I aint kilt no one or robbed no bank."

At 8 am Will was at the Willet's Pay Stable. He told Mr. Willett he wanted to check his mare's left foreleg. "May have picked up a stone," he said. "Yes, she did, no damage done, willet said.. I always walk the horses before taking them out back to the pasture. That way I can tell if any damage was done before or after putting them out, she's fine now." "You're a good stable man, Mr. Willet, Thank you. Now I can have breakfast without worrying." He ordered a steak, mashed potatoes, three eggs and two flapjacks. The waitress smiled, "You must be very hungry, mister." "That I am, Miss. Haven't eaten since breakfast yesterday." Will was on his second cup of coffee when a male voice asked, "Mind if I sit here?" Will looked about and saw empty tables. Then he looked up and saw the badge. "I don't mind, Sheriff, have a seat." "Do you intend to stay here in Jason's Ford for a long-time Mister Baker?" "Haven't made up my mind Sheriff, seems like a fair place to live." The sheriff said, "The town council appointed me to inform you we don't want you here." He smiled. "Is that your sentiment too?" "It doesn't matter. I have to go along with them." "That's too bad. I haven't decided to stay. I have to look around a bit more. Tell your council that Mr. Baker is not intimidated, and will make up his own mind. Now that's the reason I quit the law after a dozen years. I got tired of the council telling me who to arrest and who to set free and overlook. That is not the kind of law I signed up for. I don't appreciate the town council making its own laws for who goes and who can stay. Oh, sorry to have spouted off at you, you haven't even ordered breakfast yet." "I ate earlier." the sheriff said. "I just wanted to hear your side of it. I'll tell them just as you told me. Maybe they'll fire me, maybe not. I'm on duty 24 hours a day, that's a hell of a lot more than what they do, yet they make more money than I do, even though they raised my pay to $50.00 a month." The men finished their coffee in silence, shook hands, and the sheriff left.

Once inside the Jason Ford Bank, Will removed a money belt from his waist and counted out the money. The total came to $17,000. "You must have sold your business," questioned a smiling clerk. "Nope," answered Will. His next stop was at the land office where he asked about ranches for sale. The clerk opened a large volume and flipped through the pages. "Yeah, here's one, it's 22-acres and a house for $8,000." Do you have something that could feed more than two cows?" The land agent said, "Oh, this one has prime grass and a creek that runs all year long, sir, besides, the property that borders it is for sale. Most of that is prime grass too." Will wasn't satisfied. He told the man to find him about 160-acres with a house, not a shack, then said, "I'll look it over and you give me a price, OK?" "OK sir, where can I reach you?" Will answered, "I'll reach you." Will's next stop was the saloon. He was nursing a beer when the sheriff sat at his table. "I have some questions for you, Will." "What's your name, Sheriff?" "Oh, I'm sorry, I'm Paul Jamison." "OK, Paul. Where I got my money is no one's business. You tell the town leaders that they're trodding on my rights, or maybe they never read the Constitution they swore to uphold." Paul smiled, "It'll probably scare hell out of them." "Hope so, Sheriff."

Will slept well that night and awoke at 8am. The church bell was ringing, but it was not a call to services. Will noticed the sheriff going into the bank. He emerged with the bank owner Mr. Fairchild, who looked very worried. The sheriff saw Will and motioned for him to go to the saloon. Will had waited a mere five minutes when the sheriff sat at his table. "The bank was robbed, Will." "When?" "Sometime late last night. Mr. Snell stayed late to get the books up to date. He usually leaves before 11:00 pm. He was there last night and was found dead this morning by one of his tellers. I can't see how the thief got into the bank. All the doors and windows were secure. The only way to enter would be with a key. "Why are you telling me this, Paul?" "I heard that you helped a sheriff up in Wyoming Territory and put three killers in prison, and that you deposited a large sum in the bank yesterday. They stole your money too." "OK, how was Mr. Snell killed?" Will asked. Paul said that he was told that the man was hit on the head with a pistol, "but I think he was hit with an iron bar. I saw it under one of the benches, but I didn't tell anyone; it looked like it had some dried blood on it." "OK, Paul, I need that bar, but no one should touch it. I want it to talk to me." Paul smiled broadly, "I'll go get it. I'll pick it up with my bandana, Ok?" "That's fine, Paul, I want to hear it talk." The sheriff returned in a few minutes with the metal rod wrapped in his bandana. His brow was wrinkled with unasked questions. "Now, where can I get some powdered graphite?" Will asked. "The hardware store stocks some for the mine machinery." "OK. Meet me in the saloon in about an hour." The sheriff went about his duties and closed the bank for an audit. The banker had insurance to cover theft, but Will wondered if he would even get back 50 cents on the dollar. Will asked Paul to have the five bank employees (who had a key to the bank door) come to his table at the saloon. Will nodded his head knowingly and stated, "That iron rod spoke to me Paul. It seems that a workman put up some shelving the other day. That bar you found was part of a bracket left over. It had some hair on it too."

Each of the bank employees went to Will's table and was asked to show his hands. They each complied. Will studied the fingers of each. "Well, do you know who robbed the bank?" "I do, Sheriff. Tell the men if the money is returned, the law will be lenient." The five men were seated at a nearby table. Paul spoke with them then returned to Will's table. "No one's talking. They don't believe you, Will." Will shook his head and said, "Tell Mr. Fairchild to return the money. He's the thief." "How the... He's the bank owner. Never mind, tell me later." The sheriff took Fairchild aside. In a short time, the man confessed. The money was where Mr. Fairchild had put it, in the bottom drawer of his desk. The bank would reopen after an audit by the Territorial Banking Association.

"So, how did you do it, Will? I know damn well that iron bars can't talk." "I used the powdered graphite to raise a fingerprint on that metal bar. There was a good one for the left thumb. That print had a scar running lengthwise along the finger. All I had to look for was a matching scar, and our banker was the only one with that scar. I didn't do anyone a favor. I just wanted my own money back. I worked hard at earning it at the card tables. Did you know that the Chinese have been using fingerprints on contracts for centuries?" "No, I didn't" "I read an article in a Chicago paper a while back. It was about some Englishman named Sir William Herschel in India. He was asking that all civil contracts have fingerprints of the two principal persons along with signatures on all contracts. It was suggested that fingerprints could be used also to identify criminals in the absence of witnesses or other evidence. I just put some graphite on that bar and spread it out with a soft artist's paintbrush. The slash was easy to see. They say that no two people have identical fingerprints, "I think the town council will now approve of you staying here as long as you like, Will."

# A SIMPLE CHANGE OF MIND

Allow me to tell you something about Dr. Connor Kyle Cassidy, as he is known in medical literature. He is a brilliant man who has dedicated his future to helping others. Yes, he is one of the good guys. Shortly after completing his residency, he invented and patented a medical instrument used in heart surgery. His invention has aided in saving the lives of innumerable patients. Doctor Cassidy is now the leading heart surgeon at Ste. Mary's hospital. As a young man, he was quite proficient in the use of computers and in hacking into other computers. This knowledge was a great help when he was building his "machine." He had a shed delivered to his backyard and he uses it as his private lab. His goal was to build his machine, using parts from an EEG machine, a computer, and parts from the local Radio Shack. His premise is to extract information from a person's mind, digitize it, download it, save, copy it, and store it and anything else one can do with computer data. He had some idea that he could help people, but was not too sure of how it could be accomplished. As he proceeded with his work, he kept in touch with Christine, his fiancée, advising her of his progress. She is a general practitioner and a fine surgeon whom Connor had met at Ste. Mary's. "We could have saved all the information from Einstein's mind, maybe even downloaded it in someone else's mind, and Einstein would still be with us," he said. Christine wanted to know where he would get another mind for downloading it. "Hell, I don't know, maybe from someone under a death penalty? OK, here is another use for it; millions of people worldwide truly believe they were born in the wrong sex. Maybe I could get a male and female together and switch their minds. They would wake up in the other's body. Today they undergo a medical sex change through surgery, and that cannot be undone. Then there is the problem of infection as well as the healing time and high cost. My machine may be capable of switching minds. It could mean no operation, infection, hormonal therapy, and so forth. It could bring happiness or satisfaction to millions of people. My procedure is also reversible. Then there is the possibility that the machine could replace the current IQ testing procedure. Christine eyed him in admiration and said, "But then as your dad says, what could possibly go wrong?"

## MIX OF STORIES

"This actually is a topical subject Christine; scientists around the world are discussing the possibility of switching physical brains. That is far beyond the horizon as far as I am concerned. Think of all the problems associated with that procedure; the nerves of the spine are mere millimeters apart. Of course, they must be cut to remove the brain, but then they must be reconnected to the new nerves. Added to this is the problem with infection, and how about tolerance and acceptance? The problems are many. There is a lot that could go wrong, so much in fact that I believe digitizing is the better way to go."

Christine and Connor often collaborated on their problems. They had known each other since they first met several years earlier. She viewed him as a handsome man, six-feet tall, about 180 pounds and entirely involved with his work. She was in love with his personality, more than his looks. Connor viewed Christine as his girl, a lovely woman who could easily be a model, but preferred medicine. He loved her little crooked smile and how she walked. He considered himself a very lucky man to have his love returned by her.

Connor kept busy in his backyard lab, a 20-foot-by 20-foot shed. He had told Christine that he sometimes felt that he was playing in a treehouse when he was in his shed. That is where he eventually built his machine. Although he kept it as small as possible, it was arduous work. The human brain was claimed to use about 2.5 terabytes of memory. He believed it was safer to overcompensate so he built into his machine 6-terabytes of memory. He worked in secret except for Christine and his father, Dr. Desmond David Cassidy, a recently retired general practitioner. In one trial, Connor taught rat no.15 an intricate maze, put it to sleep and exchanged its mind information with rat no. 16. When the rats awoke, he tested rat no.16 in the maze. It was a surprise to see the rat run, not walk, through the maze, which it had never seen before. He boasted of this to Christine that evening, but in the morning, both rats were dead. He double-checked the small encephalography-cap he had made for rats, and then decided that the problem was there. When he discussed the problem with Christine, she wondered why he had contact points in his cap for the autonomic system because she believed it was not involved that much in new memory, but was used more for stored memory than previously believed. He reduced the electrical input in that area and made some other changes. When he repeated the experiment and the rats lived, he celebrated by taking his girl and his dad to dinner.

Christine was in a playful mood. "Let's see now, if I had your infernal machine, I'd download a bank president's mind and come home with a trunkful of hundred-dollar bills." Connor's father wanted to know what he could do with his machine if it was working like it should. Connor explained and his father smiled his approval. However, the machine could fall into the wrong hands. He asked for their silence about the machine. "If someone wanted information from a subject, he could download that person's mind. At this time, he couldn't decipher the electrical impulses, but it would not be long before that could be accomplished."

From tests he had performed at the hospital he knew that much of people's memory and societal beliefs are stored in the pre-frontal cortex, and then is sent to the hippocampus for longer-term storage. These were the areas of concentration for his experiments. The intricacies of the mind had always intrigued the good doctor. Further testing served to validate his findings. All his tests with pigs and four dogs seemed to leave no ill effects on the mind or body. He could store the information and replace it. The animals indicated no distress of mind or body; but then, pigs and dogs are not humans, although they share much of the DNA of humans, in fact, the DNA of a knuckle-walking chimpanzee is more than 98.5 percent the same as humans, and the blood of chimps and humans can be cross transfused if care is taken for the blood type. Chimps also have 32 teeth, just as humans have, and some are right-handed, some are left-handed.

It was a Monday evening when Connor went to his lab. The red indicator light on his computer was on. He thought he had turned it off the evening before. As he approached it, a message appeared on the computer. "I need your help. Please don't turn me off. I am one of the FOREVERS you may have read about. This is a term applied to those who chose to "live forever." We could not do this in our physical bodies so we were reduced to only thoughts, the ability to move, to hear and see, and that is all. I did not know it would be like this. I was dying, that is, my body was dying. An ad in the paper offered a life forever for a high price. I paid a little more than a million dollars for what? I am actually in Purgatory. I want to taste food, I want to touch and smell a woman again, but my body is dead and buried. I am a blob about five inches in diameter, and I can be seen in a fog or smoky room, but I am a ghost. I have seen your work with your machine. It is exactly what I need. If it's a matter of money, don't worry. I have millions left. Doc, I want to live. A few nights ago, it was foggy and some brat of a kid could see me. He was screaming for the entire world to come look at what he found, a thing from another planet. I slid under your door and found all your information. I can see what you have been doing Have pity, Doc. I've been this way for two-years; if I have to live this way much longer, I…I think I'd kill myself, but I don't even know how the hell I could accomplish that. All I did was answer an ad. I was dying, or my body was. I had to go down to Mexico City to have the work done. The doc told me I wouldn't have lived out the night if I didn't have the job done. He was right. My body died that night. I gave them a check before I died for over a million bucks. They buried my body under a false name, so I still have a chunk of money in several banks. It's worth a lot to me to be a man again. Hell, I don't have arms or legs. I'm in Purgatory for sure. It's terrible, Doc. It's like Donovan's Brain, no feeling or smell or touch. It's awful. You're supposed to go to Heaven or Hell when you die. I'm in Purgatory, and I'm stuck in this God-awful situation. Can't you please help me? I just now realized again that I don't have a physical body, and could live forever like this."

"I can't see any way around my oath, Mister er…" "Oh, I'm sorry. My name is Carl Watson." "Well, Mr. Watson, I still can't see any way to help you." "Look, Doc, what if I find someone willing to give up his body, maybe wanting to die, and I promised to support his family for life. Could you then reconsider the switching of my mind to his body?" "I doubt that such a person exists. If you could find him…No, I still don't know." "I'll let you know, Doc."

## MIX OF STORIES

Connor relayed this information to Christine and his father. The elder Cassidy agreed with Connor's decision. Christine said she would have to look at the situation before making a decision. When she visited him that evening Connor suggested that they try to get what information they could on Mr. Watson. He sat at his computer. It took a very short time. "Look here, Hon," he called to her. "This article says there was such a place in Mexico City two years ago, but it burned down and those knowing its operation were killed in the fire. This data was on a police report printed in a local paper. It was called The Forever Institute. Well, thank God there were not many people taking advantage of what it offered. The institute was open for perhaps as long as six months. What would you do, Chris, if faced with this dilemma? "I've been mulling that over and I'm sure you are right. I would not want that responsibility. We are supposed to help people." Connor left his machine on in case Watson returned, although he hoped he would never hear from him again. It was three nights later when the man did return. The message on Connor's computer made him grimace: "I found a man who is willing to give up his life. That is just about what it amounts too. I did not tell him the truth about me taking his body because the wrong people might get wind of it. This person blames himself for killing three people. It seems that he was the bus driver when his bus skidded on a patch of ice and slammed into a tree. Three people were killed and several were hurt. Investigations by state and local police cleared him of any fault, but he will not accept their findings. His only family is his mother, and I promised to take care of her. He is willing; how about you?" "Mr. Watson, I was hoping I wouldn't hear from you again. That poor soul could not make a proper decision because of his state of mind. My answer is the same as before. I feel sorry for you, but I cannot help you. Can't you see that?" "Yes, I can see that from your perspective, but I see a man willing to give up his life. He is willing to die, he wants to die, but you cannot see that. This guy's body would still live. It is only a half murder, isn't it? All joking aside, why the hell did you build your damn machine?" Mr. Watson was evidently angry. "I had a number of reasons, but they were all methods for helping people. I can't use it, especially for the first time, for murder, not even a half murder."

"I guess I'll have to go back to square one. If I find a better candidate, I will let you know. See ya, Doc." Connor did not hear from Watson for two weeks. He and Christine were busy preparing for their upcoming wedding. It was Saturday morning when Connor went to his lab. His machine was gone! The first words he said aloud were. "That son of a bitch!" His safe had been broken into and all the plans for his machine were missing too. He asked his neighbors if they had seen anything. Mr. Nagel said he and his wife were walking their dog when they saw some stranger coming out of Connor's shed. "The man was carrying a box about the size of a computer, but about three times thicker," said Cathleen Nagel. They did not think much of it at the time, especially because the stranger wished them a good evening as he left.

Connor would not report the theft for fear of information about his machine getting out. He would not take the chance. He seemed to take the loss in good humor, but Christine could tell that he missed it after all the time, thought, and worry he had put into it. He seemed to be more fidgety is what she told Connor's dad. Two-weeks after the theft, his doorbell rang. Connor answered it. A stranger stood on his front porch, a man about six-feet tall, thin, and clean-shaven. He spoke as though he knew Connor. "Now don't go getting all crazy on me, Doc. I'm Carl Watson. Well, my mind is Watson. My body belonged to that fellow I told you about. He wanted to die. I caught him with a gun to his head. That is when I had your machine taken. My doctor did the work you refused to do; of course, he had to read the instructions until he knew them by heart." "And you're walking around just like everyone else. My machine works! How are your reflexes, having any problems...?" Watson interrupted Connor's questioning. "Hold on, Hoss. I feel fine. My reflexes are perfect. I can run and jump and I gained two years. This guy was two years younger than me."

"Where is my machine now? You don't need it anymore." "We dumped it in the ocean about 20-miles out. Oh, we had all the proper papers and a physician in attendance for burying Watson." Connor said, "You stole from me, destroyed my work and my safe. You treated me something awful and by God I'm going to take it out of your new hide." Connor advanced toward Watson. "Hold on friend." Watson asked, almost pleading. "Here, take this envelope; it'll pay for your troubles and more." Watson pushed the envelope into Connor's hand and then began walking away. "Connor called after him, "I'm glad I didn't have a hand in any of that." Watson stopped and said, "Doc, you're clean. I learned later that the man was not a bus driver at all. He was a gangster and hit man. I went from the fire to the frying pan. I had to arrange for a face-lift. I'm flying to Cuba tonight. The doctor said he could fix my eyes, nose, and mouth so even my mother wouldn't know me." He began backing away again. "So, you open that envelope and call me stingy." He hurried to his car.

Connor went back inside his house and tossed the envelope on the dining room table on his way to the kitchen. He returned with a cup of coffee. He sat down and absent-mindedly fingered the envelope then said aloud, "Aw, what the hell." He opened the envelope and a look of surprise spread across his face when he saw the amount of the check. It was made out for one and a half million dollars. As it turned out, Mr. Watson did not make the flight to Cuba. The police arrested him that night at the airport. A radio news report claimed the capture of a notorious killer dubbed Butcher Evans. On a different channel, the newscaster reported that Butcher Evans was claiming he was not the person involved in those murders of two-years ago. He claimed to be using another person's body, the REAL butcher of those people. The newscaster then went on to explain the case: Butcher Evans was involved in an invasion of a home owned by a pharmacist, his wife, and nine-year old daughter. When he found no drugs, he murdered the three people, putting two bullets into the head of the child. Miraculously, she lived long enough to finger the butcher. She died two hours later despite all the doctors' efforts.

Donald Carver, attorney for Evans, visited Connor for information. "Is there any proof that Mr. Watson was telling the truth about switching minds with the real killer?" Connor told him the results of his trials with animals. "Would the machine work with people?" Connor could not be positive, but believed it would. "How did they get your machine if you weren't involved?" "They stole it." Connor said this with unmistakable anger. "Look, he had my machine and a doctor who evidently trained himself in its use. They stole my notes too." "Do you have any proof of the alleged theft?" "I'm not bringing any charges, Watson more than paid for the safe, and I may be able to rebuild my machine."

The media were having a field day with the court case. Watson's attorney was busy acquiring summonses and subpoenas. Connor believed it would be wrong to imprison Watson. He tried to prepare himself for the trial. He would answer all questions honestly, and he would address his answers to the jury. When the time came, he was the first one called to testify. He told how he first met the defendant and how the defendant met Mr. Evans. Most of what he had to say was declared hearsay by the judge, but Watson's attorney managed to get the information out to the jury. He had to explain the workings of his machine, but he made sure to tell that such a machine could not be replicated, and it lay at the bottom of the Atlantic Ocean. When finished, Connor was permitted to sit in the courtroom. willing to take the chance even if he died. He is a very brave man, nothing like the cowardly Butcher Evans." A Doctor Constantine was called on for testimony. He told of learning the operation of the machine, then using it on Mr. Watson and Mr. Evans. No one knew that the police wanted Mr. Evans. He placed Mr. Evans in an induced coma, but could not do this with Mr. Watson. He had to switch minds with Mr. Watson fully awake. It was a very iffy situation. "What became of Mr. Evans?" "He responded after the transfer of minds took place, but he was out of his mind. The following day I found a wet spot on his bed. When I placed my hand near it, I could feel the globular mass that had been Evans, but he was dead. The mass did not move for 24-hours. I reported the death as the physician present at the time of death. I made out a death certificate and we buried Mr. Evans at sea when we tossed Dr. Cassidy's machine in. I have all the papers and permits. Mr. Evans had told us that he spent some years in the navy, and we have his oral request to be buried at sea."

The defense attorney asked the doctor if he had witnesses to back up his testimony. "Yes," answered the doctor. Each of the defense witnesses later told the same story. The assistant D. A. called on laboratory workers who testified that Mr. Watson's fingerprints and DNA matched those of butcher Evans. The defense attorney protested. "We have already stipulated to the fact that the suspect's body is that of the killer Evans, but his mind is that of the innocent Mr. Watson. You cannot imprison the killer's body and free the mind which does not belong in prison."

The trial took four days. The jurors did not agree from the start. Two women were for a not-guilty verdict. A taxi driver was griping about losing fares while he was working with two bitches. A large juror stood in front of him and said, "Now you will apologize to all the jurors or I will change the geography of your face!" The man apologized. The following vote showed eight not-guilty, four guilty. The taxi driver's demeanor may have had something to do with it, but within the hour, there were 11 votes for not guilty. The holdout was the taxi driver. Again, the big man confronted him.

"You were bitching about losing fares while here. Now you are holding up the decision and losing more fares. I wouldn't force your vote either way, but don't hold out just to get even." "You know, maybe you guys are right. I really thought he was guilty, but that doctor's testimony started swaying me to the other side. Here, I'll go along. He's not guilty." When they left the courthouse, the big man bought the taxi driver a drink.

The following day Connor was shopping and found himself close to Mr. Watson's hotel. He had an urge to congratulate Mr. Watson. He took the elevator to the second floor and found room 216. He raised his hand to knock on the door, stopping abruptly when he heard a loud, angry voice from within. It was Watson's attorney. Connor listened as the attorney shouted, "YOU CAN FEED THAT CRAP TO THE GOOD DOCTOR, CASSIDY, BUT NOT TO ME. I KNOW WHO YOU REALLY ARE. I KNOW ALL ABOUT THAT CRAP YOU AND YOUR PHYSICIAN FED TO THE JURY ABOUT SWITCHING MINDS. I KNOW YOU KILLED THAT FAMILY AS WELL AS OTHERS. I'M NOT SETTLING FOR LESS THAN ANOTHER HUNDRED AND FIFTY GRAND.... I, I'LL YELL WHEN I WANT TO...OK...OK... I'LL SETTLE DOWN..." Connor could not hear any more. He left abruptly. He had a lot to think over.

He went home in a very confused state. He had been starting to feel pity for the butcher, now he hated him with every fiber of his being. He wondered who could dream up such a plot and involve him. The man, the attorney, the doctor, they had all lied to get a murderer off. Now the killer could not be tried again. He felt that he had been used, dirtied, and thrown away like a dirty rag. The good doctor was not a vengeful man, but this was the limit. The following morning's newspaper had an item about attorney Donald Carver. He had been mugged and killed, the item said. Connor was sure he knew better. The butcher just saved himself a bundle of money through another murder. The butcher did not know what Connor knew about him. Maybe Connor could make use of that.

The afternoon of the following day found Connor parked in an area where he could watch the front door of Evans' hotel. He had some thoughts of beating the man, but he fought to subdue them. He also wanted to search the man's hotel room. He was not sure why. He was still confused. Actually, he could not even recall why he parked there. When he was readying to leave, he saw Watson leave the hotel and get into a car with two men. Connor left his car and made his way to Watson's hotel door. He thought it better to knock before picking the lock. A tall, bald man answered. "Hi Doc, what can we do fer ya?" The doctor replied, "The boss is waiting downstairs for my machine, his machine, I mean." The big man asked, "How 'bout a drink, Doc?" "I don't want the boss angry at me. I just need the machine. The boss is in a hurry." "OK, Doc. It's right in the bedroom. I'll get it." Connor left as soon as he had the machine in his arms. He was not surprised that the machine was not on the bottom of the ocean. He drove to Christine's house. His father was in the kitchen making a pot of coffee. "Visiting my girl, are you?" Connor joked. His father said he was not feeling well and wanted to be with someone. Then, Connor dropped his bombshell. "Watson had lied to everyone! He really is the butcher. He killed his attorney because the man demanded more money. I heard the conversation. He is a cold-blooded artist at his work, as the DA said in court. He never did use my machine. I have it now and he knows it. And now his doctor is missing." "What can you do, Son?" "Actually nothing; no one, not even the law can touch him." "Maybe you're free of him for good. He knows you have your machine, and you have his money. Offer him his money back. Maybe he'll leave you alone." "Let me think on it for a bit. I cannot just jump into an answer at this time. I want to get that murderer too. I want to see him suffer like he made a lot of good people do." "What happened to your oath, Son?" "The oath is for good people. I don't think it is supposed to be for killers."

It was early in the morning. Connor was shaving. The phone rang. It was Dr. Sullivan from Ste. Mary's. "Your Dad has just been admitted, Con. He was found unconscious on his front steps. You should come down." The doctor sounded worried. Connor was there within minutes. His father had been put under a sedative. Dr. Sullivan told Connor that X-rays showed a mass in and around the abdomen. "It's too widespread, Con. We can't do much except keep him comfortable and free from pain." "Can I take him home? I'll see the administrator about some time off." "Anything you need, Con. Just ask. Your dad knows the severity of the case."

Christine arrived at the hospital and Connor gave her the information he had. She held back her tears as much as she could, but they escaped and cascaded down her cheeks. Connor wiped her eyes with his handkerchief, and then wiped his own. They went into his father's room and read the chart for Dr. Desmond David Cassidy. It was bad. He was 80-years old, and usually looked younger, but not today. An ambulance brought the sick man to Connor's house and two men carried him and put him into one of the beds in an upstairs bedroom. He was under morphine so he did not feel any discomfort. Connor had taken some time off from his hospital duties. His dad was not expected to live for a month at most. Connor picked up the jangling telephone. It was Mr. Watson. Connor's jaw tightened. "Hi, Buddy," Watson said cordially. "I heard your father is sick and I just wanted you to know how bad I feel about it. Is there anything I can do to help? I know you got your machine back. I'm happy that you did. I was trying to come up with an excuse to return it to you. Don't worry Pal, I am not angry at all. I hope your dad gets better soon. I'm sorry about lying to you about that machine. I guess you don't have much to say… Well, good luck, Pal." Connor hung up and said aloud. "What the hell was that all about? The bastard is trying to soften me up for something." Connor tended to his father and tidied up the house, then sat and twiddled his thumbs. He was fidgety. His father was asleep so he went shopping.

He returned within a half-hour. As soon as he opened the front door, he smelled the gas. He quickly dropped the groceries on the living-room table and ran to the kitchen. The jets on the stove were wide open and the pilot flame had been snuffed out. He turned off the jets then went about the house and opened all the windows and doors to clear out the poisonous gas before he went upstairs to do the same. His father was still sleeping. Connor was cursing to himself and promising all sorts of things he would do to Evans. His hands became fists then relaxed. He calmed down before he dialed Christine's phone number. He had a large pizza in his shopping bag, so he invited her to dinner at his house. When she arrived, she first went upstairs to the father's room. He was awake. "Hi, Des; how are you feeling?" "I could use some more water. I am feeling poorly, but you always make me feel better. I will need some paper and a pen too. I have to make out my will. Please tell Connor not to give me any more morphine until all my arrangements are completed." His breathing was labored. It took him all afternoon to write his will. When he finished, he fell asleep again.

Connor and Christine were smiling as they enjoyed their coffee, smiling because they had agreed on a decision as to when they would get married. He told her about the gas jets, and how much worse it was because his father was in the house. Again, his fist tightened. Then they sat down to discuss their plans. They were well aware that Watson was not finished with his dirty work.They made plans. According to those plans, Christine phoned Watson and told him of her plan to marry Connor. Connor listened in. "We want to celebrate with a dinner because Connor can't leave the house that long. It looks like his dad turned on the gas jets today when Connor went out; could have blown up the house. I will cook dinner at Connor's house and we want you to celebrate with us. No. He is not a bit angry. He is so glad to get his dumb machine back. Can you come? Oh, that is wonderful, I will tell him, six o'clock tomorrow evening. Oh, he'll be so glad." Connor was looking at her and grinning as he showed her his fist. It was 20 minutes after six when Watson arrived. He gave no excuse for his lateness. Connor believed he had driven around the block to make sure there was no gang waiting to beat him.

They enjoyed a delicious turkey dinner although Connor had to cover his inner anger several times. Then they enjoyed a glass of wine. Watson looked about him and said, "Hey, are your lights going off and on? There they go ag…" His head thumped on the table. "I thought he'd never pass out," Connor said. Together they carried the unconscious man up the stairs and into the bed across the room from the sleeping Dr. Cassidy. Christine found the doctor's will on his bed. "He's very bad," she said sadly. Connor said, "I'll do this as fast as I can, without inducing coma. Watson will be out for about six hours because of that mickey. We'll have it done in four." The transfer of minds took exactly three hours and fifty-six minutes. Watson's mind was now in the old body and Cassidy's mind was in the body of a 32-year-old. The body of the doctor made it through the procedure, but the strain was too much. It ceased to function only twenty minutes after the transfer was completed. Watson's body would not awaken for a couple of hours, if indeed it awakened at all. There would not be a second chance to transfer minds if this did not work. Connor and Christine sat at the side of his father for another two hours before Desmond stirred. He then opened his eyes and looked about the room. He saw the two worried faces scrutinizing him. "How are you feeling, Dad?" His father smiled and said, "Son, I'm starving. Don't you ever feed a sick man? The pain is all gone. I feel like a million bucks. What have you done?"

"Dad, I've got something to tell you." This must have been the understatement of the century. As he talked, he was conducting reflex tests on his father's arms and legs. "Everything seems normal," he said with a bit of surprise evident in his voice. His lips tightened and he could no longer hold back the tears that welled in his eyes. The elderly doctor viewed his son and said, "What the hell?" Desmond had many questions during his son's explanation. When brought up to date he cried "So that's my body in that bed? Son, I'm dead, dead." He threw the blanket aside and was on his feet, but almost toppled over. Connor and Christine were smiling. "Who put these clothes on me? They have to go." He was brought back to reality and said, "Geez, I've got to get used to living in another body. How old am I, anyway?" Christine said she believed he was 32. "Oh, man, I feel so strong, so alive, and wide awake. I've got muscles again. Your machine works fine. I'm taller than I was too; I'll have to get used to that. Do you realize that I'm only six years older than you, Son?" He smiled.

Someone was knocking on the front door. Connor opened the door and was facing two police men. They wanted to know if he had seen Mr. Watson lately. One of them said, "He was reported missing this morning." There was a sudden movement on the stairs and Desmond called out," I'm right here officers I stayed the night. I thought you people didn't check on a missing person for at least 24 hours." The officer answered, "That's usually true, but you've been in the papers lately, giving you a high profile, so the chief thought it best to check on you." The officers thanked Connor and left.

Three days later, the good doctors were not so chipper. They were at the graveside when Dr. Desmond's body was buried. They were very sad to see the end of Desmond's body, yet they were very appreciative that Desmond stood and watched his own burial. There were 118 people at the gravesite. There were many doctors and nurses and yet more ex-patients. Desmond was a happy man, yet a saddened man. He was further saddened by the fact that he was no longer practicing medicine.

During the following days Desmond lived at Watson's apartment while he was learning Watson's habits and how best to impersonate him. He had Watson's goons take him to the several banks where Watson had accounts because he did not know their location and they did. When he totaled his accounts, they came to a little over six million dollars. He paid off the goons with a nice retirement plan. He had thought to change his name to Desmond David Cassidy, but soon gave up that idea. It would create more problems. Another of the doctor's problems was the fact that he had life-long friends whom he now had to treat as strangers. His new life had given him many more years, but it contributed to his sadness and aloneness. However, the good doctor was a resilient man and would surely overcome these obstacles during the following months.

Connor and Christine were married the following week. Desmond served as best man. He also went with them to the Bahamas with a beautiful blond at his side. The good doctor Desmond had not yet told his son that he had enrolled in a medical course and was getting very high grades on his tests. He may be qualified to take some of the state tests in one year if he continued getting such high grades.

EDWARD MCCARTHY

# BOUNTY HUNTER

The only dead body that Dan Wilson had seen before the rebellion was his grandfather. Now Sergeant Dan had seen many since the war in the north. He joined the army, and for almost a year saw no sign of the war. When war sought out his company, he could count the bodies by the score after score. When his officers were killed, he was promoted to captain. His company was restored to full strength, and then decimated again. He was finally returned to his former rank of sergeant, then rumors of peace spread across the land for a week and more. They proved true in April, 1865.

Dan could no longer march with his troops. A string around his neck carried two Minie balls; one had been removed from his right shoulder the other came from his thigh. He could no longer farm either, because of the damage they did. This is why he accepted his discharge. He took his savings from the bank and roamed the country for a time. Feeling sorry for himself brought no relief. He became deathly sick on arrival in Jason's Ford. He rested and had a drink at the saloon, took it to a table, and then passed out. He awoke in a bed in a private house a few minutes before a woman entered the room. She held his forehead and said, "Thank heavens your fever is gone." Dan seemed confused, "Where am I," he asked. "You're at Dr. Williams' house. You came here two days ago, or rather, you were carried here." He shook his head, "I recall being in the saloon." The woman said, "Yes, that's where you passed out. The doctor said you had a bad case of pneumonia. It was iffy for a while. He said you almost drowned when your lungs filled up. He stuck you with two hollow needles to drain the liquid from both lungs." Dan said, "I'm better now, where are my clothes?" She said, "You're not better yet, not for traveling. One more day in bed is the doctor's order. Oh, I'm Carol Williams, the doctor's sister. He's out with the posse searching for those who held up the bank two days ago. Three thieves made off with $35,000. One was wounded, but still in the saddle. The sheriff said they might find him dead on the road if he slows his partners down." Dan said he was leaving in the morning. "How much do I owe the doc?" Carol answered, "I think $12.00 is enough." He said he would leave the money on his side table.

In the morning he dressed and walked out the front door. Miss Williams seemed to come from nowhere, but she followed him and said, "Your horse is at Masons' Livery. If you feel weak, you come back, hear?" "Yes, I heard. Thank you, Miss Williams." Dan ordered a whisky at the saloon. He carried it and the bottle to a table after the bartender drew a line on his bottle to show the level of whiskey. Dan was on his second drink when the sheriff sat at his table. "What's your name, stranger?" "Hello Sheriff. I'm Dan Williams." The sheriff repeated the name, and then said, "Oh, I know, you're the guy who passed out here the other day." Dan said, "Yep, that's me." The sheriff told him that was the same day the bank was robbed. "Have a drink, Sheriff?" "Sure, Dan. I've been out for two days now and I'm tired as hell. I've been sheriff here for 21-years and I don't think I'll be staying much longer. I'm Jim Johnson." Dan called, "Bartender, another glass please." Sheriff Johnson said, "Followed them out to Pine Ridge. The trail just petered out. It's so rocky out there a horse doesn't leave much of a trail. Didn't find the body of the wounded man either." Dan said, "I was a pretty good scout in the army. Maybe I'll have a look tomorrow." "It's worth $2,000 if you find them, plus 10 percent of the stolen money," the sheriff said.

Dan was on the trail in the morning. He felt a bit stiff from inactivity, but that didn't slow him down much. He arrived at Pine Ridge; the ground there was covered in flat stones. He scanned the area, looking for overturned stones, flattened grass, etc. He followed a trail of overturned stones and those misplaced by a horse's hoof. They led to a grassy area which then led to larger stones and boulders. Very dim trail markings were followed for about four miles until Dan looked up and saw a shack in the distance. No smoke came from the chimney. He waited and watched, then saw a movement. A window curtain was raised and lowered. When darkness came, Dan stole closer to the shack. Suddenly, light spilled from an oil lamp as the front door was opened wide and a man exited. Dan lay flat on the ground. In a few minutes the man reentered the shack. Dan approached and listened at the side of the house. Two men were talking about dividing the loot between them, and leaving in the morning. Dan stole up to the front door, slowly turned the doorknob, then yanked open the door as he yelled, "Reach!" The men had been playing cards. They stood and were disarmed. Dan followed the men back to the sheriff's office. Once there, he locked the men in cells and dropped the bag with the stolen money on the sheriff's desk. The sheriff had been sleeping in one of the cells, now he was fully awake. He emerged from the cell and asked Dan, "What the hell is going on?" "I put the thieves in a cell. I don't know where the wounded one was buried, if he was. How far is the next doctor?" "Monroe has one. It's a day's ride from here." "He can't be there, it's too far. I think he's hiding over at Doc Williams' place; he wasn't at the shack." Dan and the sheriff mounted their horses and rode to the doctor's house. Miss Williams opened the door a bit and shook her head at Dan. She said, "Oh, Mr. Wilson, tomorrow is your appointment, not today." Dan knew that no appointment had been made. He acted on this immediately. "Oh, hell, I get my days mixed up. I'll come back tomorrow." The men rode back to the sheriff's office. Dan said, "I'll wait 'til dark, then go back and check out the house." "I was thinking the same thing Dan. Someone was watching us from the front window. I saw the curtain and someone's hand." Dan said, "Maybe it was the doc's sister." "This hand was holding a .45," the sheriff said.

They played cards and drank whiskey, limiting their drinks to two each. When darkness covered the town, the men left the saloon, made a wide circle and came to the back of the doctor's house. The sheriff listened at the wall, but heard nothing important.

They edged their way to the back door, but it was locked. Dan opened a kitchen window and prepared to clamber through it when someone inside the house yelled, "Shut that damn window, woman." Miss Williams appeared. Dan pointed to the door. She nodded. Before she returned to the large room, she quickly unbolted the kitchen door, and returned to the room saying, "I closed the window, can we have coffee now?" "Sure. That sounds good," said the strange voice. Dan could hear the stranger sipping his coffee. With gun drawn he entered the doorway saying, "Don't do anything foolish. Get his gun Jim." The sheriff cuffed the man and led him directly to a cell at the jail. When Dan entered the sheriff's office, the sheriff asked, "Do you know why I let you take the lead?" "No, why?" "Because a lawman here can't get a reward; he's paid for what he does. You have more than $5,000 coming. I know where there's a ranch you can get for less than that, or let me make you a deputy, no, you can't get the bounty here as a lawman. Look, I can give you all the information on wanted people. You bring them in and take the reward. It's worth a try, Dan."

Dan spent the whole day poring over wanted posters. He and Sheriff Jim went for dinner at the Mama Jane Restaurant, then to the saloon for a nightcap. They rose from the table to leave when a large man at the bar shouted, "Have a drink on me." "Thanks, but I'm too tired, gotta get some sleep," Jim said. "Too good to drink with me Sheriff?" Jim was not in a good humor. He said, "I told you I'm going to bed. You be good Henry." Henry was insistent, "You don't wanna drink with me?" Jim's jaw tightened as he said, "I told you I was tired, now I'm getting tired of you." The man called Henry stepped away from the bar as he faced the sheriff. Dan stood to the side of the sheriff. Henry said, "I heard about you Dan. You're the best bounty hunter in these parts. I'm not drawing against you." Dan said, "You shouldn't think about drawing against Jim either. He's faster than I am." Henry turned and was speaking with the bartender when the two men left.

Dan did check out the ranch he and Jim had spoken about. The owners said they were saving money to go west to California. They gave him a special price because they could go earlier and the owner wouldn't have to take the time to sell his cattle and horses around town. The ranch was good for 60 cattle, but the owners had raised as many as 86 on it. Dan told this to Jim, and then surprised him saying, "I bought it and an adjoining 164 acres! "Going into the cattle business, Dan?" "No, well, not right away. The owners are leaving in the morning. The Apaches have been quiet lately. I'm pretty sure they'll make the trip safely. Carol said she would be there tomorrow to figure out what I'll need, you know, linen, a bed, food and other necessaries. It's only four miles out of town." "Carol? The doc's sister? You two already?" Dan smiled and said, "Oh, it's nothing like that, well, not yet anyway. Did you know the sellers have a water pump in their kitchen? Mighty handy. The owner said he has a good well too, never went dry in six years and his windmill keeps the water trough filled too." The sheriff received a wire that afternoon from the sheriff of Tucson. "Watch for two members of Charley Comber's gang heading your way." "Charley Comber is one of those bank robbers in my cell. I can't get rid of him until the circuit judge comes and someone's sent here to take him away. The two who are coming may try to break him out of jail," said Jim. "Do we have anything on them?" "You checked the wanted posters. Remember anything about them?" "Nope!"

"One of us must cover the office every day until this matter is settled, Dan." "OK by me, Jim."

That day Jim watched as two strangers rode into town. He followed them to the saloon. They ate lunch and left town. Two days later three men rode into town, two were in their thirties, and the other was perhaps 17. Jim was convinced that one of the older men looked much like his prisoner. He returned to his office. "They're here," he told Dan. Dan said, "Jim, I've been very selfish. I spent most of the reward money on things for me, but if it weren't for you, I'd be broke." Jim said, "Dan, when we made that deal, I had no intentions of sharing your reward money." "That's neither here nor there Jim, I want to make you a partner in my ranch. I don't know much about cattle besides getting them fattened to sell them." Jim said, "I'll think about it. Sounds good to me, I was raised with cattle. There's much more than getting them fat involved." Suddenly the front door opened. Dan's gun was in his hand. One of the two strangers said, "I came to visit my brother." "Unload!" the sheriff said as he patted down the men, finding a small .32 in the other man's jacket. They visited for ten minutes and then left. Dan went to lunch at the saloon and saw the men there. They were becoming drunk and loud and often looked at Dan with narrowed eyes. He finished lunch and returned to the office. Now the sheriff went to lunch. Jim was gone only a few minutes when Dan heard the shot. He ran up the boardwalk, someone pointed at the saloon door. Dan entered and faced a man with a drawn gun. Dan jumped to the side as he pulled his gun and fired. The armed man dropped his gun and fell to the floor. Another man was seen running out the side door, and then Dan heard a horse galloping through the street.

Dan ran to Jim who was seated in a chair looking as though he had fallen asleep. Blood ran down the back of his shirt. "They shot him in the back," someone said, "then waited to shoot you, if you're Dan." Six men were carrying Jim when Dan ran to his horse. A man and woman pointed west. He turned his horse and galloped away. Three miles ahead was a split in the road, but it was surrounded by trees. He slowed his pace and was making plans when a shot thumped into a tree near him. He dismounted and ran into the wooded area to circle around the shooter. His quick judgement was accurate. He came behind the man. "Drop the rifle." Dan shouted. The man turned quickly and fired. Dan felt the sting of the bullet as it burned a rut in his thigh at the same moment the man grabbed his belly. The man was ten minutes from death. Dan stayed with him until the end.

He rode into town with the shooter slung across his horse. He stopped at the doctor's house. Carol was relieved to see him. "How is Jim," he asked. The doctor entered the room just then and said, "He's doing fine. I took the bullet out. He's lost a mite of blood, so he'll be in bed for a few days. It was close; however, the bullet just nicked his intestine. Don't talk too long." Ten minutes later Dan came from the room and told Carol, "Jim said he'll try ranching. We'll build another room onto the place. Would you also like to try ranching? I'm asking you to marry me, Carol." She looked shy when she said, "I'm just an old maid, Dan." "But a beautiful one, he added. "Well, will you marry me? It doesn't have to be now, maybe this afternoon or tomorrow?" He joked. She smiled, "Let me catch my breath. When I know more about you, I'll give you my answer. He said, "I'll tell you everything you want to know, he said. "My shoe size is eleven. I have two brothers. I'm from Nebraska. I'm not wanted anywhere." The wedding was two weeks later.

MIX OF STORIES

# THE BAILIFF

The rebellion ended on Sunday, April ninth, 1865. Some of the soldiers were so tired they lay on the ground among fallen men from both sides, and fell asleep. There was no enemy as far as they were concerned. President Lincoln called for state and territorial governors to put down all rebellious talk and actions as well as criminal actions. The territorial governor of Arizona sent out word that statehood could depend on reducing crime. He wired Judge Matthews, asking him to look into the recurring murders of young girls in the town of Mason. Judge Matthews and his bailiff, Linc Chambers, arrived there shortly. Mason was a small town of about 215 people. The bruised and beaten body of Judy Moran had been found recently on the desert lightly covered in sand. Hers was the third such body found in the desert home to coyotes, scorpions, and cactus. Like the others, who were younger, she had also been molested. Linc agreed to investigate the case and promised his boss and friend to keep his anger in check. His first move was to ask directions to the murder site, then ride to it and study the terrain. Footprints were all over the area. The sheriff's men had walked all over the site and people were visiting the area. In spite of this, he found a print in hard ground. After checking the area, he could tell that those size 9 prints were not among the newer prints. He told the judge, that they could belong to the killer.

Linc worked closely with Sheriff Josh Logan who said he had four residents in mind as the killer. Linc was determined to check into them himself. He spoke at length with each one and was satisfied that they were not guilty. When he told the sheriff, Logan cursed, "I don't know where to go now." Linc answered, "We do what we can, Josh, and none of the men wore size nine boots." Linc went to the Happy Times saloon and ordered a beer. He stood at the bar so he could listen to the various conversations going on about him. One man was trying to sell a milk cow; another was looking for a horse for his son. There was nothing unusual in the talks until a young man at the bar said to his companion, "Geez, I was shaking when I looked at the sight. I was thinking that a person had given up her life on this very spot." The companion, a younger man, said," I started shaking the minute I looked at the spot. It was spooky. I could almost hear Judy's watch chiming the hour. I think it was an old Irish tune. I couldn't away from there fast enough."

Linc hurried out to his horse and to Judy's murder site. No one had mentioned a watch, and no watch had been found. Some souvenir hunter could have taken it home. After reaching the site he worked his way in an ever-enlarging circle, peering at the ground. About 50-feet from the circle center he saw something red. It was a small purse made of red and white cloth. Inside was a man's watch, a lace handkerchief and 27-cents. The watch had wound down and was stopped, but it started ticking again when he wound it. He was thirsty from all his labor, so he rode back to town. At the saloon he ordered a beer and took it to a table. One of the saloon girls asked if she could sit with him. He ordered a drink for her. They spoke of the weather and other mundane topics. Her name was Molly. As they spoke, Linc reached into his shirt and withdrew the small purse. Molly saw it and suddenly paled. "That's Judy's purse." Linc removed the watch from the purse and put it on the table. "Oh God," Molly said. "She never got home to give that to her dad for his birthday." Linc said,"I'm at a loss, Molly. You'll have to explain what you're talking about." Molly looked very serious as she explained: "Judy and I were good friends. When she told me she was looking to buy a gift for her dad's birthday I offered her that watch. You see, Jerry Komar tried to sell it to me, and then finally settled for 5-dollars, but he was going to retrieve it when he earned the money. Well, he fell off a train and was killed, so the watch was mine, but I didn't want it. She bought it. I didn't cheat her. It's a forty-dollar watch, 17 jewels and all." "I believe you, Molly. Who else knew about the watch? Maybe someone tried to steal it from her?" "I don't think so; no one else knew about it." "Except the killer," Linc said as he watched the young man at the bar who had visited Judy's murder site and "could almost hear the watch chiming." Linc rose and walked to the man. He held the watch in his hand and shoved it toward the man. The man jumped back. Linc said, "Can you hear the Irish tune better now? Maybe you can even hear Judy calling you a murderer. You're the lowest kind of human being on Earth but you 've killed your last little girl." Suddenly, the man jumped aside and grabbed at his sidearm. Linc shot him and saw the look of surprise on the man's face as he died. Linc took the watch to Judy's father. He could not speak. He handed the watch to the surprised man and mumbled, "Judy's gift for your birthday." He could be seen wiping his eyes as he hurried to his horse. When he mounted his horse, he wiped his eyes and said to himself about being a baby.

# MIX OF STORIES

# CALICO

Jeff's mare walked haltingly as she approached the doctor's house. It was dark, but the light from inside the house lit the front yard dimly. Jeff dismounted slowly and held on to the fence posts as he made his way to the doctor's house. He entered the yard, walked up the path, and fell. He picked himself up and continued to the porch, then passed out. The doctor and his sister appeared at the front door. They had heard the noise. Doctor John Ward almost tripped on the prone figure, He and his sister, Marie, carried Jeff into the house and into a bed in the spare room. The doctor made an examination. Jeff had a scalp wound, a hole in his upper arm and one in his left thigh. Doctor John worked until two in the morning as he cleaned and sewed up the wounds. In the morning Jeff was awake. He was told to be careful when using his wounded arm and leg. "We don't want complications. That head wound will keep you from straining yourself. You may get blurry or double vision for a time, but that won't last long." Marie was questioning him and writing notes in a small pad. He was 26, unmarried, place of work? He was a US marshal, but that must be kept secret. As she left the room, she said "Get all the sleep you can, Mr. Crowder. Sleep is a great healer."

On the following day, while eating lunch, he sat in the bed. The doctor sat in a chair beside the bed and asked, "Why did you want it kept secret that you are a marshal.?" "It isn't only to protect me, but also to protect you and Marie. There are people in Calico who do not like the law. That is why they ambushed me when I arrived. They also stopped the stage coach and searched for me. They don't know what I look like, so you tell everyone I'm an old friend of yours who came here to regain my health. Is this OK?" "It's fine with me and Marie, too. Oh, by the way, your horse made it to Green's Livery all by herself. Just walked in. Mr. Green wants to see you when you're able to walk." "If you see him before I do, tell him, yes, I will pay the bill." "Mr. Green said she had a wound on her left hip, but it was healing fine after he cleaned it."

It was three days later when Dr. John was going near the livery in his wagon. Jeff said he would go with him. He wanted to see his mare and get some news at the saloon. The livery was at the other end of town. The doctor dropped him off there. It would have been a straight walk, if Jeff could walk that far. Jeff paid Mr. Green and checked his mare's hip. It had been shaved and cleaned, and was mostly healed. Jeff was grateful. The saloon was about half-way back to the doctor's house, Jeff dropped off for a drink or two and to listen for any news. The saloon was almost empty except for a few men at the bar. Jeff ordered a beer and sat at a table. When the bar man took him his drink, he said, "You're Mr. Jeffords, aren't you? John said he had an old friend visiting him."

"I have a lot of faith in John. I came all the way from Wyoming to get his help. I was hurt three years ago and my leg still hurts when I walk." Jeff had placed his cane on the table, Now, two men at the bar began shoving each other. One was shoved into Jeff's table. Jeff held his beer safely off the table, but his cane went clattering across the floor. Jeff asked if someone could pick up his cane. The man who had knocked it to the floor said. "Pick it up yourself,." then returned to the bar. Another man returned it to Jeff and whispered, "Be careful, he's a deputy and mean as hell." When Jeff told Dr. John about the incident, John said, "I know you could have clobbered the man, but then we'd find your body in an alley." In another three days, Jeff could walk without his cane, but he continued using it. He did not want to be a continuing burden to the doctor and his sister, so he checked into the Calico Hotel. He bought a new shirt and pants at the mercantile shop and visited the saloon again. The man who had picked up his cane days earlier, entered and sat at his table. "Aren't you Jeff Crowder? You can tell me. I'm the one who wrote to the marshal's office pleading for someone to come here. Those people have murdered four men in the past month and they've beaten up the barber because he asked for his payment. They never pay for a drink at the bar either, and that eats into Mr. Morgan's profit. It does no good to tell the sheriff, either." Jeff told him that he had a plan in mind set for the ninth of the month. What I need from you is as many honest men as you can get together. The man was the town accountant, Henry Madison, and he knew many men in the town because he worked on many of the shopkeeper's books.

Jeff saddled his mare and rode to Tatum Crossing to send a wire to headquarters, alerting his boss as to the need for four deputies on the ninth, then he returned to the saloon. He ordered another beer and sat at a table. There were 5 or 6 other men in the saloon when the two previously rowdy men walked in. It wasn't long before the brothers were shoving each other again. Other customers walked away from the bar to sit at tables, where they would be safer. Mr. Madison walked in and sat at Jeff's table. "I've got two men out of the six I talked to." "And how many does the sheriff have?" "About thirty. not counting the entire town council. The sheriff told us many ways we could make money, all crooked. Watch out for those Foley brothers at the bar, they're fast with a gun. I heard them bragging about gunning a marshal not two weeks ago too. Well, gotta go, they're giving me the evil eye." As soon as Madison was out the door, one of the brothers approached Jeff's table. The other brother watched Jeff with an evil grin on his face. The closer man reached down for Jeff's cane. Jeff grabbed it and stood. "Oh, ho," the man said. "We got a live one here." Jeff drove the cane into the man's middle. The man doubled up as he grabbed his stomach. The brother at the bar slapped leather. Jeff beat him to the draw and shot him in the chest. His gun clattered to the floor. The nearer brother straightened up, looked at Jeff with widened eyes, and drew his weapon. Jeff hit him in the throat with his cane. That was their game, one man distracted their target while the other man killed him. Both men were dead within ten minutes.

However, it didn't take that long for the sheriff to walk into the saloon and demand of Jeff, "What the hell's going on here?" A customer said, "They asked for it, Sheriff, Weren't his fault no how." Four others nodded. "Well, OK. Come to my office later to sign some papers."

It was the ninth of the month. Mr. Madison met Jeff at the saloon He told Jeff that his men, five of them, were waiting at the barber shop. Jeff reminded him that he had already gone over the plans with them for retaking the town. Jeff walked the short distance to the sheriff's office. In the office were the sheriff and three of his men. Jeff pinned on his badge and placed the sheriff and his men under arrest and into a cell. One-by- one and two- by- two the sheriff's men came to the office after being told that the sheriff wanted them. When it was all over, there were twenty-seven men in cells, and not a shot fired to retake the town.

Court was held on the following morning, convened by Judge Randolph and four deputy marshals. The judge sentenced two men to be hanged, four received ten-year sentences, six received one- year sentences, and four were fined fifty dollars each, which the judge pocketed. The freed men had to be out of town within an hour or face a year in prison. Once the prisoners had been taken away, Jeff called his men together. "You did a wonderful job. I've been checking over some flyers I found in the sheriff's desk. So far, I've located a total bounty for those men remaining in the cells amounting to $4,340.00, and there's probably more. There are six of you to share in that reward. You do the math. Hold a vote tomorrow. One of you should replace the sheriff, another the mayor, and so on. I've gotten my reward, six honest men. I feel like Diogenes." Mr. Madison asked, "A friend of yours?" Jeff said, "No, he's a guy who lived in Greece a while back. He was looking for one honest man." "Lived in grease?" Jeff smiled, "Not that kind of grease. The country of Greece, far, far away, in another town," he grinned.

EDWARD MCCARTHY

# RETIREE

Jim and Carl were the owners of the Double D ranch. Jim was Carl's nephew. He was 26; his uncle was 52. The ranch was of considerable size, including a bit over a thousand acres. The former owner was Jim's dad who died six months ago. Every time he had a dollar to spare, he bought more land. There was a bit of land, about twenty acres, set aside for a small Apache band of peaceful Indians. They could use this land as long as they remained peaceful. They had been living there for about thirty years, hunting and fishing for their food. Buffalo. deer and antelope were becoming very scarce, so the tribe recently voted to farm the land. They could stay on the property as long as they remained peaceful.

Times were very hard immediately after the uprising. Many old-time residents were pulling stakes and leaving for the promised land in California. Carpetbaggers made the living harder. Rents, mortgages, prices rose, but wages remained the same, so did the price for cattle and horses. Carpetbaggers were raking in money under the guise of working for the government. They were buying the property of those who were forced to leave, but they were paying only one-quarter of the original price, sometimes less. Some people sold their property, then returned at night and burned down their former home because of the way they were treated by the carpetbaggers. Jim and Carl were forced to pay five percent of their sales prices for the cattle and horses they sold. Shops in town were no longer dealing in credit. They had lost too much money already.

Jim drove his buckboard into town (four miles), and left his list of necessaries with the shopkeeper while he visited the saloon. He ordered a beer and sat at one of the empty tables. He nodded to several ranchers he knew as he wondered why so many were visiting the saloon instead of working. He was well liked by the town folk and ranchers he knew since he prevented a robbery at Taylor's Mercantile. A stranger had pointed his .44 at the store keeper and said, "Put your hands…" That's when Jim hit the man on the head with the ball of his fist and knocked him out. The store keeper spread the story about town.

# MIX OF STORIES

The would-be thief had a $100.00 bounty on his capture. It was payable to Jim. One of the carpetbaggers approached him and demanded his five percent. Jim cursed the man and told him he wasn't paying it. The sheriff later told the carpetbagger he was not entitled to a percentage of bounties or any other state or territorial payments. This is when Jim decided to become a bounty hunter. Sheriff Charles tried to talk him out of it. He knew of four others who had the same idea. Two were now dead, the others were just as poor as before. "You're very good with your gun, but I advise against it." Jim said that he wasn't serious about it. Some of those men in the saloon were once hard-working ranchers, but now seemed to have given in to the hard times, and joined with other losers, playing penny- ante poker and swapping rumors. Jim finished his beer, loaded his necessaries, and drove home. He could see the friendly Apaches as he drove onto the ranch. They were eager to tell him, "Three white men, they come to steal. They hit Mr. Carl. Him in house. Him sleep." Jim jumped from the wagon and ran into the house with the Apaches behind him. Carl was awake and seated in a chair as he held his head in his hands. There wasn't much anyone could do to ease Carl's pain. Jim set about making a pot of coffee as the Apaches unloaded his necessaries, then sat at the table enjoying the coffee. The Apaches explained that they were there to sell Jim some fine furs for three hoes. Jim or Carl would get the hoes in town. They also brought Jim an elderly Apache who was about to die. They had found him sitting on a hillside singing his death song. The man was Carl's age, but looked much older. Carl said, "OK, we'll patch him up and send him home." They learned that the man was starving himself so the women and children in his clan would have more to eat. The man's name was impossible for Jim to say. He called him OK. Jim wanted to take after the two men who beat Carl, but Carl told him it takes planning to go after a man. Carl could recall that the two men spoke of going to Mexico, and having to split $27,000 they had stolen from a mine payroll.

Carl awoke early in the morning to some noise outside. The sun was just rising as Jim was saddling his mare. Jim saw Carl at the window, and went to him saying he was taking some time, maybe four days, to search for the men who beat him. "Take care of yourself, Jim," was all Carl could think of saying. On his ride south Jim asked several people if they had seen two men, one with a mustache, the other much younger. No one had seen them. Jim went into Mexico and asked the same question. Nobody saw them. He took a room at the Frontier Hotel and walked through the small town, stopping at the cantina to listen to the talk. Every day seemed to be the same. He decided he was wasting his time. Carl was having some problems at the ranch with the Morgan brothers, (the carpetbaggers), as well as two gunnies. Carl refused to allow them into the house. They had a reputation for stealing when invited to anyone's house. They wanted Jim and Carl's ranch. They already owned much of the property around the ranch, even threatened to shut off the road to the ranch. Carl told them that the final decision was Jim's. The brothers didn't like the answer, but said they would be back. OK was in his spare bedroom holding a rifle aimed at the brothers in case they started something.

Jim returned to the ranch that afternoon. He found that OK had painted his face with a death mask. Jim told him to wipe it off, "Cause you aint dying, not here, not now. Make up your mind. You can retire here, but you can't die." "What means retire, Mr. Jim?" "Why, it means you don't have to work anymore. It means you rest and get strong."

"You let OK retire here? I find way back off death road." OK cleaned his face. He went out that afternoon on Carl's horse, and brought home a large deer. Then he went out again and brought another deer to his tribal people. Jim said. "So much for rest. The man looks younger already."

In the morning, Jim rode to town and bought ammo for his rifles and pistols. He was sure that the Morgans would be back. As he was leaving town, he noticed two men entering the saloon. They fit perfectly the description of the robbers. He entered the saloon and ordered a beer. He chose a table and sat down as he kept an eye on the two men. After finishing his beer, he rose to walk up the street to the sheriff's office. He decided it was too much for him. This was a job for more than one man. It was too late. One of the men rose and faced Jim. "You got nothing better to do cowboy, except gawk at strangers?" It was do or die time. Jim slapped leather and beat the man to the draw. He did not fire because the man removed his hand from his weapon, letting it fall back into the holster. Jim ordered the two men to put their weapons on the table and head for the sheriff's office. The sheriff searched them, finding two more guns before putting them in a cell. They fit the description on the wanted posters, but the sheriff wanted Carl to eyeball them before he put in the papers for a four-hundred-dollar reward. Most of the stolen money was found in their hotel room. Carl later identified the men as the ones who beat and robbed him and had talked about robbing a stage coach.

By the end of the week, the judge had sentenced the men to twenty years in prison. Each man had a bounty of four hundred dollars. Jim would also be entitled to twenty- seven hundred dollars for the return of the stolen money. When he went to collect the money, he was met by the Morgans. They wanted their percentage. Jim said, "Do I have to get the sheriff again?" When he returned to the ranch, he was told that OK had walked to his clan and came back all tuckered out. "He almost fell at the door," Carl told him. Jim returned to town the following day and returned with a horse in tow for OK as well as a brand-new repeating rifle. OK was at a loss for words. He almost cried.

OK felt much better in the morning. He mounted his horse and rode off. A while later the Morgan brothers and their two gunnies showed up. They wanted to buy the ranch. Carl ordered them off the ranch. One of the gunnies stepped down and was about to punch Carl when Jim aimed his pistol at the angry man and told all of them to get the hell and gone. The men had a pistol aimed at them from the front. OK was aiming his new rifle at them from the side. The men left, but didn't go far.

Jim and Carl sat down later in the day to enjoy a cup of coffee. That is when a bullet shattered a window pane and clunked into a wall. "Hey, that's a twenty- cent window pane," said Carl. Another shot shattered an oil lamp. "Your mom bought that lamp some forty-years ago. It's a dollar lamp. There was a long wait before the next shot, but it sounded different. In the dwindling light they could see one of the gunnies lying on the ground. He was not moving. Carl and Jim could see flashes of light each time one of the thieves fired his weapon. That is where they aimed. Jim brought one of the gunnies down by firing at that flash. Carl was adding another dollar to his mental tally because a bullet put a hole in one of the cooking pots. Jim was about to fire at one of the Morgans when he heard the sharp sound of OK's rifle. Morgan fell. His brother came from hiding and was tending to his fallen brother when the sheriff asked. 'What the hell is an Injun doing here?" OK answered," I retire here. I tire now…go bed."

The sheriff laughed and wished OK a good night. Then he said, "Hell, Jim, I bet those gunnies have a price on their heads and you didn't even have to leave home to make money as a bounty hunter." Jim laughed and shook his head as he said, "No more, I'm retiring too."

EDWARD MCCARTHY

# NAMES

Before the Middle Ages (500-1500), people got along fine with only a given name. As the population grew, this caused confusion among John the baker, John the cook, and John who lived on the hill. It took time, but people began to identify a man's name with where he lived, any special qualities, his trade, etc. Thus, John, who lived on the hill, became John Hill, John the cook became John Cook, etc.

In the year 1545 the pope ordered all Catholics to name their children after people in the New Testament. Not to be outdone, Protestants were told to name their children after people in the Old Testament.

In Ireland and Scotland, some family names are preceded by Mc, Mac, or O'. Mc and Mac refer to children who are direct descendants of a person, such as MacHenry. An indirect descendent (nephew, cousin, etc.) would be named O'Henry, or "of the family of Henry." An illegitimate child would be named FitzHenry. This was a terrible way to burden an innocent child.

Esq. (Esquire) written after a name denotes someone much respected. An esquire was one rank below a knight, a gentleman was one rank below an esquire. Goodman was a title used for the head of a household, and the feminine counterpart was Goody, sometimes good woman.

# WWII
## LOST AND FOUND

     I met George Cowell when I joined G Company. He was born in Brooklyn too, so we hit it off right away. We walked along the Autobahn Highway until the captain told us it was time to take over a house and bunk down until sunup. I was put on guard outside the front door. A wire was tied to my wrist and to the wrist of the man at a side door. If attacked, the captain would know it when our rifle fired. I noticed George leaving the house with another man. He said. "Patrol" as he passed me. He had been gone about 45 minutes when the other man returned and asked if George showed up. I told him I hadn't seen George since he left.

     I began to worry about my friend because it was a very dark night, no moon, no lights anywhere. Another ten minutes passed, then somebody came onto the porch and stumbled into the wire tied to my wrist. This caused me to fire the carbine I held. I had the carbine only because a Lieutenant told me to take care of it while he went back to regimental HQ to complain about cold feet. In less than 5 seconds the top sergeant told me to see the captain as soon as I was off guard duty. No sooner had I begun to worry about myself, I heard a noise. I aimed my carbine and George appeared, "I knew some jerk GI would lead me home. Man, it was so dark, I

got lost. I couldn't yell or even whisper loudly because there were German patrols out in our area. Who's the jerk who fired the shot?" I answered, "You're looking at him." Later, I reported to Captain Mike as ordered. He asked why I fired the rifle. I told him that someone pulled the wire on my wrist or bumped into it in the dark. He asked if I pulled the trigger hard or easy to cause it to fire. I was confused, but I answered. "Very easy, Sir." When the lieutenant returned from his trip, he was chewed out for filing down the sear in his carbine after the captain told him not to do it. He was also told that everyone in the company had cold or frozen feet. "Why should you be different?"

EDWARD MCCARTHY

# THE BOSTON TEA PARTY

What we know of the Tea Party of Dec. 16,1773 actually started many months previously. It began with the pleas of the East India Company to save it from bankruptcy. King George lll came to the rescue of his friends on May 10, 1773. The Tory (Republican) British Parliament passed a law giving the East India Company exclusive rights to sell tea in the colonies. It also increased the tea tax. The tax itself amounted to only to 300 pounds annually for the British. The company then decided to sell the tea directly to the people instead of to wholesalers, thus bankrupting many colonists. On Nov. 26, 1773, three East India ships put in at Boston Harbor with enough tea aboard to last an estimated 7-years. The ships captains were aware that a customs fee was due. They had 20 days to pay it. Many believed it would never be paid. Colonists prevented the unloading of the tea casks until the fee was paid. Royal governor Hutchinson prevented the ships from leaving the harbor to avoid payment of the fee. It appeared that the fee would not be paid voluntarily.

Sam Adams, a cousin of John Adams, organized what was humorously called a Tea Party in the back room of a print shop. Paul Revere was said to be among the 150 or so men who kept warm on applejack. The men split into three groups, some were half naked and dressed as Indians on the rainy, cold night of Dec. 16, 1773. They dumped 342 chests of tea into the cold waters of the harbor. The governor would have seized the cargo on the following day for non-payment of the customs fee.

# MIX OF STORIES

# SHORTY

Shorty did not appreciate his station in life. He lived with his parents and nine siblings in a house that needed repairs in every room and the roof. He felt sorry for all the family. He also wanted some action in his life. He felt awful for his brothers and sisters, but couldn't do anything about the situation. If he left home, maybe the kids would have more to eat, at least he wouldn't have to sleep three in a bed. He was determined and quite self-sufficient at 11 years of age. He headed west and joined a wagon train as a hunter when he was barely twelve. The wagon boss was quite surprised when Shorty brought back deer, antelope and even two buffalos. He had to return to the ranch, then drive a wagon back to the buffalo after quartering them. It was not easy work to load the buffalo. His hunting ability kept the wagon train well-supplied, even for the dogs and cats.

The train reached San Francisco and Shorty was paid for his work, but needed a job. There wouldn't be a need for a hunter until spring. He hired on as a seaman with Captain Rogers, and he did as much work as anyone else. He saw much of the world on his voyages He had been around the Horn twice, and to China India and Japan. His ship returned with tea, olive oil, and spices. The seamen returned with stories of pirates and how Captain Rogers outwitted them. After two years he could spin yarns with the best of the spinners because he lived the life.

When the Jolly Star was wrecked on a reef, it ended his sailing days. He would not sign on with any other captain. He headed east and took a job as sheriff's deputy in a Wyoming town for several years. He was twenty-four when he tried his hand at prospecting. He bought a burro and all the equipment he would need, although he didn't know how to use most of it. He headed for the hills of California.

It was getting dark when he found a suitable camping site among the trees. He was stirring the campfire when some movement caught his eye. He rose and walked to the spot. What he had seen was an arrow. It was sticking out of a man's back. He quickly searched the area with his eyes, but saw nothing of interest except a shovel. Why was a shovel there? He searched the area for freshly turned earth, but found none. Then he turned over the dead man and saw fresh soil. He dug into it and brought up two pouches of gold. It appeared that the dead man was hiding his gold when some Indian killed him, or so Shorty guessed. He moved his camp some three hundred yards downhill. He would have to notify the sheriff of his discovery in the morning. He must be careful because of the fear of being blamed for murder.

    Noise and shouting awoke him in the morning. Someone had found the body of John Hastings. "An Indian did him in," someone yelled. Shorty learned that John Hastings was much loved by the people. They were prepared to hang anyone who had a hand in his death. Shorty kept his mouth shut. He knew he would receive some notoriety by notifying the sheriff, but the mob could also blame him, and when they discovered the gold, he was sure to be hung. Now, dishonest people would be searching all over Hastings' claim to steal any hidden pokes of gold.

    He expected to be questioned about Hasting's death, but wasn't, because there were always strangers and visitors among the prospectors. He gathered his belongings, mounted his horse and rode up stream surveying the area for a place to make his claim. The sheriff had not questioned him, and did not plan to. That evening he settled down in a wooded area and began to heat his coffee. The sun was just setting when he saw a man on a horse slowly approaching the creek where prospectors were still working. He saw an elderly man panning near him in the creek. He studied the man's actions to learn how to pan. Then he noticed the horseman nocking an arrow in his bow and aiming at the man in the creek. Shorty drew his pistol as fast as he could and shot the man, who fell dead from his horse. Again, he looked for the elderly man and saw him trying to remove an arrow from his upper arm.

    People came running from every direction. Someone grabbed Shorty's arms until the elderly man yelled to let him go. "He saved my skin," the man said. On closer inspection, it was clear that the dead man was not an Indian and would now be blamed for the previous killing also. Shorty felt better about keeping the pouches of gold when he learned that the murdered man had no known family. The wounded man thanked Shorty and offered to make him a partner since he would not be able to work on his claim for a while. He would sign the papers after seeing the doctor in town. The new partner's name was Ray McGrew. The men got along very well together. Ray removed some equipment from his tent to make room for Shorty. He was surprised by the great amount of work that Shorty was doing. Shorty also cooked most of the meals, something he learned from the cooks on the Jolly Star. In two months, their combined labors filled a pouch with $700.00 in gold. Ray's highest total previously was only $137.00. One morning, Ray and Shorty rode to town to bank their gold. This was a good time for Shorty to rid himself of the two pouches now belonging to him. The bank offered the best amount for the gold. The market price was about $20.00 per ounce. The bank offered $16.40. per ounce because there were many impurities mixed in with the raw gold. Their claim wasn't that rich, to account for all the gold that he sold, so Shorty told of a claim he previously had at the Powder River in Wyoming. He actually did have a claim there two years ago, but he was scared off his claim before he worked it.

## MIX OF STORIES

    Someone didn't know the partners had banked their money because two men came skulking around their claim at about three in the morning. The slight sound awoke Shorty. He tip-toed to the tent doorway with gun drawn. He shouted, "Drop your guns and put your hands in the air." The men froze and were soon surrounded by a group of prospectors who pummeled the two thieves until they were unconscious. Shorty was a hero again. The sheriff took the two thieves in tow. When the claim had been worked dry, Shorty had a total of $8,000 banked. He was a wise investor. He also owned shares in three other claims. The bank owner, Mr. Clarence Wilmer, talked Shorty into buying a share of his bank. He did this. Within two years, the bank's value quadrupled. Shorty could now wear the latest fashion and drive the fanciest Grade A Michigan Under Cut surrey with the fanciest matched horses, but what pleased him most was the fact that no one called him Shorty anymore. Now it was Mr. Bill or Mr. Murphy. Of course, he had grown several inches since he was seven, but now he felt ten feet tall.

EDWARD MCCARTHY

# ATTORNEY AT LAW

Tom Matthews was born in Yuma, but chose to settle in Clay City when he received his law degree. He bought a small ranch with money left to him by his father. He won a two-story building in town in a poker game, but swore off gambling when he married. Gold was found on his ranch, but the assays were all one notch above Poor. He earned more money practicing law than his other enterprises, but he did keep some people working at his mine, and his friend, Jose, ran his ranch. Jim was born three months before his mother died. He had promised his father he would become a lawyer too. His father had plans for a law firm called Matthews and Son, but he died three years before Jim received his law degree.

The sun was setting as six stout horses stopped the coach at the S. and R. Clay City depot. The passengers numbered two, Mrs. Ann Marty, the mayor's wife, and Jim Matthews, the young man who recently won the title of attorney at law, esq. Jim followed Mrs. Marty off the coach. He collected his carpetbag, tipped his hat to the mayor, and walked to the Golden Cage Saloon. He ordered a glass of beer, and carried it to an empty table where he sipped the cold liquid, thoroughly enjoying its cooling effect. When his glass was empty, he left the saloon and walked down the boardwalk to Andy's Bake Shop. He and Andy were great friends. They grew up together and had respect for each other. He reached the shop as Andy was closing for the night. He was invited to the rear of the shop and was soon enjoying coffee in the kitchen. Yes, he was now a lawyer. Yes, he had high grades. He answered all the questions. Andy was truly proud of his friend, but he could see that Jim was very tired after his long ride. Andy gave him two doughnuts and shooed him home to his own shop in the building left to him by his father. Once there, Jim sat on his bed in the rear of the shop to remove his shoes. He awoke ten hours later.

Someone was knocking on his back door. Jim answered the knocking. It was a young man named Frank Winslow. He claimed to have information of help to Jim. For 45 minutes Frank and Jim sat in the kitchen drinking coffee while Frank outlined how his mine foreman was taking the money for every tenth load of Jim's ore sent to the smelter. Frank was one of the freighters who hauled the ore. Caswell, the mine boss, was also very friendly with Jones, one of the town's bankers. Frank said there was something

## MIX OF STORIES

cooking between Jones and Caswell, but he couldn't pin it down. Caswell became suspicious and fired Frank. Jim thanked the man, asked him to stay mum, and Jim would work on it. Frank said, "Be very careful of Caswell. He's fast with his gun and he killed a man in a town 30 miles away two weeks ago." Jim relayed this information to Andy, who suggested, "Take it to the judge." Jim explained that Judge Worth was a stickler for evidence, but all he had was one witness, and no evidence. "I'll do what I can," he said.

Jim learned that Frank had been arrested earlier that day because of an argument he was in at the saloon. The fine was ten dollars. Frank had the money, but would not pay the fine. Before sundown, Frank paid his fine and was released. Sheriff Casey told Jim that a man came to his office and said that Frank's mother was sick. Frank paid his fine and left. Jim rode out to Bekes Road. Before he reached Frank's house, he spotted a dark mass by the side of the road. On close examination it was found to be the body of Frank. There was a bullet hole in the back of the young man's head. Jim believed that Caswell had hired a killer to shut up Frank. Yes, Jim now had evidence, but it was a long way from being tied to anyone. He and Sheriff Casey looked all over town for the stranger who claimed Frank's mother was sick. They had no luck.

Early on the following morning there was another young man knocking on Jim's back door. He introduced himself as Bill Stanton. He was no older than 21, but knew everything to know about mining. His father had been a graduate in mining engineering. Bill had no college experience. He learned from his dad. He was working for Caswell a month previously when he overheard a conversation between Caswell and Banker Jones. Caswell had boarded up a north wall of Jim's mine because it looked very promising and he didn't want Jim to know about it. He continued working on an eastern wall, which was a poor prospect. Caswell and Jones were going to work on Jim to get his mine for as little as $15,000 at most. Jim warned the man to keep this information to himself if he wanted to keep living. When Jim visited Andy later in the day, he told of a field trip that his class had taken to some Chicago court houses. He recalled a café that baked bread and cakes, but it also sold coffee and tea. "You could try that out with a table or two. You've got plenty of room." Andy was unconvinced, he murmured, "Maybe."

After leaving the bake shop, Jim joined the sheriff in peering into every shop on the street, in search of the man believed to have murdered Frank. They had no luck until they looked into a saloon for the second time. Casey whispered, "There he is, the young man with the brown shirt." The men entered the saloon. The young man gave them a casual glance then returned to his beer. Jim made his way behind the man and lifted the man's pistol from its holster. The man then saw the sheriff and smiled. Then he saw that the sheriff was not joking with him. "What's the beef, Sheriff?" Casey answered, "Remember that young man you told his mother was sick?" The stranger was obviously puzzled by the question. He said, "That's what I told him. Wait a minute…You don't think I killed him? You do! I didn't even know the guy. I was told to say his mother was sick. That's exactly what I said to him. Then I left him outside the sheriff's office." Casey asked him, "Who told you to say that?" The young man seemed tongue-tied. "I don't know his… his name, the guy who…who bosses the miners at the Jim Matthews mine." Jim and Casey looked at each other and nodded their heads. Casey was a bit surprised but he held back on arresting Caswell. Jim promised to get some written evidence to cinch the case.

    It was early in the morning when Jim rode to the smelter. He was warmly greeted by the owner. Jim asked for an accounting of the ore delivered as well as the payments from the foundry. The staff was happy to supply what he requested. Jim had the sense that the staff had some idea of crooked dealings, but they said nothing. On his way back to Clay City, Jim was fired at twice by someone hiding in the rocks. He buckled on his .45 when he reached home. Then he rode out to his mine to ask the whereabouts of Caswell. One of the miners said, "He hasn't been here all day."

    Jim visited his friend Andy. He was surprised to see two tables and eight people sitting and enjoying their coffee. When a table was empty, he and Andy sat down. A pretty, young woman rolled a tea cart their way. It was loaded with a coffee urn, tea pot, cream, sugar, various cakes, and cookies, etc. Jim brought Andy up to date. Andy answered Jim's questions. They all concerned the young waitress. Jim asked, "I'm not stepping on your toes, am I?" Andy answered, "Heck no, she's too skinny for me." Jim was quite relieved. In the following days Jim found the waitress, Eileen, to be very naïve. He could have taken advantage of this, but he wouldn't. He was smitten.

    When Jim left the bake shop, he walked to the saloon. He noticed some new faces at the bar. They viewed him with obvious anger. The bar grew silent. Jim ignored the men and asked for a beer. He took it to an empty table and sat down. One of the angry men approached his table and asked, "So, you're the galoot that got our brother killed?" Jim was very surprised. He asked, "Who was your brother?" The stranger smiled as he said, "Frank Winslow." Jim remained calm as he explained that Frank had been a good friend who gave him information on a crooked scheme." He was believed to have been murdered by a Mr. Caswell." The stranger motioned for his three brothers to join him at Jim's table. After ten minutes the men had a totally different outlook concerning Jim. One of the men told him that Caswell had lied to them about him. Before he left the men, Jim cautioned them about Caswell. "He's fast and he's good.

    Jim visited several shops and ordered office furniture. The mayor visited him and surprised him with an offer for the position of City Attorney. "It's not a full-time position yet, but you never know when we'll need an attorney." Jim accepted the position and requested a certificate to hang on his wall. "It makes you look important," he said. The mayor smiled. Suddenly the mayor's expression changed. He said, "Your upstairs renters have complained to me about their high rent. Well, I checked with the bank that handles it for you. The bank owner said that rents are increasing all over the territory." Jim was surprised. "I haven't changed their rent since they moved in four years ago." The mayor whispered, "Someone is giving you a bad reputation."

    Jim went to the bank and spoke with the owner, Mr. Jones. Jim looked at the books and saw that the rent had not changed in four years. "Mr. Caswell had orders only to collect the rent, it looks like he's been holding out ten dollars a month from me. Jones said, "I hear that your mine is barely making a profit, Mr. Matthews. I can offer you ten thousand dollars for it, but I don't know how long I can offer that much." Jim's anger was getting hotter. He said, "You and Caswell make a really ugly pair. From now on I will not bank here, neither will my friends."

Jim had had enough. He walked the boardwalk toward the saloon where Caswell would be this time of day. Suddenly a shot sounded and Jim whirled about to see a rifle fall to the ground behind him from an upstairs window, a body lay across the window sill. One of Frank's brothers stood on the boardwalk holding a smoking rifle. They waved to each other. Jim entered the saloon as new thoughts suddenly filled his brain. He wasn't that fast with a gun. His accuracy was only fair. And Eileen... He thought of backing out, but he couldn't. A cold sweat dampened his forehead and seemed to melt away the bravery and anger he once felt. Caswell stood at the bar, seemingly cool and calm, even smirking. Caswell's hand moved swiftly for his pistol. Jim noticed the movement and said, "Dammit," as he dropped to the floor while drawing his gun. He felt the sting of a bullet tear into his lower leg muscle, but he was still alive! He aimed and fired. Caswell fell to the floor. He died within two minutes. Jim was helped to a chair and someone fetched Doctor Perry and Sheriff Casey. The doctor stitched up his leg and was bandaging it when Eileen came rushing to his side.

Judge Worth learned that Caswell had $14,000 in the bank. He confiscated all of it, then ordered a payment of $1,000 to Jim, and another $1,000 to Jim's upstairs renters. The remainder of the money was set aside for assistance to needy children. Jim hired the self-taught mining engineer, and work soon started on that north wall. It was a rich lode that held up for four years. Jim and Eileen were married. They moved into his ranch house when Eileen became pregnant. Andy was getting rich on his bake shop He soon had 5 tables and a counter that seated 5 people. Jim made plans for a law firm he would name Matthews and Son.

# COPS

    Back in the 1930's most kids never heard of a weekly "allowance." We had to earn our own money to go fishing, bike riding, or to the movies. I sold newspapers, delivered the Saturday Evening Post, and shined shoes. I built my own shoe box, bought the black and brown shoe polishes and I could snap that polishing cloth with the best of them. What made it tougher to earn money that way was detective McCarthy (no relation). He had a bad reputation because he had shot and killed two men. When he was in the area, I hid out until he left. He would grab up a kid's shoe box and toss it into the air, then smile when it smashed on the sidewalk. No one could find out why. Why would anyone stop a kid from helping his family get food?

    I recall other cops who were nice. While walking his beat, officer Stevens called out, "How's your wife, Mr. Russo? Officer Stevens never had to use his weapon. I believe that bad cops create a basis for some crimes because of their ill treatment of people. The criminal would call it "Getting even" or "Teaching him a lesson." When cops treat everyone as a possible or real criminal, people will be getting even. No one likes to be put down or embarrassed.

MIX OF STORIES

# DREAM WIFE

The sign on the door read "INTERROGATION ROOM #1. Inside the room were police sergeant Tom Rosen and lieutenant Jim Ryan. Tom Rosen was explaining that he had no idea why the odd dreams started. "I have notes that I started to write on the third morning after having a recurring dream. I didn't know the dreams would recur, so I didn't take notes at first." Tom had written the notes as soon as he awoke after having a dream The first note read: May 18 "Chicago." In this dream he said he was married to a beautiful blond woman. His real wife had brown hair, and she too was beautiful. There was nothing familiar about his dream surroundings until he dreamed he saw a newspaper on his front porch. It was the Chicago Clarion. Chicago? He and his real wife lived in Miami.

The next notation was: May 20. "Husband". In this dream he looked in a mirror and saw a police sergeant, but it wasn't him. That sergeant had a totally different face with a small mustache. On the bureau was a wedding picture dated a year earlier. Lieut. Ryan reminded the sergeant that he had more important things to do, and they weren't getting anywhere. "What made you go to the captain with your dreams?" The sgt. wondered if he was doing the right thing. The note for May 21was "WOW"!! "So, what does that mean," the lieut. asked. "Look Jim, don't mention this to Sarah, but I was enjoying sex with my dream wife, and man, it was good, but suddenly in this dream, the thought hit me that I wanted my dream wife killed, and I was making plans to have it done. I was so agitated for making love with someone I hated that I dressed and walked outside the house. That's when I noticed the house number was 2240. I also saw a street sign for Leslie Street. So now we have an address. The name on the mailbox was Harrington. Tom and Ellen Harrington." The lieut. was busily writing in his notebook.

The next dream was on May 22. The notation was: "Locker room." Lieut. Ryan was becoming, antsy "I haven't seen anything that calls for police action so far." Sergeant Rosen bit his lip and said, I'm getting to it, Jim. In this dream I was sitting in the police locker room with my good dream friend, Bob Cary. Bob said he would take care of it in the very near future. I stopped him from speaking more, and said, "Don't give me any details. When she's dead, I have to be surprised."

Lieutenant Ryan reported this latest information to Captain Williams. He was ordered to phone the Chicago police precinct. "Tell them we have a snitch who reported some information, and we're checking some details." The lieut. returned to the interrogation room because he did not know the precinct where Harrington worked. He told Rosen to go back to the dream where he was looking in the mirror. "I have to know what precinct Harrington works in." Rosen answered, "Yeah, I recall it was on his collar, precinct 17." The lieutenant phoned the 17th precinct captain in Chicago and asked if he had a Sergeant Harrington working there. He told the captain the cover story about a snitch. He was fully prepared for a negative response. Without hesitation, the captain answered, "Yes, we do." The lieutenant then asked if Harrington lived at 2240 Leslie Street. The answer was positive. Ryan then said, "This problem may not involve Harrington at all, so please don't mention this to him. "Okay," the captain answered. Lieut. Ryan then said to Rosen, "The plot sickens. We've got a magician in the Miami police.

The next dream note was for May 23. The notation was: "Tomorrow." The dream was in the locker room again. Harrington sat with his buddy, Bob Cary. Cary said, "One more day, partner. for the big bang, then you'll be a widower." Rosen said. "Jim, that dream was this morning; we've about run out of time." Lieut. Ryan banged his fist on the table and said, "There's nothing we can do. We can't have a man arrested because of a dream. I know you'll feel guilty, but so will I if anything bad happens."

On the following morning Sgt. Rosen was relating his latest dream to Lieut. Ryan. "I left My dream house and drove away in my dream car in the morning. My wife would leave a few minutes later in her car. I drove slowly so I could hear the explosion, then grinned widely when I heard it. Captain Cassidy phoned Lieut. Ryan that morning. He said, "I guess your snitch had some good information, Mrs. Harrington's car was blown up this morning. We'll have a hell of a time finding the killer." Lieut. Ryan said, "So far, our snitch has had the right information. Maybe you should check out Harrington and Sgt. Bob Carey." Captain Cassidy agreed.

Later in the day, Captain Cassidy again phoned Ryan to let him know that Mrs. Harrington was not found in her car. The police interviewed a neighbor who saw a police sergeant put something in Mrs. Harrington's car very early in the morning, but it wasn't Sgt. Harrington; it was Sgt. Bob Carey, whom she met when invited to a cookout months earlier. We learned also that Harrington's half-brother (with a different name) and Cary's brother were involved in a bank robbery. Mrs. Harrington was a witness. Back then she was Miss Evans. She was in the bank that morning. Her testimony put the robbers in prison for five years. This is when Sgt. Harrington decided to marry her and get revenge. Those two sergeants will probably get 8 to 10 years to mull over their crimes. Thanks for the heads-up. And no, I didn't go for that crap about a snitch. No, don't tell me. Thanks again. Now we have to find Mrs. Harrington before her husband does. We're checking all the hotels in the city, but there's a hell of a lot of them."

Sgt. Rosen slept fitfully that night. He was worried about Mrs. Harrington. He had grown fond of the woman, he also felt sorry for her although he never met the lady who lived 1,000 miles to the north. In the morning he had news for Lieut. Ryan. He had believed his dreams were over, but he had another one. He saw Mrs. Harrington in room 303 of the Carlton Manor. Although it was 7:19 in the morning, his watch in the dream read 4:10pm. He saw the watch through Sgt. Harrington's eyes. He was in the hallway leading to his wife's room. "This means the bastard found his wife and will kill her this afternoon," he said. Lieut. Ryan left the room and phoned Capt. Cassidy again.

Sgt. Rosen was ordered to patrol duty. Lieut. Ryan promised to call him if anything happened.

There was no call. When Rosen's duty ended, he went to Ryan's office. Ryan was on the phone and motioned Rosen to have a seat. Ryan said into the phone, "Yeah, I understand, Captain. If I told you, you wouldn't believe it. Good bye. Captain." Ryan turned to Rosen, "They got him good. They put cameras in Mrs. Harrington's rooms and have the whole thing on tape. Sgt. Harrington was mad as hell. He terrorized his wife. When he reached for his gun, the cops collared him and Carey. He'll get extra time for carrying an unauthorized weapon. Harrington allowed his need for revenge to overcome his good sense. He swore revenge. All the crazy people are not in a hospital. Go home, Tom. You have a nice wife. Stop mooning over your dream wife. She's safe now. You deserve a medal, but we can't give you one, not even a letter of commendation. No one would ever believe it. Go on home, and have some happy dreams."

EDWARD MCCARTHY

# JEB AND DAVE

Jeb Walker helped drive a herd of cattle from Texas to Kansas. Now he was in need of a job. He had $47.00 left from his pay when he entered the town of Black Rock. He was drawn to the Saloon because of his thirst. He could stand a little rest too. Tonight, he would sleep in a bed at the hotel. He viewed his image in the saloon mirror and saw a 25-year-old, about 6 feet 2, and about 187 pounds. He also noticed some odd behavior from the barkeep who seemed to be signaling a scar-faced man seated at a table. The beer had a cooling effect on Jeb. He drank about half of his beer then was unable to raise the glass to his lips. The clock behind the bar read 11:15. It was dark outside. The darkness crept into his head as he swirled into a black pit.

He awoke with a hammering in his head. It was daylight. His pocket watch read 8:17. He was on the ground in an alley next to the saloon. A quick search of his pockets showed they were empty. Without hesitation he entered the saloon and walked behind the bar. He bent low to view the contents of the low shelf under the bar. He saw several glasses. In one were several small paper packets, He took two and emptied them into a glass of beer. He ordered the barkeep, "Drink it!" The barkeep whined, "I can't drink that. It could kill me. Those are knockout packets." Jeb drew his .45 and told the barkeep to empty his pockets on the bar. The barkeep complied. Jeb counted the money. There was a total of $52.00. Jeb pocketed $47.00 of it and returned the remainder to the barkeep. The frightened man said he had received only $5.00 of Jeb's money. Jeb told him to get the rest from his boss, Scarface.

"What's going on here," a man said as he entered the saloon. Jeb turned with his hand on his .45. "No need for gunplay, young man. I'm not armed." Jeb poured himself a beer and sat at a table. The stranger sat and told Jeb that he was mayor Johnson of Black Rock. "How can I help you, Mayor?" Jeb asked. Mayor Johnson said he needed a sheriff. Black Rock had 4 sheriffs in less than 3 years. The latest one took off for California two weeks ago. The other three had been killed. No one would take the job. "We can pay 40.00 a month, you can receive rewards, and you can have a small share of fines and free board at the hotel. You look like you can take care of yourself, that's why I'm asking you. A lesser man wouldn't last a week." Jeb answered, "You mean you found the fool you looked for." Johnson shook his head, "No, a lesser person would be the fool,

## MIX OF STORIES

not you." Jeb insisted that no one was to tell him who to arrest and who to ignore. Johnson nodded his head then swore in Jeb before he was called back to his office. Before Jeb left the saloon, he told the barkeep he was posted out of town. "Don't be here tomorrow or it could mean 5 years at Yuma prison."

Jeb walked to his new office and found his sheriff badge in a desk drawer. He pinned it on and walked the boardwalk to each of the shops, introducing himself to the shopkeepers. Mr. Murphy wasn't as cordial as the other businessmen. "How much do you get, Sheriff?" Jeb answered. "My salary is a public record, Mr. Murphy." Murphy shook his head, "I mean how much off the books." Jeb became angry and let Murphy know that he never accepted a nickel of dishonest money in his life. Murphy apologized. "I thought you were in with that crowd who's been forcing us businessmen to pay for their services. I can't tell you any more. I've got a wife and two kids they need me alive.

Jeb left the shop and walked to Pointer's Saddle Shop. He was checking out a saddle in the back room when two men entered the shop. One of them said, "It's payday. Get it up." Mr. Pointer went to his cash box as he said, "This has been a bad week." He handed over the cash reluctantly as the teller counted it. "See ya next week," he said as he and his partner left the shop. Jeb asked, "How much did you pay him?" Pointer answered. "$22.00." Jeb asked the questions and Pointer was angry enough to answer them. He had been paying this gang for more than a year and was making plans to move to another town or city. The gang had caused four shops to move out of Black Rock. The gang leader was Scarface. Jeb put a calming hand on Pointer's shoulder and said, "It won't go on much longer. Let's see if we can get your money back."

There was a new barkeep at the saloon. He was telling a customer that the other barkeep left town in a wagon with all his furniture. Seated at a corner table was Scarface. He was eying Jeb with so much anger that Jeb was forced to say, "I posted him out of town." He saw Scarface through narrowed eyes. A glass smashed on the sawdust floor behind the bar. Everybody turned to look. The anger that seemed to permeate the saloon soon disappeared. Jeb visited the town's judge, then returned to the saloon and put Scarface under arrest. Within thirty minutes the entire gang of six, including the town's tax collector, was in jail. The trial was two weeks later. Five of the gang received a sentence of 8 years, Scarface received 12 years without parole. Territorial guards took them away the following day. Everyone in Black Rock felt relieved for the first time in years. The leader was also fined a tad more than $18,000. The town's shop keepers shared this money.

The congratulations did not last long. In the morning a telegram notified Jeb that 4 of the men had escaped from the police wagon, among them was Scarface, and they were seen heading toward Black Rock. The townsfolk again shunned Jeb. They were aware that Scarface was coming for revenge and they feared for their safety. Jeb was not going to wait for them. He didn't want them in his town. He prepared to meet them on the road with a posse. However, there was not a man willing to join him. Jeb tightened his jaw and remained silent. He mounted his horse and set off alone. Half-way out of town Murphy caught up with him. "I'm going with you," he said. "You're putting yourself in danger," Jeb told him. "Well, I wasn't always a shopkeeper. I spent a year as a deputy marshal up in Colorado. I'm fair with a gun too." Jeb told him he was welcome. "Call me Dave. My sister is working in the shop while I'm gone. I can't afford to lose any money. I have a mortgage to pay off plus some loans in two weeks and I have no idea where I can pick up $600 before then. If I can't pay it off, I'll lose my house and 165 acres, but I'll still have about 400 acres to build on if times get better. I had the money practically in the bank before 30 of my cattle were stolen, but that's life. Jeb planned to wait for the 4 escapees at a boulder-strewn area called Dyson's Ditch.

  They camped that evening by a stream. Early in the morning they were about to mount their horses when they saw 4 figures in the distance coming their way. They walked their horses deeper into the wooded area and waited for the escapees to pass. Again, they were mounting their horses when they heard horses approaching, then saw 3 horsemen dogging the escapees. These men were Apaches, and they had rifles. Jeb told his partner they would wait, "Maybe the Apaches will take care of the escapees," he said. Then they would wait until the Apaches cleared the area before making a move. In the meantime, they found some higher ground from which to view the events about to enfold below them. The escapees stopped among the boulders and prepared to eat the mid-day meal. The Apaches moved silently on foot, surrounding the escapees on three sides. They opened fire and downed two of the escapees. They moved forward and engaged in a firefight for about 15 minutes. Then there was an eerie silence as The Apaches moved forward carefully. There was more silence, then a shot was fired. An Apache was on the ground, wounded. The 2 other Apaches had Scarface targeted on two sides. They opened fire and Scarface fell dead. Jeb and Dave would now wait until the Apaches cleared out. This was a good plan, but the best plans of mice and men oft go awry. An Apache noticed fresh hoofprints where they shouldn't be. Soon two Apaches were following those prints to Jeb and Dave, There was no place to hide. Jeb and Dave fired at the approaching Indians, killing both. They began to ride to the road when suddenly the Apache who had been wounded came galloping and screaming toward them as he fired his rifle. Both men fired as one. The Apache fell from his horse. He was dead.

  Dave set about collecting the horses, side arms and rifles of escapees and Indians. He told Jeb he would auction them off in town and see how close to $600. he could come. Jeb wished him luck. They returned to Black Rock. That night Dave auctioned off seven horses, 4 saddles and tack, 4 sidearms and belts, and 6 new repeating rifles. He kept one for himself. In total, he collected $216.00. He turned over half of it to Jeb, who returned it, as he told Dave that he just heard that a reward was offered for the escapees, $200.00 each except $500.00 for Scarface, "Sharing that reward and the auction money will pay off your mortgage and then some," Dave said, "Call on me when you need someone."

# ABOUT THE AUTHOR

The author, Mr. McCarthy, was born in Brooklyn, NY in Feb, 1926. He quit school in the eighth grade and found a job to help support his family of eight siblings and two parents. No one else in his family was working. When he was eighteen, he went into the army and served in combat in Europe, earning a Bronze Star, Purple Heart, Combat Infantry Badge, and the French Knighthood and Legion of Honor medal from the President of France. He later attended the University of Wyoming at Laramie and earned a B.A. degree in psychology in two years. He is retired from Orange County, N.Y. and now lives in Florida. He continues to write at the age of 96. He says he was born during the transition between the horse and wagon and the automobile. And now we are at the beginning of the space age. That is a mere 100 years from horse and wagon to moon flights. Hang on for the ride. Where will we be 100 years from today?

# EDWARD MCCARTHY

# DEDICATION

When reading a story, whether a tale or a true experience, use your imagination, put yourself into the action.

If reading about a sea voyage, smell the salt water, feel the dampness on your face, hear the sea gulls and the wind in the sails. No, don't get sea sick. Enjoy the story. Listen to the man aloft. He may be shouting above the wind, "Whale ahoy, off the port beam." If you were really there, your blood would rush through your body in anticipation of the chase. Enjoy the thoughts as well as the words. Lose yourself in the story; become a part of it. I guarantee it will increase your enjoyment tenfold. Stories are written for you, the reader. Therefore, I dedicate the stories herein to you.

www.ingramcontent.com/pod-product-compliance
Lightning Source LLC
LaVergne TN
LVHW010216070526
838199LV00062B/4604